What readers have to say about *Jessica's Secret*

"If you are a Jack Beale fan, you already know that you are in for a wonderful read. If you aren't already a Jack Beale fan, *Jessica's Secret* will convince you.in just the first few pages of the book. When I look for a book to read, I want to be taken away on a journey; become someone else; and have some excitement, danger, and even a little bit of romance. That can be said of ANY of the Jack Beale Mystery Series by K.D. Mason. From the first book, *Harbor Ice*, to his most recent, *Jessica's Secret*, you will be kept captive in a little coastal town in New Hampshire and you won't want to leave . . . even when you close the book at the final words."
—Missi Stockwell, Missi's Book Reviews

* * *

"Mr. Mason,

I have read all of your books and can't wait to read your latest, *Jessica's Secret*. Jack and Max and their friends have become my friends and the way that you tell their stories, I get completely swept up into their world. Over the years you've taken me from the town of Rye Harbor to Belize, to Camden, ME and the Isles of Shoals. Whenever I finish one of your books, I'm left with a little feeling of emptiness as I know I will have to wait patiently for the next.

Thank you for creating these wonderful stories and keep writing."
—Laurie Pare, email from a fan

* * *

"Once again, KD Mason has written another page turning Jack Beale mystery. From the first page of *Jessica's Secret*, on a stormy night in 1942, until it's conclusion in today's world, I could not put it down. I was hooked. I cannot wait for the next installment of the Jack Beale Series."
—Carrie Aubut, a New Hampshire fan

* * *

"I'm a lush for entertaining books, and *Jessica's Secret* met all of my expectations. The opening chapters present a harrowing start off the NH coast in 1942, and I was pleasantly surprised at how easily K.D. Mason shifted his tale to present-day New Hampshire. This book, like the rest of K.D. Mason's books, pulled me into the world that Jack, Max, and Courtney inhabit. They have become my friends who live just down the road, and I can't wait to run with Jack or sail on *d'Riddem*. If you are looking for a fun read with mystery, suspense, and—of course—romance, *Jessica's Secret* is for you."
—Andrea Vomacka

JESSICA'S
SECRET

JESSICA'S SECRET

K.D. MASON

The author may be reached through www.kdmason.com

Jessica's Secret is a work of fiction. All of the characters, places, organizations, and events portrayed in this novel are either products of the author's imagination or are used fictitiously, and any resemblance to any actual persons, living or dead, business establishments, events, or locales is entirely coincidental.

ISBN-13 978-1540770264
ISBN-10 1540770265

Cover and book design by Claire MacMaster, barefoot art graphic design
Copy Editor: Renée Nicholls | www.mywritingcoach.net
Back cover photographer: Richard G. Holt
Proofreading : Eileen Frigon, Nancy Obert

Printed in the U.S.A.

Dedicated to my good friend RAY BOLDUC 1942–2016

* * *

THANK YOUs

*As with each of my books, I can't thank enough
all the people who have helped and encouraged me in this endeavor.*

*This year I would like to offer a special thanks to Edso Harding,
who, as the top bidder in last year's NHSPCA Auction,
became a character in this latest Jack Beale Mystery.*

CHAPTER 1

BEN INHALED DEEPLY, TAKING IN THE RICH, salty smell of the ocean. Then, as he blew out his breath, he shivered. Standing at the end of the small dock, which ran into the harbor from behind his house, he looked out toward the horizon. Without thinking, he took his hands out of his pockets, holding them to his breath for warmth even though he knew the effect would only be fleeting at best. He tugged his collar higher and hunched his shoulders up in an effort to pull his head down into his coat. For a long moment he stared out into the dark. *Time to go.*

It was going to be a rough night, but he had known that all day, since the hours before sunrise. The first hint had been the sound of the surf breaking against the shore. Instead of making the usual shooshing sound, waves too large for a calm sea had started slamming themselves against the shore with a resounding thud that could be felt as much as heard.

He had recognized the signs. Only a storm far out at sea could make that happen. Wind, blowing continuously over water, created waves, and in the deep sea, they were nearly invisible. However, as the depth decreased, the wave's energy began to consolidate until there came the inevitable collision with the unmoving land. He had always felt that it was not unlike the way a steam locomotive would start. First there were the slow, ponderous strokes whose power would begin to move the locomotive. Then, as it gained momentum, those slow, powerful stokes would increase in speed as they worked to keep ahead of the momentum until all that could be heard was a single, loud roar.

As the sun had risen, it had shone beneath the clouds that he could see far out over the ocean. Those moments of early sun had illuminated a calm, flat sea. Only the thud of wave on rock had hinted at something else. Once the sun had risen above those clouds, a glorious late-September day had presented itself. The day remained sunny as the sun, moving west, stayed just ahead of the approaching clouds while he had spent the day preparing for the night's work. By sunset, the clouds covered the sky and the wind had started to pick up. The large Chinese Elm tree that grew majestically next to his house had begun to sway, its leaves making a steady whooshing sound.

He looked up one last time now and took another deep breath, what little light the new moon might have provided had been eliminated by the heavy cloud cover. He turned and walked back toward the house, steeling himself for his night's work.

CHAPTER 2

"I'VE PACKED A SANDWICH FOR YOU, and the coffee's hot—ready whenever you are."

"Thanks," he mumbled, not really listening to what she was saying. His thoughts were elsewhere. He was sitting at the small writing table in the parlor, staring at the secret log that held notes from all his missions. He flipped the pages back and forth as he reread what he knew all too well.

There were two missions that the German U-boats were perfectly suited for. One was sinking ships heading for Europe with arms and supplies. With that they were having great success. The other was potentially much more deadly. If they could land spies and saboteurs, the fear and panic they might cause could be devastating. Just in the last few days, he had heard about a U-boat sighting out on the fishing banks, and another near the Cape, both too close.

To counter these threats posed by U-boats, private yachts and many of the larger fishing schooners had been organized into what was called the Picket Patrol or Corsair Fleet. Because their crews were often a ragtag group of beach bums, young men from college, boy scouts, ex rumrunners and bootleggers, it was also called the Hooligan Navy. Fast and silent, these sailing schooners patrolled the fifty-fathom curve offshore watching for enemy activity, with orders to report any sightings. Even though many of the boats were armed with machine guns and depth charges, their radios were far and away their most potent weapon.

Nearer to home, many of the lobstermen and fishermen who worked the New Hampshire coast and whose boats were too small for that kind of offshore work wanted to contribute too, if not officially, then unofficially. Many had honed skills during prohibition that, in their minds, could be invaluable in combating this threat to America. Not sanctioned by either the Navy or the Coast Guard, they formed their own unofficial "Picket Patrol" and went out on the darkest of nights, the nights most suited to smuggling, and patrolled close to shore. They faced not only the danger of running into a U-boat but also the chance of being mistaken for the enemy by the US Navy or Coast Guard.

He had watched the weather all day. He knew that it was going to be a perfect night for a U-boat skipper intent on putting someone ashore. He and several of the other fishermen in Rye Harbor had taken up patrolling their little piece of coastline on nights such as this, determined that none of the Bosch bastards would ever make it to their shore. None of them ever considered what a small, unarmed fishing boat could actually do if it did run into a fully armed, hostile submarine. After all, wasn't the Navy just a few miles up the river in Portsmouth? The thought gave them courage. Tonight was his turn.

He picked up a pencil. Writing was a challenge. Were that pencil a hook, needing to be tied on a line, or a bobbin for repairing a net, his thick, weather-toughened fingers would have nimbly handled the task. But he had never liked school and quit when he was fifteen, preferring a life on the water over time spent behind a desk. His reading and writing skills were rudimentary at best, but they were sufficient for the life he had chosen. So with slow, deliberate strokes he began this night's entry. His penmanship, while legible, was far from fluid.

29 September 1942 8pm. Wind NNE force 4, rising. Seas building, Heavy cloud cover.

He stopped and put the pencil down. That was how each entry began: date, time, wind speed and direction, sea state and visibility. He would fill in details when he returned. It was time to go.

* * *

"Did you put on your sweater?" she asked, even though she clearly knew the answer. They had been friends and even lovers for most of their lives; marriage had just never seemed an option. Of course she knew he had his sweater on, but she asked anyway, knowing he wouldn't answer.

"Here's a thermos of hot coffee. I made it extra strong," she said as she handed it to him. "And here's a sandwich." She handed him a small paper bag, which he put in his pocket. "Please be careful."

"Looks a bit nasty, but I've been out in worse."

As he took it from her, he knew that she would have put an extra treat inside with his sandwich, but he said nothing.

She smiled back silently, her eyes betraying her true feelings, wishing he wouldn't go out on such a night, but knowing that he would, and that nothing she could say would dissuade him.

CHAPTER 3

WHEN HE REACHED HIS BOAT, THE *DOROTHY KAY*, she was tugging hard at her mooring. It had been a long, hard pull rowing out to her, made all the more challenging by the fact he couldn't even see her from shore, but that made no difference.

On board, he looked around. Because of the recent sightings, the blackout that was in effect was being strictly observed. It made his sojourn that much more dangerous since anyone spotted out on the water would be considered hostile. There were no lights anywhere on shore, and even the lighthouse out on White Island was dark. He wedged his thermos next to the windshield by the helm, then took the bag with his sandwich out of his pocket and placed it next to the thermos.

When he pressed the ignition button, the engine groaned and coughed several times before finally catching. He cocked his head and listened to her distinctly deep, throaty rumble, and he smiled. "It's going to be a rough one tonight, sweetheart," he said softly, staring out the window into the blackness while holding onto the wheel with a tenderness that contrasted with his rough and powerful hands. He always talked to her before setting out, no matter what the journey. Sailors all had their superstitions, and whether or not there was any validity to them, he reasoned, why take the chance?

Dorothy Kay had a reputation of being the fastest boat south of Portland, Maine. It had been nearly ten years since prohibition's repeal, but as was often true, reputations—once earned—were hard to deny. On this night he wondered if he would be thankful for that reputation.

While the engine warmed up, he opened the small companionway door that led below and climbed inside. Inside this small space it was blacker than black, but in his mind's eye he could see everything. Pulling the door closed behind, he took a small flashlight out of his pocket and turned it on, directing its beam forward, inspecting the space.

It was a stretch to consider it a cabin, since it lacked living accommodations. It was impossible to stand straight, and what could be called a berth was more a bench covered with fishing gear. Another set of oilskins swayed from a hook. A spare pair of sea boots were on the floor. All the way forward in the bow was a bin in which the anchor rode lay coiled. It passed through the deck via a hawse pipe, which even when capped still allowed for a steady drip of water into the boat whenever it was raining or waves crashed over the bow. It was dry now, but he knew that before the night was out, that would change.

On the bulkhead, next to the companionway door, was a rack in which he kept a large-caliber hunting rifle. It was a holdover from his days running liquor during prohibition; now, he kept it more for show and to shoot the occasional large shark. On the floor by the rifle was a metal box in which he kept its shells and a pistol. Having both on board gave him a sense of security during these nightly patrols, even though deep inside he knew they would be mostly ineffective if he actually came across a German submarine. Taking the rifle out of the rack, he inspected it, making sure that it was loaded and ready to fire. Then he opened the box and did the same with the pistol. Satisfied that all was as it should be, he repacked the box, doused the light and returned to the deckhouse, taking the rifle and the box with him. It was time.

CHAPTER 4

HAD THE TIDE BEEN LOW, leaving the harbor might have been impossible because of the waves created by the shallow bar at the mouth, but it was mid-tide and he knew that while it wouldn't be easy, neither would it be impossible. He cast off and smiled as he pressed the throttle forward and felt the power of *Dorothy Kay's* engine. Motoring forward, toward the mouth of the harbor, he checked his compass. The faint red glow of the compass's light, while just bright enough for reading it without destroying his night vision, was at the same time dim enough that it would remain invisible to eyes outside the deckhouse.

As he neared the mouth of the harbor, *Dorothy Kay's* bow began to rise and fall more sharply as she powered her way through the entrance. Once clear, he was able to increase his speed until he found that sweet spot where he was making steady headway without excessive pounding. He pointed her bow toward the Isles of Shoals and, taking the waves just off the port bow, began his patrol.

His plan was that before reaching the Isles he would turn back toward the coast, beginning a zigzag pattern parallel to the coast as he worked his way south until he reached Hampton Harbor. When he reached Hampton Harbor, he would turn north, running parallel to the coast back to his starting point before turning back toward Hampton Harbor again. The rest of the night would be spent cruising parallel to the coast until just before dawn.

Memories of nights spent out on the water before the war flashed through his mind. The occasional summer evenings out on the water to escape the heat could be quite magical when the ocean was calm, the night was crystal clear, and a canopy of endless stars filled the heavens. During those times, the moon and stars provided more than enough light to be able to see for miles, their reflections dancing off the water.

This night would not be so pleasant. Visibility was near zero because of the nearly complete darkness, and the ocean was roiled up, which made the ride uncomfortable. His first pass south to Hampton Harbor was uneventful, as was the first leg returning to Rye Harbor along the coast. Everything changed after he made the second turn south.

With the waves off her stern quarter, *Dorothy Kay's* motion eased from the hard bashing of driving into the waves to a more wallowing pattern as her stern lifted with each wave and then settled into the trough before being picked up again. The motion may have seemed easier, but it required extreme vigilance and care to avoid broaching. Fortunately, she was a good boat and he knew her well.

He was nearly halfway to Hampton Harbor when there was a resounding thump against the starboard bow. It wasn't the hard, sharp sound that hitting a log or some other solid object would make, and it wasn't the sound of a wave slapping her hull. It was softer, but it was still hard enough to leave no doubt in his mind that something had been hit. Without thinking, he immediately pulled back on the throttle and turned slowly to port, all the while looking for whatever it was that he had hit. With the bow pointed directly into the waves, he set the throttle so his forward speed matched the wind and waves against him, and he lashed the wheel to hold course.

Satisfied with the way she was riding, he looked around again to see if he could see whatever it was that he had struck. Black waves continued to rush by, making it impossible to see anything. Opening the companionway door, he stuck his head inside and listened for any indication that the hull had been breached.

Between the incessant crashing of the waves against the bow, the wind whistling, and the steady *chugga, chugga* of the engine, it was impossible to see or hear anything just by looking inside. He'd have to go in and make a visual inspection. He was about to squeeze through the companionway door when *Dorothy Kay* rose up on a particularly high wave and he thought he heard a voice call out, followed by the clang of metal hitting metal. He stopped, and his heart began to pound as he imagined the worst. He stared out into the inky blackness of the night, hardly daring to breathe.

After pausing for what seemed an eternity, and not hearing those sounds again, he returned to the companionway door and squeezed below. As before, he pulled the door closed behind him before turning on his flashlight. Temporarily blinded, he briefly closed his eyes. Then he slowly reopened them, looking around for any signs of trouble. All was tight, and in a low voice he said, "*Dorothy Kay*, you're a good girl."

He closed one eye for a few moments before shutting off the flashlight so that when darkness returned, that one eye would be ready for the dark while the other readjusted. Returning to the helm, he quickly took stock. Satisfied that she was still holding course, he began to scan the inky blackness in the hope of seeing whatever it was that he had hit.

CHAPTER 5

AT THAT MOMENT, THE CLOUDS THINNED just enough so that the uniform blackness of the previous hours was broken by shades of gray. As *Dorothy Kay* rose and fell with each passing wave, he slowly turned and began scanning the ocean, searching for any sign of what he had hit. While staring aft, he watched the continuous procession of waves moving away from him. About fifty yards and three waves behind, he saw something, but it disappeared as quickly as it had appeared. He continued to stare at that spot long enough to begin to have doubts. Then he saw it again. This time it was even further away, but he was certain. There wasn't a moment to lose.

He unlashed the wheel and pressed the throttle forward. The distance between him and that object grew, but he needed to have way on in order to be able to maneuver. With the increased speed, *Dorothy Kay's* motion became more violent. Her bow drove into the waves and sheets of water flew over it, making visibility even more difficult. Intending to run down toward whatever he had hit, he was just beginning to turn the wheel to port when he reached the top of a wave and saw a large, dark shape off his starboard bow. If the waves had not been crashing against it, creating slashes of white, he might never have seen it.

He stared in disbelief and wondered if his eyes were playing tricks on him. Then *Dorothy Kay* fell off the top of the wave, and as she descended into the trough, the small gap in the cloud cover closed. As she rose up on the next wave, whatever he had seen had disappeared into the impenetrably black night.

A chill went down his spine. "U-boat?" he thought to himself as he stared out into the darkness. He tried to convince himself that that was impossible—after all, it had only been a fleeting glance at best—but the hairs on the back of his neck stood up as he remembered that thump. If indeed it was a sub, then there was only one reason for it to be so close to shore. And if that was so, then whatever he had hit had probably come from it, and somewhere, out in the dark, the enemy was near.

Without thinking, he pulled the throttle back and hove to once again, reasoning that he would be less visible if he was not moving. As *Dorothy Kay* settled, his hands began to shake, and suddenly the night felt really cold. He reached for the thermos and poured a cup of coffee. It was hot and as strong as she had said it would be. He could feel that first sip as it warmed him all the way down to his stomach. A second sip and his hands stopped shaking.

Without thinking he felt for his rifle, then he touched the box containing the pistol and extra ammunition, reassuring himself that they were within easy reach, but the courage that they had given him when he began his patrol was now replaced with fear and caution. What good would an old hunting rifle and a pistol really be against a marauding, enemy submarine? Still, if whatever he had hit had been launched from a sub, he had to find it and stop it from reaching shore. For that job, he was confident that his guns would be perfect.

CHAPTER 6

DECISION MADE, BEN SWALLOWED HIS LAST SIP OF COFFEE. Once again, he pressed the throttle forward and spun the wheel, feeling *Dorothy Kay* respond, turning away and putting her stern to the wind and waves. Again, he had to be vigilant as wave after wave rolled under her stern, lifting it before she surfed down the face of each one. His only opportunity to look around was that split second at the top of a wave before the plunge down into the trough.

He knew that the odds of finding whatever it was he had hit were slim to none. Too much time had passed, and unless the clouds thinned again, it was unlikely that he would have any chance of success, but that didn't stop him. He kept *Dorothy Kay* heading down the wave train, knowing that his progress was faster than something that was just drifting. When he was just south of Little Boar's Head and about a mile and a half off shore, the clouds thinned again. Looking toward shore, he could just make out the distinctive high bluff.

That's when he saw it. Only a few waves ahead of him, there was a dark shape. That had to be it. He touched the throttle, increasing his speed, and watched as the distance to his target decreased each time *Dorothy Kay* rose up on a wave. Then it was there, right in front of him.

He stared at it, hardly daring to breathe. It was obviously a rubber raft, black and small. A thousand thoughts flashed through his head as he felt his heart rate increase. He took the pistol out of the box and cocked it, all the while never taking his eyes off the rubber raft. It didn't appear large enough to hold more than a single person. Pistol in hand, he carefully guided *Dorothy Kay* closer until they were riding next to each other. He uncocked his pistol and set it back down near the helm when he saw that the raft was upside down and there was no sign of its occupant. Taking a deep breath, he began planning his next steps.

Pushing the throttle forward, he motored past the raft, spun his wheel, and turned until he approached it again, this time with his bow to the waves. Maneuvering until the raft was close to his starboard side, he adjusted the throttle and lashed the wheel, heaving to for the third time. He could see that a rope ran around the outside of its tubes. After several tries, he was able to catch hold of it with his boat hook and pull it alongside *Dorothy Kay*, thankful that it was upside down. Had it been right side up, it would have been full of water, making its recovery that much more difficult, if not impossible.

The thinning in the clouds had now become a hole through which the new moon shone. What little light it provided was more than enough for him to see the dark shoreline, and he knew that he needed to gain more sea room. Concerned that the raft would break free if he tried to drive forward against the waves, he felt that the only option was to bring it on board.

There was no way that it should have weighed more than one of the lobster traps he hauled daily, he reasoned, but it seemed to. Struggling against the wind and waves, and with a final heave, he finally managed to pull it into the boat, where, with a resounding thud, it landed on the deck. He stared at it while he caught his breath.

CHAPTER 7

TAKING THE WAVES OFF HER PORT BOW, *Dorothy Kay* rose, fell, and rocked from side to side as he motored away from the shore and steadily gained sea room. When he was finally far enough off the coast, he began to turn to the south again, resuming his patrol. With each passing minute, visibility improved as that small opening in the clouds increased in size and he could see stars. Several times he glanced back at the raft that lay in the back of his boat. He wanted to inspect it more thoroughly, but that was impossible as long as he continued heading south with a following sea.

Finally he reached the southernmost point of his patrol and turned *Dorothy Kay* into the wind and waves for the trip back. Her motion was much sharper as she rose and fell with each wave. Her bow split the water, sending most of it in great sheets off to port and starboard while the remainder washed over the foredeck. What wasn't deflected splashed up against his windshield.

Adjusting the throttle, again he found the sweet spot between too much speed, where she shuddered as she drove her bow into each wave before finally splitting it, and too little speed, where the waves seemed to win the battle. As her motion became more settled, he looked out over the water. It was black and menacing, with slashes of grey that gave definition to the breaking waves. Taking a quick glance up at the sky, he could see that the hole in the cloud cover was closing and soon all would disappear into the inky blackness once again.

His stomach rumbled. He had been so busy that he hadn't realized how hungry he had become. He decided to eat first. Then he'd try to inspect the raft.

In the bag with his sandwich, he found a slice of apple cake. He ate the sandwich, washing it down with another cup of coffee, but he decided to leave the cake for later. Enough coffee remained in the thermos for one more cup, and he decided to save it for the cake. Checking his course again, and satisfied that *Dorothy Kay* was running true with little guidance from himself, he finally turned his attention to the raft.

Again, the clouds had closed, and since the raft was black, his hands became his eyes. Running them over the outside of the raft, he estimated it to be about seven feet long and less than four feet wide, just large enough for a single man to sit deep inside. The dark shape he had seen before, the sound of voices above the storm's roar, and the clang of metal on metal now felt very real.

As equal parts excitement and fear washed over him, he began to understand what had probably happened. While not exactly an invasion, it had likely been an attempt to set ashore an agent intent on harm. *Dorothy Kay*, quite by accident, had hit the raft, probably sending its occupant overboard to drown in the frigid waters of New England.

"Serves 'em right, the Nazi bastards," he mumbled under his breath. Then he smiled. The sub may have escaped, but its mission was a failure, he had the raft.

CHAPTER 8

HE MANAGED TO FLIP THE RAFT OVER and began to run his hands over the inside of the raft. He was nearly finished when his hands found something lashed securely deep inside it.

"Well, well. What have we here?"

It seemed to be some kind of a valise or sea bag. Unable to tug it loose, or untie the rope holding it to the raft, he reached for his knife. With his last stroke, the bag came free—but at a price. He must have slashed the raft, because it began losing air.

"Damn."

Whatever it was, it was not only wet and slippery, it was also heavier than he expected. Unable to find any kind of handle, he finally managed to pinch enough of one end that he was able to lift it out of the swiftly deflating raft. Now he knew why the raft had seemed so heavy. When he dropped the bag on the deck next to the helm station, it landed with a thump.

He checked his compass and estimated that it would be several hours before he'd be back to Rye Harbor. He began to consider his options. Should he report the incident to the Navy and the Coast Guard or not? If he did, and if they believed him, by the time a response could be mustered, chances were good that the sub would be long gone and he'd be the one in trouble since he wasn't supposed to be out there. If he didn't, he'd be the only one who knew what had happened.

Curiosity over what was in the bag from the raft won out over making a decision. Besides, he had time. Course holding, he opened the companionway door, picked up the bag, and, after pushing it inside, followed, closing the door and turning on his flashlight. He made space on the berth to sit and dragged the bag over until it was at his feet. The bag was made from the same dull, black rubber as the raft. It was closed securely by some stout lashings, and he didn't waste any time trying to untie them. A few quick slashes with his knife and the bag fell open.

Inside, there was a sealed packet and two metal boxes, also sealed so as to be waterproof. The packet didn't weigh much, and he opened it first. Inside he found several packets of papers—maps, documents, train and shipping schedules, and several passports. Any questions that might have lingered about where the raft came from evaporated in a heartbeat. His hands shook as he stuffed everything back into the packet and set it aside.

He picked up the smaller of the two boxes. Prying its lid off, he found inside a pistol and a box of ammunition. He took a deep breath. If the man in the raft had made it to shore, things might have gone very badly for anyone he might have encountered.

The last box was the largest and the obvious reason why the whole bundle had weighed so much. There was a handle on each end, and not only was its lid sealed, but also a padlock hung off its latch. He used his knife to break the seal, and a hammer and screwdriver made short work of the lock. He lifted the lid and found inside two more boxes. He picked up the smaller of the two. It didn't weigh much. Shaking it by his ear, he turned it over in his hands, studying it before pulling the lid off.

"Son of a bitch," he exhaled as he stared at its contents. It was tightly packed with US dollars, all neatly banded together. Not since he ran liquor during prohibition had he held that much cash in his hands—and quite possibly not even then. Quickly he snapped the cover back on the box and put it down with the others.

He looked down at the last of the contents of the bundle he had taken out of the raft. His heart pounded in his chest, and he hardly dared breathe as he looked at the last unopened box. *Dorothy Kay* continued to force her way through the waves, but he hardly noticed either her motion or the noise of the storm outside. His thoughts turned dark. From the bag he had already taken a gun, enough cash to support someone for quite a while, and all the necessary identity papers needed to disappear into America. What was left?

"Oh, shit," he thought to himself.

Gingerly he reached down and began to pry the lid off the box. As it came free, he froze, and when nothing happened, he let his held breath out. His heart pounded even harder. Slowly, he lifted the lid, and peered into the box. He sucked in his breath.

"Oh my god," was all he could say.

CHAPTER 9

IN THAT SAME INSTANT, *DOROTHY KAY* FELL OFF A WAVE and heeled sharply. As he tried to avoid getting knocked off the berth, he dropped both the cover and his light, which went out, plunging the cabin back into darkness. He knew by her motion that he needed to get back to the helm. He groped his way to the companionway door, opened it, climbed out, and took control of his boat.

The night was still black, and for the few minutes it took him to get *Dorothy Kay* back on course, he gave little thought to what he had seen in that last box. Finally, settled back on course once again, he allowed his thoughts to return to the raft and its contents. As her bow rose and fell, he glanced back at the now mostly deflated raft in the back of his boat. A plan began to form in his mind.

To begin with, he now knew that he wouldn't report the incident. The U-boat had crept in near shore and had launched a raft, its occupant intent on harm, but the attack had failed. The proof of that failure was lying in the back of his boat. He rationalized that since the submarine's only success was its escape, only he would know what had really happened this night.

His next move was to return to the cabin, where he repacked the gun, resealed it into the bag, and tied the bag back into the raft. He checked his position and estimated that he was just south of Little Boars Head, near the spot where he had found the raft. He hefted the raft over the side, and in an instant it disappeared into the darkness of the night.

Knowing the waters as he did, he was confident that by morning it would wash ashore. The surf pounding on the rocky coast would finish the job his knife had started. Someone would find it, and then its condition, along with the gun, would tell a story very different from what had really happened. Maybe whoever had been in it would even wash ashore, further confirming the evidence of a failed mission. Most important, he knew that nobody would be the wiser about his role in what had really happened. Instead, the discovery would become part of the lore of the seacoast, a story to be told and retold over countless beers for many years to come.

CHAPTER 10

THE CLOUDS REMAINED IMPENETRABLE and the night inky black as he worked his way back to Rye Harbor. As he drove *Dorothy Kay* toward home, he realized just how tired he was. Remembering that he still had a slice of apple cake, he offered a small thank you and poured the last of the coffee from the thermos. The cake tasted better than any apple cake that she had ever made before, and it was just what he needed. And the coffee, while no longer tongue-burning hot, was still hot enough to take away the chill of the night.

Ever since he had relaunched the raft he knew that he had some additional, difficult decisions to make. First and foremost was whether or not to tell her about what had happened this night. He knew how much she worried about him whenever he went out fishing, and even though she remained silent, he knew how much more these nighttime patrols worried her. He decided that she did not need to know how close to a German U-boat he had come, which meant that he could not tell her about what he had recovered from the raft. No one could know.

By the time he reached the point where he would begin the final approach to Rye Harbor, he had decided that he would leave the cash on the *Dorothy Kay,* taking from it only occasionally and in small amounts so as not to raise suspicions. He estimated that it would last for many years, providing just enough to make his life and hers a little easier. That only left one problem remaining—the gold. That last box was filled with small, gold bars, illegal to have, and more valuable than cash. What he needed was a way to hide them, and for that he had no solution this night.

As when he had started his night's mission, the tide was halfway between low and high, only now it was dropping. He glanced up at the sky, hoping to find some small break in the clouds that would allow for just enough light to make negotiating the entrance a little more certain. There was none.

"Well, old girl, let's hope we didn't use up all our luck tonight," he said to *Dorothy Kay*.

Only his years of experience and knowledge of the local waters kept him off the rocks. As slow as time had seemed to move while he fought the helm to keep his boat on course, that all changed as they passed into the harbor. Expertly he nosed his boat up to her mooring and carefully secured her. As soon as she was secure and he shut the engine off, a wave of fatigue washed over him. All he wanted to do was sleep, but that would have to wait. He had things to hide and a long row to shore before he would be able to sleep.

CHAPTER 11

MAX WALKED OVER TO BEN'S FOR HER SHIFT two days after the Labor Day weekend. The haziness of heat and humidity that had so dominated the weather throughout August had disappeared overnight. The atmosphere was scrubbed clean, revealing a perfectly blue, cloudless sky, and a sun so bright its light made the ocean sparkle and dance.

As she walked into the bar, she was met by a strong, cold breeze because the doors to the deck were open. She shivered. It had felt warmer out in the sun. Rubbing her hands over her bare arms, she regretted that she hadn't brought a sweatshirt with her. She walked over to shut the doors.

As she approached the deck, she could see Courtney, the restaurant's owner, standing out by the railing, holding a cup of coffee in front of her mouth with both hands, staring out over the harbor.

"Morning, Court," she called out.

Courtney turned her head. "Good morning, Max."

"Beautiful morning," said Max as she walked out toward Courtney. "You're in early."

"Yeah. There's a lot to do in the bar."

"You got a minute?" asked Courtney.

"Uh, sure. Let me get a cup of coffee first."

A couple of minutes later Max joined Courtney out by the railing. "So, what's up?"

Without turning her head, Courtney said, "Well, we made it through another summer."

Max waited for more words, but they didn't come. After an awkward silence, she responded, "Ye-es . . . we did."

"How're you holding up after that stuff out on the Isles?"

"*What an odd question*," thought Max as she looked out over the harbor toward the Isles of Shoals and took a deep breath, remembering how Sylvie had once again impacted their lives. "Fine. Why do you ask?"

"No reason."

"Come on, Court. What's going on?"

"Nothing."

Then, suddenly the boss's voice changed, and she turned and looked at Max, a smile on her face. "Isn't it a glorious day? I was really getting sick and tired of that heat and humidity. Hey, we're going to be busy today. We better get our asses in gear."

And with that she spun around and walked back into the bar, leaving Max even more perplexed.

* * *

By the time Ben's had officially opened, the temperature had risen to near-summertime levels, only without the humidity. The crystal clear sky made the sun seem even brighter, and the breeze off the water remained fresh and pure, tempering the sun's heat. More than half the tables were already full, as was the bar.

With two lunches in hand, Max had just stepped out onto the deck when she thought she heard Jack's voice. She turned her head and looked back, but because of the bright sun outside, the inside of the bar was lost in the shadows. It would be a minute before she would know for sure.

After delivering the two lunches, she returned to the bar. It seemed even darker now—just shapes and shadows. It wasn't until she was nearly at the bar that she was finally able to see clearly. Jack was sitting in the corner seat, turned so he was facing the door to the deck.

"Hey, babe."

She smiled and paused to give him a quick hello kiss. Then she asked, "What're you doing here? I thought you'd be going out on the boat or something."

"I was, but I saw all the cars so I thought I'd stop first to see if you needed any help."

"That's so sweet."

Before she could say anything her register started chattering, and she turned from Jack and tore off the slip. She quickly and efficiently made those drinks, then tore off another slip that came in.

Out of the corner of her eye, she saw the boys come into the bar. That was how everyone referred to Leo, Ralph, and Paulie.

"Hey, Jack." Leo spoke first.

"Guys." He acknowledged them.

"Hi, Max," said Ralph. "Could we get a round?" Her shoulders tightened. She had never found them as charming as everyone else seemed to, still, they were paying customers. She reached into one of the coolers, pulled out three beers, opened them, and with a slightly forced smile, placed one in front of each.

"So, what kind of trouble are you three into today?"

"What makes you think that?" said Paulie. As she watched, he feigned hurt feelings while his two friends lifted their bottles to drink.

"Oh, I don't know," she replied. She allowed a bit of sarcasm to creep into her voice. Then she rolled her eyes.

He just looked at her, smiled, and took his first sip of beer.

Before any conversation could get rolling, her pager went off indicating that she had food up in the kitchen. "Behave yourselves," she said as she left the bar.

CHAPTER 12

"SO, HAVEN'T SEEN YOU THREE IN A WHILE," Jack said. "What've you been up to?"

He saw Leo start to open his mouth, but a slight nudge from Ralph stopped him. Then Leo answered—a bit too quickly, Jack thought.

"Not much, really. Some fishing, odd jobs down by the harbor."

While the boys sipped their beers, Jack helped Max as much as he could, clearing tables, getting food from the kitchen, and talking with the boys so she wouldn't have to. He knew how much they annoyed her. After only three rounds of beers, Leo, Ralph, and Paulie said their good-byes and shuffled out of the bar.

Jack was sitting at the bar sipping an iced tea when Max finally had a minute.

"Boys gone?" she asked.

"Finally."

"Thanks for your help."

"No problem."

"So, what were they up to?"

"Not sure. Got a sense that something's going on, but with them, you can never be totally sure whether it's for real or imagined."

Max looked at him.

He continued, "Funny thing was, it was obvious they didn't want to tell me anything directly, but they talked amongst themselves loud enough to be heard by everyone."

"What were they talking about?"

"As best I could tell, there was some guy hanging around the harbor, asking questions about Ben's. Mostly about what it was like here during World War II. But two things struck me from what they were saying. One, it didn't sound like he was really interested in history but more like he was looking for something and two, he asked them not to mention any of this. They also talked quite a bit about his voice."

"Looking for something? From World War II? That's bizarre. Why wouldn't he stop by the historical society? Why just randomly stop at the harbor? And, why would anyone ask those three about anything, especially if it were to be kept quiet?"

"I know. Makes no sense. Maybe they were the only ones around."

"I suppose."

"What was that about his voice?"

"They were arguing whether it was growly or raspy. Go figure. Either way, they did agree that he was someone they would not want to cross."

"Interesting," then she pointed at the glass in front of him. "Iced tea?"

"I was thirsty."

"You want a beer?"

"Sure. Doesn't look like you need my help now, so what the hell."

When Max returned with Jack's beer, he had a grin on his face.

"What?" she asked as she put the beer down in front of him.

"Nothing."

"Jack, don't *nothing* me. You have this stupid grin on your face. What's up? Do I have something on the back of my shorts?"

He started to laugh as she twisted around, brushing at her rear. "No. I was just thinking about what someone would think when it's those three they talk to."

She stopped, then chuckled. "Ooo, I see what you mean." Then with a *chikka, chikka, kchuk*, her register spit out an order.

"I'm sure that it was nothing," she said as she turned from Jack, tore off the slip, and began making the drinks. "You know how people always stop in here asking random questions. That's probably all it was. Happens all the time here. Guy comes in, you talk with him, you act interested in what he's talking about, answer a few questions, and then all of a sudden, he thinks he's a regular. Maybe for his one- or two-week vacation, he is, but then vacation's over and he's gone and forgotten. It's a cycle. No big deal."

"True, but there was something about the way they described him and his questions—it just seemed different."

"Well, no one's been in here asking about the place. At least, no one I can remember."

"Thanks for the beer. You're off at five, right?"

"I am. Why?"

"I thought we might go out for a bite to eat."

"Where?"

He shrugged and slid off his bar stool. "I've got to get going. You okay here?"

"I'm fine. See you later."

Jack walked out of Ben's still thinking about what the boys had told him—or maybe more accurately, what they hadn't told him.

CHAPTER 13

JACK SPENT THE REST OF THE AFTERNOON OUT ON *D'RIDDEM*. There wasn't anything specific that needed his attention, but he found enough little things to keep himself busy. It wasn't until he heard the throaty sound of one of the whale watch boats returning and *d'Riddem's* reaction to its wake as it went by that he realized just how long he had been out there.

"She's gonna' be pissed," he thought as he rowed back in.

The sun was getting lower in the sky, not quite sunset, but close. Jack glanced at his watch one last time as he hurried up the front steps at Ben's. The bells hanging on the door clingled as he pulled the door open. A man who must have been reaching for the door just as Jack pulled it open stumbled forward and nearly fell into Jack.

"Sorry," said Jack as he moved to the side.

"No harm done. Have a nice night," he said with a deep, raspy voice as he hurried past.

Jack, struck by the abruptness of the man's departure, stood and watched him as he walked away.

Heading for the bar, he hoped that Max wouldn't be too angry with him for being so late. As he rounded the corner into the bar, he saw that Courtney was sitting next to Max, and that they were having what appeared to be a serious conversation. Two glasses of red wine, each half empty, were on the bar in front of them. He paused a moment and took a deep breath before walking toward them.

"Max, I'm so sorry," said Jack as he stopped next to them.

Both Courtney and Max looked up at him without saying a word.

"Hi, Jack," said Courtney. Max just gave him a stony look.

"Hi, Court."

Then, focusing on Max, he said again, "I'm sorry I'm late."

"Hadn't really noticed. We're having such a nice time."

Her tone was cold, almost dismissive, and he wondered just how much trouble he was in.

"May I join you?"

"Of course," Max said in that same tone. Then she turned back toward Courtney.

Jack signaled the bartender for a beer.

Obviously he was not to be a part of their conversation so he decided to sit quietly, sip his beer, and eavesdrop as best he could.

"So Court, what did he want?" asked Max.

"He said that he was doing some research on the history of Rye Harbor for a book he was intending to write, and he had some questions about Ben."

"Ben?"

"Yeah. He was my uncle, after all," she said.

"I suppose. So what did he ask?"

"It was kind of strange. Actually, he didn't ask much about Ben specifically. His questions were mostly about what it was like here during World War II and if I had any stuff from back then"

"World War II?"

"Yeah. I wasn't even born then. I mean, I'm not even sure that I know anyone around here who was alive then."

"Why didn't he just go to the historical society or the library?"

"I asked him that. He said that he had, but all he could find were a few documents—pretty limited, according to him and they gave him my name."

"What did you tell him?"

"Not much, really. But it was funny, what struck me wasn't so much what he asked as it was the way he asked it."

As Jack continued to watch, Max looked at Courtney, her eyes full of questions.

"It just seemed a bit odd."

"Odd?"

"I can't explain it."

Jack had to interrupt. "Court, I'm sorry, but did you just say that some guy had called you looking for information about Ben?"

She nodded.

Turning, he looked at Max. "Do you suppose it could be the same guy the boys told us about who was asking the same kind of questions over at the harbor?"

"What guy?" Max said.

"Remember, I told you earlier today. The guy that the boys were talking about, but it seemed like they didn't want to tell me."

She looked perplexed. "No. I guess I wasn't really listening."

He turned back to Courtney. "So he was looking for old stuff from back then?"

"Apparently."

He sat and stared into space for a moment.

"What kind of stuff?"

"I don't know." Then Courtney added, "What are you thinking, Jack?"

"How about the boat models you have on display here. Didn't you tell me that Ben made most of them?"

"I suppose they would count," said Court.

"I bet there's other stuff too."

"What are you talking about?"

"Remember when I first arrived here?"

"What's that have to do with anything?"

"You said I could live in the barn if I did the work to turn the upstairsinto an apartment."

She nodded. "What's your point?"

"I kind of remember finding some old boxes filled with papers and stuff in the barn. I asked you what to do with them, and you said to toss 'em."

"Sorry, I don't remember."

"Well, I sorta' do, and I'm pretty sure I didn't."

"You saved that stuff?"

"Pretty sure."

"So where is it?"

"Well, that part's unclear. But I must have put them someplace."

Courtney looked at Jack. "I really don't remember any of that."

"How about if I keep an eye out for them anyway?"

"Sure. Whatever. I wouldn't waste a lot of time on it, though. Chances are I won't hear from him again."

She reached for a sweater and stood up. "Listen, I've got to get going. You two behave yourselves. Max, I'll see you tomorrow."

Before walking out she turned and with a smile said, "Maybe he'll put our names in the book."

CHAPTER 14

AFTER COURTNEY LEFT, THEY SAT IN SILENCE for a few minutes. Then Max said, "Jack, what if it's the same guy?"

"What guy?"

"The one that the boys told you about."

"So what if it is?" He looked at her and could tell that she was thinking way too hard about this stranger.

"Just suppose."

"Max, I see the look on your face. Please tell me you're not going into conspiracy theory mode."

"No!" She gave him a slap on the arm.

"Good."

Then she asked, "What do you want to do about supper?"

He said, "Your choice. I already know what I want to do after."

She smiled and slapped his arm again.

* * *

Jack slid out from under the covers, careful to not disturb Max, but as his bare feet hit the floor, he sucked his breath in. The floor was cold, and a chilly gust of air blew in through the open window. He shivered. Goose bumps covered his arms, raising the hairs. Rubbing his arms, he glanced down at Max. She was still asleep. The covers were pulled up under her chin, and she looked so warm and inviting that he nearly reconsidered his decision to get up.

* * *

Cat was curled up on her favorite blanket in a corner of the couch. It wasn't until Jack started the microwave to heat his cup of coffee that she stirred. Without lifting her head, she opened one eye just long enough to see which of her two humans had dared to disturb her slumber. Curiosity satisfied, she closed her eye, took a deep breath, and went back to sleep.

Jack, coffee in hand, moved past the couch, careful not to disturb her, and stood in front of the window looking out over the harbor. He could see that the breeze was out of the west. And from the way the boats strained at their moorings, it was quite fresh. Out toward the Isles of Shoals, whitecaps were providing a sharp contrast to the deep steel blue of the ocean. The atmosphere was so clear that even at six miles away, he swore he could see individual windows on the island's hotel. The sky was such an unblemished shade of blue that even the few white, puffy clouds seemed an insult to its purity. He couldn't not go for a run.

After changing quickly and quietly so as not to disturb either Max or Cat, he hurried down the stairs. As he stepped outside, the brightness of the sun forced him to shade his eyes with his hand. For a moment, he was shielded from the wind, and with the warmth of the sun he began to question if he might be overdressed.

He took a moment for his eyes to adjust to the bright sun, and then he stretched his arms straight up, reaching as high as he could and inhaling deeply. Exhaling, he lowered his arms and reached for the ground. Then, standing, he shook out his legs and walked to his truck for his sunglasses before slowly beginning to lope down the drive.

By the time he reached the end of the drive, and had turned toward Ben's, the west wind hit him full-on, easily penetrating his clothes like an icy needle. He shivered, but knew that once he warmed up, it wouldn't feel so cold.

CHAPTER 15

THE WIND NEVER LET UP, and as it pushed him toward the ocean, his stride became effortless. The sun, while still several hours from its zenith, was no longer directly in his eyes, and when he finally saw the ocean for the first time after miles of anticipation, he smiled. He loved that moment. It lasted no more than a stride or two, but in that instant his head was filled with dozens of memories. Each one was separate from the others, yet somehow they all muddled together into a single feeling that spoke to his connection with the sea, with Max, with life.

As the sun's light shimmered and danced off the surface of the water, it mirrored those memories. Each flash of light, each glint, twinkle, and sparkle, were all so brief as to defy study, and yet combined together they created a complete image that could be understood.

When he turned south onto the boulevard, his view of the ocean was blocked, but it was replaced by the ever-present sound of the ocean crashing against the berm of rock and stone that had been built in a mostly successful attempt to protect the road from the sea. With a mile to go, his thoughts began to wander, and he thought about those boxes that Courtney didn't remember and why all of a sudden several people had expressed interest in Ben and his history in Rye Harbor.

By the time he made the final turn off the boulevard, he was completely in the moment of the run. All he felt was his heart pounding in his chest, his feet striking the pavement, and the sound of his breath. It wasn't until he crossed the bridge before Ben's that he began to reduce his pace. Reaching the entrance to the parking lot, he slowed to a walk and, without thinking, turned in and walked toward the harbor, hands on his hips, his breath slowly returning to normal. When he came to a stop at the edge of the harbor, his breathing had slowed and his heart was no longer pounding in his chest, but he was still sweating heavily.

Even as the temperature had risen with the sun's rise in the sky, the westerly wind was still winning the battle, and he shivered. A quick look out over the harbor satisfied him that *d'Riddem* was riding nicely, so he turned and headed home.

* * *

As Jack walked past Courtney's cottage, he saw Cat in the garden beneath Courtney's kitchen window. She was in full-on hunting mode, all scrunched down, belly on the ground, her haunches twitching, ready to pounce on some poor unsuspecting creature.

"*Good. Max must be up,*" he thought.

As earlier, when he had first left his apartment, the wind, here partially blocked, was but a whisper, and with the sun higher in the sky, it was warm and pleasant. He stopped to stretch before going in, enjoying the moment. As he had before starting his run, he stretched his back and legs by alternately reaching up as high as he could, breathing deeply and holding that position, before slowly bending down until his fingertips touched the ground.

"Hey, Jack." He heard Courtney's voice coming from behind him. "Cute."

He had been in the downward part of the stretch, and his back was toward her cottage. He straightened up quickly and turned toward her voice, his face red.

"You're blushing," she continued to tease.

"Am not. It's from bending over."

She grinned. "Sure it is."

Before he could defend himself further, she said, "Listen. When I got home last night, I had a message on my machine from that guy I told you about."

"What guy?"

"The one looking for information about Ben. Remember, I told you yesterday."

"Oh, yeah. The World War II guy. What about him?"

"Well, I don't know, but there's something in the way he asks, or maybe it's just his voice, and I'm kind of weirded out. Did you have a chance to look for those boxes?"

"Not yet. Why?"

"Before I talk to him, I'd like to know if I have anything to share."

"Sure. Anything else?"

"When can you do it?"

"Next day or so. I've got some time between projects."

She paused for a split second, as if she had more to say but decided not to.

She said, "Thank you. Say 'Hi' to Max for me. See you later."

Then she turned and walked away before he could respond.

"Mrowh!" Cat rubbed against his leg.

He bent down and scratched her head and ears. "No luck?"

"Mrowh!"

"You gonna' come in?"

"Mrowh!" Then she sauntered back toward her hunting grounds.

"I guess not." He opened the door and went in.

CHAPTER 16

"HAVE A NICE RUN?"

Max was standing by the window, cradling a cup of tea in her hands. "What did Courtney want?"

"The run was great, but the wind was really strong from the west. Tough going out: a bit chilly. Great returning though. She told me she got another call from that guy looking for information."

"She did?"

"Yeah, last night on her machine. She asked me to find those boxes I think I saved."

Max just looked at him. He could tell she had more questions, but all he wanted now was a shower and some food. So when she didn't say anything else right away, he turned and headed for the bathroom.

"I need to get cleaned up."

* * *

Cat was waiting for him when he came back to the kitchen after his shower.

"Mrowh," she said, sitting by her dish.

"Gave up on hunting for your breakfast?"

"Mrowh."

"And you want me to feed you?"

"Mrowh."

He was about to get the cat food out when he saw the note from Max.

Don't take any bullshit from Cat. I fed her.
Working today, went to Ben's early.
I want to talk to Court.
Xoxoxo

Jack looked down at Cat.

She looked up at him, blinked once, and uttered a very soft, "Rowh."

"Max left me a note and told me you've already been fed, so give it up."

Cat stretched, looked up at him one more time, and then walked off, obviously disappointed that her act had failed.

CHAPTER 17

OTHER THAN THE COOKS AND THE CLEANING CREW, Max didn't see anyone else when she walked into the bar. She was early for her shift, so she
headed to the back room. She bent over to look through the backup
liquor supply, and, as she checked the shelves, she made a list of what
she would need to bring down from the storeroom.

"Max, what are you doing in so early?"

Max jumped. "Oh my God, Court. You scared the shit out of me."

"Sorry."

Trying to keep a straight face, Max replied, "I came in early because
I'm such a wonderful employee and I just couldn't stay away."

"You are so full of shit."

Max could tell that Courtney was trying hard not to smile, but she
failed.

"You're right. I'm a bitch, and I don't want to be here."

"C'mon, Max. You know it's okay if you think you need to come
in early. But honestly, there really isn't all that much extra to do today.
I checked."

"Fine. Jack told me that that guy called you again. Do you know
who he is?"

"Not a clue. I've only talked to him on the phone."

"So are you gonna' call him back?"

"Maybe later."

"Court, I know you. Don't even think you can keep anything from
me, especially if he turns out to be tall, dark, and handsome."

"Okay, we've wasted enough time. I have stuff to finish upstairs,
and you have to get set up. It's going to be busy today. I have a feeling."

With that, she turned and almost ran up the stairs, leaving Max
standing there, still wondering about the mystery man.

CHAPTER 18

AS COURTNEY HAD PREDICTED, BEN'S WAS BUSY.

"Excuse me." It was the man who had been sitting at the end of the bar for the better part of lunch.

Max looked over at him. He was not your average tourist. First of all, he had the most intense blue eyes. He was well-tanned, clean-shaven, obviously fit, and his not-quite-blonde hair was disheveled just enough to give him a devil-may-care look. In that instant, she felt embarrassed, realizing just how little attention she had paid to him.

"Oh, I'm so sorry."

"That's okay. I've had a nice relaxing time sitting here watching you work so hard." His voice would melt butter. It was warm, resonant, and impossible to ignore.

She removed the dirty dishes that were in front of him. His wine glass was empty, so she asked if he wanted another.

"That would be nice."

As she placed the new glass in front of him, he looked directly at her. "Thank you."

"You're welcome," she replied. Then she realized that he was still looking at her. In itself, that wasn't unusual, but there was something about the way he was looking at her, an intensity, that she found unsettling. Max glanced over toward the bar's entrance, hoping that a new customer would come in so she could escape his eyes. There was no one.

"This place been here long?"

She turned her head back toward him at the sound of his voice. He was still looking directly at her, and her discomfort increased.

"It has." Her eyes darted toward the entrance again.

"It's nice. Has a good feel," and then he added, "I like that boat model," motioning toward the sailboat on a shelf next to the bar.

"Oh, that's the *Jessica*. She was a local fishing schooner way back."

"Who's Ben?" It was an innocent enough question, and she had been asked it many times before, but this time it didn't feel like just curiosity.

Feeling trapped under his gaze, she gave him the short answer.

"Ben Crouse. He was a lobsterman. Started this place. It kind of just grew over time. From what I've heard, he was quite the salty character."

"How so?" Now his tone seemed more curious than interrogatory.

"Oh, I don't know. I've only heard stories."

"Such as?"

"Well, back during prohibition, a lot of liquor was rumored to have been smuggled in through Rye Harbor."

"Really? He was involved?"

"Don't know for sure, but if I were to guess, I'd say yes. But no one will really talk about it. Not even today."

He stopped staring and sipped his wine. Then he said, "Interesting. He still around?"

His voice had softened and she began to feel less wary.

"Oh, no. He died long before I came to work here, and even the new owner, his niece, hardly knew him. She was away at college when he died and left the place to her."

"His niece? Maybe I could talk to her."

Max's guard went back up. "She's not here today."

He must have noticed her resistance, because he changed the subject and again softened his tone.

"I travel a lot, and I enjoy learning stories about local areas that aren't in all the tourist publications."

Max's uneasiness began to wane again, and she was curious. "Like what?"

He hesitated and took a sip of wine. "Let me think. Like, did you know that during World War II there was quite a bit of German submarine activity in this area?"

"Really?"

"Of course. And it only makes sense. There's a major navy base right next door in Portsmouth."

"I suppose. So how do you know all this?"

He set the wine glass down.

"When I'm in interested in a place, I make it my business to find out."

CHAPTER 19

THE MAN AT THE BAR HAD BEEN GONE TWENTY MINUTES when Courtney walked in.

"Lunch busy?"

"It was. What have you been up to? I half expected you to be down here helping."

"Sorry. I had a lot of office work that had to be dealt with, and then I began digging around to see if I could find any old stuff from the early days of Ben's."

That caught Max's attention. "Why? Because of that guy who called you?"

"Maybe . . . I'm not sure."

"But he got you curious."

"I suppose. I got to thinking and I realized I don't know much about what went on here during Ben's time."

"So, did you find anything?"

"A whole closet full. I pulled a couple of boxes out, but they mostly looked like old business records, nothing too exciting."

"You know Court, today at lunch a guy was here asking about Ben. He told me some interesting things about this area." Then, in a more serious voice added, "What if he was the guy who called you?"

Court froze and gave Max a look that was a mix of curiosity and wariness. As well, her answer seemed just a bit too sharp. "What do you mean?"

Court's reaction caught Max off guard. She looked at her friend, paused, then said, "Take it easy, I'm sure he was just some tourist. I'm sure he would have told me if he had already called you. I didn't mean anything."

"I'm sorry. Tell me what took place."

"Well, it was busy, and I kind of ignored this guy who was sitting at the bar through most of lunch. I mean, I did get him food, but after that I really didn't pay much attention to him. As things quieted down, I apologized, and he asked me who Ben was."

"What did you tell him?"

"Not much. Salty character, lobsterman, started this place, died long before I got here, left the place to you. The usual."

Before Max could resume her story, Courtney cut her off.

"You didn't tell him my name did you?"

Max stared at her friend, startled by her reaction.

"Relax, Court. I didn't, but I'm sure he could find it out if he wanted."

"What else did he ask?"

"I thought it was a bit strange, but he seemed particularly interested in what went on around here during World War II."

"What?"

"Yeah. He told me that he traveled a lot and when he got to a new area, he liked to find out things that weren't usually in the regular tourist information. He mentioned smuggling during prohibition and U-boat activity off the east coast, particularly around here."

"What was he like?"

Max smiled. "Well, he had the most intense blue eyes. He was well-tanned, clean-shaven, obviously fit, light-brown hair." Then, with a sly grin, she added, "I'd say just about right for you."

Court did not take the bait. "But what was he like?"

"What do you mean?"

"What was he like?"

Max thought a minute before answering.

"Intense."

"Intense?"

"I don't know how else to describe it. At first he seemed like every tourist who comes in here, but there was something about the way he looked at me when he talked. I mean, he was nice enough, polite, but there were moments when I felt like I was being interrogated."

"In what way?"

Max thought a moment before answering.

"Well, his voice was warm and disarming, but there seemed to be an edge to the way he asked questions. Kind of like he already knew the answer and was testing me."

"Did he say his name?"

"You interested?"

"No!"

"He didn't. Sorry, Court." Then, before Courtney could say anything else, Max added, "You're wondering if he's the man who keeps calling you, aren't you."

"Am not."

CHAPTER 20

"JACK, I'M TELLING YOU, I'm sure he was in the bar today, and when I told Courtney she got all weird."

Jack had showed up at the bar at five, just as her shift ended, with a cooler and an invitation that they row out to *d'Riddem* to have cocktails and watch the sun set.

"Max, you're letting your imagination run away from you. I'm sure that there's nothing to any of this. He's probably just some schmuck tourist who thought he was connecting with you."

"What are you talking about?" She feigned indignation.

"I know guys hit on you all the time in the bar, and if they aren't actually hitting on you, then in their minds they are."

"Jack Beale, you are such a perv."

"Well, it's true."

"Are you hitting on me?" She smiled over the rim of her wine glass as she looked at Jack.

"You can't tell?"

"Of course I can."

As the final sliver of orange slipped below the horizon, Jack said, "Well, no green flash tonight." He stood, leaned over, and kissed her on her forehead. Then he whispered, "Come down below," and disappeared into the cabin.

Max swallowed her last sip of wine and pulled her sweater close. The west wind that had blown throughout most of the day had died, but it was still chilly. The tide was slack, having paused before reversing, so the harbor's surface was now a mirror and with no wind or current to align the boats, chaos became the rule as each began to drift about, pointing in different directions, some closing and others separating. She could hear faint sounds of laughter from the deck at Ben's. An occasional duck fussed, several seagulls argued over a scrap of fish, and a lone outboard engine propelled its fisherman home. But what struck Max was the calm and peaceful silence of the moment. As the transition from day to night neared completion, she too left the cockpit and disappeared inside.

* * *

"You want to stay here tonight or get back?" Jack whispered. Her naked body felt so warm and right pressed against his that he already knew the answer to the question.

"Here," she whispered and pressed closer.

Soft moans mingled with the sound of the water gurgling against the hull as the tide began its outward flow in earnest and order returned to the harbor. Eventually sleep won out, and sunrise found them still locked in each other's arms.

CHAPTER 21

SHORTLY AFTER THE BREAK OF DAWN, Jack was reminded that the first hours after sunrise are often as noisy as those after sunset are quiet. The calls of seagulls greeting the new day, engines roaring to life, and men calling out to each other echoed across the still harbor. As he rolled over and tried to fall back asleep, he heard the distinct click and whir of the electric winch on the commercial pier that lowered supplies packed in crates and barrels from pier to deck for another long day on the water. The result was a great deal of thumping and scraping, and he found it impossible to fall back asleep.

While the commercial boats were heading out, he heard signs that the next wave of activity was well under way. The professional charter boats began queuing up at the docks to load their supplies and guests, and these were joined by the recreational fisherman who trailered their boats to the harbor and launched them with varied degrees of success, often causing mirth among the locals. Finally, the last to load and leave were the large, so-called "head" boats, packed with tourists eager to spend several hours on the water in the hopes of seeing a whale.

As each passing vessel added its wake to the assault against those boats still moored, *D'Riddem* shimmied and tugged on her mooring. She didn't wallow from side to side in the way single-hulled boats did; her motion was more jerky, and it was that invisible hand that shook Jack more and more awake. Eventually he looked over at Max, who was still sleeping soundly. He slipped out from under the covers and sucked in his breath as his bare feet hit the cold cabin sole. He grabbed his sweatshirt and pants and then, as quietly and quickly as possible, he tiptoed out of the cabin and pulled on his clothes before going up into the main salon.

He needed coffee. Ignoring his cold feet, and blinking because the early morning sun was so bright, he put water on for coffee. Still barefoot, he slid the cabin door open, stepped out into the cockpit, and inhaled deeply. Yesterday's west wind, now gone, had left behind clear, clean air, which now had the barely discernible overtones of salt, seaweed, bait, and diesel. He watched as the *Sea Witch* slid by, her powerful engine seemingly at idle, barely disturbing the water's surface. Art looked toward Jack and acknowledged him in a classic workingman's wave—a nod and a hand barely lifted from the wheel—and Jack responded in much the same way.

The water was boiling and he needed to get some shoes on, so Jack returned inside just as Max emerged from the cabin. She was wearing an old sweatshirt of his that he kept on the boat. As she climbed up the couple of steps into the cabin, he couldn't take his eyes off of her. The sweatshirt, which was way too big for her, was just long enough to maintain a modicum of modesty and yet short enough to tease. She had rolled the sleeves up so her hands were free.

She pointed at his feet. "Aren't they cold?"

"I was just coming in for some shoes."

"My feet are warm. Come here." She held out her arms and stepped into him. As they came together, she wrapped her arms around his waist and pulled him close, burying her face into his chest. He looked down and nuzzled the top of her head and forgot all about his cold feet.

As he held her, it was obvious that all she was wearing was the sweatshirt. His reaction was impossible to hide. Before he could suggest a solution, she leaned back and looked up at him, her hips pressing tighter against him, further increasing his desires and said, "Your water's ready." A bucket of cold water couldn't have been more effective.

* * *

Jack handed Max a cup of instant coffee with powdered creamer, which he actually preferred. Somehow, out on a boat, it always tasted so good.

"I've been thinking," said Max.

"*Uh, oh,*" thought Jack. "About what?"

"I'm beginning to think that Courtney has a new boyfriend that she's keeping secret."

"And why do you think that?"

"Just the way she's been lately. I can't describe it, but whatever it is, I'm sure something is going on."

Jack sipped his coffee and changed the subject.

"Hey look, over at the park," he said, pointing to an older woman with binoculars. "Isn't that Gladys?"

Max shook her head. "She's on an Audubon trip in Key West. I know you're just trying to distract me. Don't you want to talk about Courtney?"

"Not particularly."

"Yes, you do."

"I do?"

"Yes. Remember the other day when she told us about those mysterious calls?"

"What's that got to do with a new 'secret' lover?"

Max waved her hand. "Stop. Just listen."

Jack turned his head slightly and took a sip of his coffee while rolling his eyes.

"Jack!"

"I'm listening."

"For the past few weeks, she has been acting differently. She disappears upstairs into the office for long periods of time. Then, when she reappears, she rushes out. Then, when she returns, she acts as if nothing happened."

"Max. Summer just ended. She probably is way behind in office work. I think your imagination is getting the best of you."

He could tell that she wasn't about to give up.

"No, Jack. I know I'm right. She has a new boyfriend and is keeping it a secret."

"Time will tell," said Jack.

CHAPTER 22

"OKAY. LUNCH IT IS. I'LL SEE YOU THERE." Courtney smiled as she slowly replaced the handset. "Edso," she said softly. She loved the sound of his name. It was exotic and yet seemed so down to earth. She smiled.

They had met only a couple of weeks ago, at "The Pic," of all places. She had been standing in the juice aisle picking up Nellie and Joe's Key Lime Juice, the secret ingredient for their cosmos, which could only be found locally at the chain store now called Hannaford's, but formerly known as Pic N' Pay, or "The Pic." The lime juice was always secreted away on a top shelf, and as she had stretched up to coax out to the front of the shelf the last couple of bottles, she had managed to drop one.

"Damn," she had said under her breath. Then, as she had bent over to pick it up, another one of the bottles that she had already cradled in the crook of her arm had slipped out and landed on the floor.

"Shit," she had hissed as she bent down to pick them up.

"Here. Let me help you." His voice had been warm and soothing, and before she had had time to respond, he had gotten down on one knee to hand her the bottles of lime juice.

"Thank you," she had stammered. Quickly she had glanced over at him, her embarrassment prohibiting a longer look. But that brief look had been enough.

* * *

As Courtney parked her car next to Lexie's Landing at the Great Bay Marina in Newington, she looked at her watch and noted that she was ten minutes early for their date. Lexie's was a summertime offshoot of the original Lexie's in Portsmouth, and just like Max and Jack, she was a big fan.

She put her car keys in her purse, shut the door behind her, and looked out over the marina. It was not quite as grand as the one at the Wentworth, but the boats were still pretty impressive. From her car, the marina had looked full, but as she walked out onto the floats to kill time, she saw that many of the slips were empty.

"Nice day," a cheerful voice called out.

She stopped and looked around. Standing in the bow of a small open boat was an older man. A wide-brimmed hat cast a shadow over his face, but she was still able to see the mischievous quality in his eyes.

"It is."

"Too bad the season is so short. People are already pulling their boats out. You have a boat?"

"Oh no. No, I don't. I'm just meeting someone here for lunch. I'm early so I thought I'd wander around, look at the boats to kill some time."

"They won't be open too much longer. Food's good, though."

"This your boat?"

"Oh no. I'm just cleaning it up for a friend. Mine's down there. *Christine.* The trawler out on the end."

"She's beautiful," said Courtney, craning her neck to get a better look. "Do you keep your boat here all the time?"

"Yep. Been here longer than I can remember. Good spot. Bay's pretty, especially this time of year when the trees start turning."

"I can only imagine."

"If you ever want, I'll take you out to see the foliage from the water."

Before she could answer, a car horn honked in the parking lot. They both turned to see who was honking.

A man was waving in their direction.

"Looks like my lunch date has arrived," said Court. "It was nice talking to you."

"Enjoy your lunch."

"Thank you. What's your name? I'm Courtney."

"Rusty. Nice to meet you."

She smiled, then turned and walked back toward her lunch date.

CHAPTER 23

THIS WAS THEIR SECOND DATE, if you could call a cup of coffee after the Lime Juice incident a date. In her head she could hear Max reminding her of the dangers of getting involved with strangers.

"This is different," she thought in an effort to clear Max's voice out of her head.

"Hello. Who was that you were talking to?"

"Hi. Just a sweet old man. He invited me to go out on his boat with him sometime."

"So I'm late and you were ready to replace me?"

"You weren't late, I was early. And, I'm not ready to replace you . . . yet." She smiled.

"Fair enough. I'm hungry. Let's go eat."

Their shoes crunched on the gravel as they walked from the parking lot to the restaurant, which was a casual space covered by a canopy.

"Go ahead, seat yourselves anywhere you like," said the young waitress. "I'll be right over."

"Thanks," said Edso. He directed Courtney to a table in a corner.

"How's this?" he asked.

"Perfect." She noticed that he had chosen to sit as far from the others as possible, and that was all right with her.

Forty-five minutes later, they were making their way through the last of the fries on their plates.

"Thank you for suggesting this place," he said.

"Isn't it good?"

"It really is."

Throughout lunch, their conversation had remained light. He was a well-practiced listener, guiding her with questions and leaving her to do most of the talking.

"Go for a walk?" he asked after settling the check.

"Sure."

"This way or that?" He motioned first to the floats out in the bay and then back toward the mostly empty boatyard. Courtney had already been out on the floats, so she chose the boat yard. In the back area of the yard, the only boats to be seen were sitting in a sea of weeds, their covers either torn or entirely missing. Many had for sale signs attached.

"So sad, so many dreams lost," she said.

Then they walked down to the water. This time, Rusty was nowhere to be seen.

The afternoon was passing, and the light breeze off the water put a chill in the air.

"Here, you look cold," Edso said. He took off his jacket and placed it over her shoulders.

"But now you'll be cold."

"No. I'm fine." He smiled and took her hand, and then they walked back to their cars in silence.

By the time they had reached their cars, it suddenly seemed warmer, and she slipped his coat off and handed it to him.

"Thank you."

"The pleasure was mine. When may I see you again?"

She shrugged. "Call me."

* * *

After he drove off, Courtney sat in her car for a few moments longer. She was puzzled by how she was feeling. He was polite, easy on the eyes, interesting, a gentleman, but there was something that she didn't understand and couldn't quite put her finger on it. It wasn't until she was nearly back at Ben's that it came to her. She still knew nothing about him besides his name.

"Edso Harding, who are you?" she whispered. Then she parked in front of Ben's and turned off the engine.

CHAPTER 24

COURTNEY PULLED THE DOOR TO HER OFFICE CLOSED, glad to have some time alone in front of her computer so she could begin her search for some answers. She looked at the same sites she used to screen potential employees: first Google, then Facebook, then Linked In. Yet she found nothing. She visited other paid search sites with the same result.

"What are you hiding?" she kept whispering to herself as the hours passed by and her search widened. She knew he existed. She had just spent a delightful afternoon with him. Problem was, it seemed that no one else seemed to know that.

There were two soft knocks on her closed door, accompanied by a muted voice. "Knock, knock."

She glanced quickly at the time in the top corner of her computer screen. "Shit," she murmured. "Come in."

The door opened and Angela, one of the bartenders, stuck her head in. "Hey, Court, we're about to close up. Thought you'd like to know. You need anything?"

"Thanks, Angie. Go ahead and wrap it up. I'm almost finished, and I'll be out of here pretty quickly." Then, before the door clicked shut, she called out, "Hey, Angie, there is one thing."

Angie stuck her head back in and Court said, "Could you ask the kitchen to pack up a lobster roll for me to take home?"

"Sure." She pulled the door closed, and Courtney listened to her footsteps on the stairs as she went back down.

Courtney looked at her laptop's screen one last time. Then she bookmarked a few of the open windows from her search and printed several of the reports before closing everything down. When the screen was blank, she turned it off and sat for another minute, staring at it. All those hours spent searching should have resulted in some answers, but instead, all she had were more questions, and those questions all came down to one simple fact: she still knew next to nothing about him. The more she searched, the less she seemed to find. Questions filled her head, and her emotions alternated between fear and excitement and almost everything in between. "*What are you hiding?*" Those four little words kept reverberating through her head as she prepared to go home.

* * *

"*What is that sound?*" Courtney thought. A bell was ringing and it wouldn't stop. Even though her eyes were closed, she could feel the heat of the sun on her face. Slowly she pried her eyes open, then almost immediately dropped her arm back down over her eyes in an attempt to block the blinding light that assaulted her. The bell continued ringing. Gradually the fog of sleep began lifting, and she understood that the bell was coming from her alarm clock. Taking her arm off her eyes, she was forced to squeeze them closed against the bright sun. She rolled onto her side, and as a blind person might, she reached out for that ringing sound. Her hand brushed the clock off the small bedside table and onto the floor, where by some small miracle it stopped its incessant ringing.

Sitting up too quickly, her head began to spin. As she lay back down, returning her arm to her eyes, she heard a dozen or so sheets of paper slither off the bed onto the floor. It all began to come back to her: the lunch date with Edso, her search for clues about his identity, and her late return home, where she had continued the search. She moved her arm again and assessed the situation. She was still dressed, the remains of a lobster roll were on a paper plate beside her, an empty wine bottle was on the floor next to the bed along with those pieces of paper that had fallen onto the floor.

Then she heard a knock on the door downstairs.

"*Who could that be?*" she wondered. She swung her legs off the bed, bent down to pick up the papers, and grabbed her clock.

"Shit!" It was later than she had thought. That realization prompted her to toss the clock and papers on the bed. She grabbed the paper plate and hurried downstairs.

She heard another knock as she reached the bottom of the stairs.

"Coming, coming," she called out as she reached for the latch.

"Jack! Good morning."

"Sorry to bother you, but . . ."

"Oh, no problem."

"You all right?" he asked. "It looks like you slept in those clothes."

"Yes, fine. I fell asleep pretty late last night, that's all. What brings you by so early?"

Jack frowned. "It's not early. It's nearly lunchtime."

"I'm sorry, that's not what I meant. What's up?"

"I was rummaging through my workshop. I found the boxes I told you about, along with some other things I think you'd like to see."

CHAPTER 25

AN HOUR LATER, WASHED AND DRESSED IN CLEAN CLOTHES, Courtney walked over to Jack's workshop.

"Jack?" she called out.

"Back here." His response was a bit muffled and sounded strained.

"Where?"

A great deal of rustling and scraping seemed to be coming from within the small room off the back corner of the shop. Suddenly she heard a large crash, like the sound of a large pile of wood falling over. It was immediately followed by a string of shouted epithets.

"Jack!" She quickly worked her way through the shop toward the source of the noise.

When she reached a point where she could look inside the doorway, she saw him bent over a pile of boards that were on the floor. "Are you all right?"

He looked up. "Yeah. Give me a minute."

She stepped into the doorway and looked around. It was a small room, obviously an afterthought added to the original building, and shelves lined its walls. Dust-covered cobwebs braced the corners of the shelves, and others dangled from the exposed rafters of the ceiling. A single window opposite the doorway provided the only source of light, and that, at best, was minimal because of the heavy layer of dust and grime that coated the glass.

As her eyes adjusted, she could see that there were open spaces on the shelves, and she guessed that those spaces had been the homes of the many cartons now stacked in the middle of the floor. She watched as Jack worked to pick up the boards and lean them side by side against those boxes. Dust, kicked up by his efforts, swirled about and gave definition to the light, creating a beam that fell directly onto them.

"There," he said as he leaned the last board up against the boxes.

"Well, that was exciting. You sure you're okay?"

"I'm fine."

"So where are the things you want to show me?"

"The boxes are right here," he said, motioning to the pile in the center of the room. "But, even more interesting, I thought, were these boards. Come look."

She moved into the room and looked at the boards. They were dark, almost a honey mahogany color. She could see many nail holes in them, and several had broken edges. *"Old and junky"* came to her mind.

Singularly unimpressed, she looked at him, then back at the boards one last time. "What am I looking at?"

"The writing."

"What?"

"The writing." He waved his arm at the boards.

Before she could answer, he looked at them again and began rearranging them into a different order. When he finished, he asked, "Now, what do you see?"

Courtney looked again, this time tilting her head and moving so as to see through the beam of light.

"I see a bunch of crappy old boards with stuff painted on them."

"Court! Stand over here. They go this way." He motioned with his hands, indicating that she should tilt her head and look at them as if they were horizontal. "Look at these last names. There are still some guys fishing here in the harbor with those names."

She shrugged, still unimpressed.

"Look at the dates! Some are before 1920! Here are some boat names, and these over here are from the 1930's. I bet the guys at the harbor would be interested in seeing this. You have any idea where these boards came from?"

Courtney continued to look at the boards with her head tilted. When she finally straightened up, she said, "Not sure."

"Don't you think it'd be fun to find out? You mind if I ask about?"

She shrugged again. "I don't care."

Then she pointed to the boxes at his feet. "Could you take them and put them inside my cottage? I've got to get over to Ben's."

CHAPTER 26

"HEY, MAX," SAID JACK AS HE WALKED INTO THE BAR A FEW HOURS LATER.

"Jack. What a pleasant surprise."

"Court around?"

"She is. Why?"

"Did she seem okay to you?"

"What do you mean?"

"I don't know exactly, but I think you're right. Something's going on."

"So now you believe me," she said.

"Maybe. Remember those boxes that I told Courtney I thought I remembered saving? The ones with old stuff from Ben."

"Yeah. What about them."

"I found them in the shop this morning, so I stopped by her place, gave her the news and asked her to come over to check out some other stuff I found."

"What other stuff?"

"Some old boards with names and dates painted on them. She acted like she didn't care, but she almost seemed *too* casual about it. Plus, when I first went to find her, she looked like hell."

That got Max's attention, but before she could say anything her register spit out an order.

"Hold on, let me get this."

While she began making the drinks, Jack walked to the back of the bar and looked out over the harbor where Art was expertly maneuvering his boat, the *Sea Witch*, up to the commercial pier. Then he sensed Max's presence behind him. He turned his head back to look just as she slipped her arm around his and pressed up against his side.

"Now, what were you saying about Court?"

"Well, it was almost noon. She looked awful, like she had just woken up after having slept in her clothes. "

"Hungover?"

"Maybe. Anyways, I told her what I found and asked her to stop by and take a look. It was over an hour before she got there and seemed totally disinterested."

"In the boxes?"

"Those too. But what I wanted her to see were the boards. Some of the names on them are the same as some who are still fishing here in the harbor. I'm guessing, relatives. I thought she'd find that interesting, but she could have cared less. I asked her if she knew where they came from and she said no, but I think she probably knows. She asked me to take the boxes and put them in her cottage and then she left. I'm telling you, she was acting strange."

"That explains it."

"Explains what?" Now it was Jack's turn to look puzzled.

"When she came in, she was totally somewhere else. I didn't pay much attention, I was busy, but thinking back, she hardly said Hi and went right up to her office. Haven't seen her since. Good thing things are quiet here."

"What do you suppose is going on?"

"Well, you know I suspect a new boyfriend. Rumor has it that yesterday she had a mysterious lunch date. Everyone was talking this morning, but Courtney didn't say a word."

The register came to life again, and she released his arm, gave him a quick kiss on the cheek, and said, "Gotta' go."

Jack remained standing there, looking out over the harbor for a few more minutes before returning to the bar. "How long 'till your shift is over?"

"Maybe another hour, hour and a half. Why?"

"I think I'll walk over to the harbor and talk to Art."

"Want me to wait here for you?"

"Don't have to. I'll see you at home. Think about what you want for food tonight."

With that, he turned and slipped out the back door.

CHAPTER 27

"HEY, ART," JACK CALLED DOWN TO HIS FRIEND, who was giving his boat a quick wash.

"Jack, what's up?"

"You got a minute?"

"Come on down."

By the time Jack reached the *Sea Witch*, Art had finished rinsing her off and was coiling up the hose.

"So, what's up? You in some kind of trouble?" Art asked, but his smile told Jack he was kidding.

"Nah, not this time."

"Beer?"

"Sure."

Art turned and leaned through the doorway into the small forward cabin. Jack could hear a cooler creak open and the sound of ice being pushed about as his friend rummaged about for their beers. Then Art returned with two cans.

"Here you go."

"Thanks." Jack took one of the cans. It was wet and cold, and he wiped it against his pant leg in an attempt to dry it off before opening it.

Ka-psht. Art pulled the tab on his can. Beer began to foam out, so he quickly lifted it to his lips, sucking in the froth. Jack pulled on the tab on his beer, and he too had to quickly inhale escaping froth. Finally, with beers under control, they nodded toward each other, lifted their cans to their lips, and took a long sip.

Art lowered his beer first. "Okay, Jack. What's up?"

"Couple of things. You know anything about some guy who's been down here asking about Ben's and what things were like here way back?"

Art took another sip of his beer and gave Jack a puzzled look.

"What do you mean *way back*?"

"Forties, World War II. Back then."

Art took another sip of his beer, obviously thinking about what Jack had just asked. "About all I know is that's about when the breakwaters were built. Why?"

"Leo, Ralph, and Paulie were in the bar not too long ago talking about some guy who had been hanging around down here asking questions about what it was like here back then."

"Not that I noticed, but it's still silly season, and there's always someone new down here asking stupid questions. I don't pay much attention."

"Here's where it gets a bit weird. Turns out Court had been getting phone calls about much the same things. Never says who he is. And ever since then she's been acting a bit squirrelly."

"You think it's the same guy?"

"Don't know, but it wouldn't surprise me. After the calls started, she began to look around and I know she found a closet full of old stuff upstairs at Ben's."

"Anything interesting?"

"From what I understand, looks like mostly business records. I found some boxes in the shop as well, but even better, I found a bunch of old boards with some names and dates painted on them. I'm guessing they were relatives of guys from around here, some of whom are still fishing."

"No shit."

"Yeah, the dates were all in the twenties, thirties, and forties. Plus there were some other numbers and names I didn't understand. Want to come take a look? Maybe it will mean something to you."

"Of course. You around tomorrow? I've got some things to take care of today."

"That works. Just give me a call. I should be around all day."

CHAPTER 28

"BYE, MAX."

Max turned from the bar just as Courtney's hand touched the doorknob. She hadn't heard her boss come down the stairs.

"Court. Wait. Come here a minute!"

"No, I've got to get going."

Max thought she sounded distracted, almost sad, and she had no intention of letting her friend escape.

"Where? What's so important? Bank's already closed. And I know there's nothing we need."

Courtney stopped, took her hand off the knob, and faced Max. She looked tired. Not the tired people get from hard physical effort, like putting in an hour at the gym, but more bone weary, like the weight of the world was just crushing her soul.

"What's the matter?" Max softened her voice.

Court remained silent.

"Come on, come sit with me. My shift's nearly over. We'll have a glass of wine and talk."

To Max's relief, Courtney gave an imperceptible sigh and surrendered. She followed Max out through the bar, took a seat, and waited while Max prepared for the shift change.

* * *

Max walked back to the table with two more glasses of wine in her hands. When her replacement had arrived, she and Court had moved to a more private, corner table, away from the bustle of the bar itself, and it had taken their first glasses of wine to get the conversation started.

"Here we go," said Max. She placed the glasses on the table and then sat back down.

"I'm sorry, Max."

Max looked at her and took a sip, giving Courtney time to compose her thoughts.

"Remember, I told you that I've been getting those calls asking about Ben and the harbor and what it was like here during World War II?"

"I do."

"Obviously, I don't know anything about what went on then. I mean, I wasn't even born then."

Max nodded.

"He keeps calling. At first I didn't give it much thought. I get so many random calls with stupid questions that I never give them much thought. I mean, Ben's has been here for so long, I think that people just expect me to know everything. But, I don't."

"You told him this, I assume."

"Of course. I thought after the first call that would be it. He was pleasant, thanked me, and that was that, or so I thought. Since then, he has called back several more times."

"He has?"

"Yeah. Same basic questions. He's still polite, but each time it feels like he's a little more insistent, but it's obvious that he thinks I know something." She paused and took a sip of her wine. "But I don't."

"What's his name?"

"I don't know. I've asked, but before I can press for an answer, he hangs up."

"So, you have no idea."

"None. And now I'm even wondering if these calls might be coming from the guy who the boys said was asking around over at the harbor."

"Leo, Ralph, and Paulie?"

She nodded.

"Court, you know those three. Almost anything that comes from their mouths is probably bullshit."

"I know. But still, I can't help but wonder."

"Okay, let's leave this alone. What else is going on? Who's this new man you're slinking about seeing?"

Max saw Courtney's eyes brighten for a split second. Then her answer was muffled as she took another sip of her wine.

"I'm sorry. I couldn't hear what you said," said Max. She smiled as she tried to goad her friend into an answer.

"He's nice. And I'm not 'seeing' him," she said, adding air quotes as she said the word *seeing*.

"So, how many times have you not 'seen' him?" Max added her own air quotes.

"Actually, just once for lunch. We met at Lexie's Landing out on Great Bay. It was nice."

"How'd you meet him? What's his name?"

"We met at the grocery store when I was picking up lime juice. I dropped some and he helped me out."

"And it just seemed like a good idea to go out to lunch after?"

"It wasn't like that," Courtney protested.

"His name?"

"It doesn't matter."

"It does."

"Why's this so important to you? All I did was have lunch with a guy. End of story."

"It's important . . . because, well . . ." Max struggled to come up with an answer. After a moment she blurted out, "It's important because what if he's some kind of a psycho and he kidnaps you—or worse. If I know his name, it'll be better when I talk to the police."

Courtney stared at Max. "You're insane. You do know that, don't you?"

"I may be insane, but you know it's happened." She flushed. "Come on, Court."

"Fine. His name is Edso Harding."

"That's an interesting name. So where's he from? What's he do?"

"I don't know."

Max looked at her friend with an open mouth before saying, "You don't know." Her giddy curiosity was shifting to concern.

"I don't know," Courtney repeated.

Max started at her.

"He was nice. We had a good time. Hey, it was just lunch and a walk. Still, something seemed a little offbeat. Then later I realized he never really said anything about himself. Heck, he could be married with twelve children for all I know. So when I got home, I went online to check him out. But I didn't find anything at all."

"Nothing?"

"Nothing. He doesn't seem to exist."

CHAPTER 29

MAX OPENED HER EYES. The blackness of the night was tempered by the faint light of the night sky, which created a kaleidoscope of deep blue and purple shadows that filled the room. She was lying on her back, Jack next to her, his breathing deep and steady. Sleep had come fast and easy for both of them at first. It always did after sex, but now, several hours later, Max was awake.

Through the skylight above the bed, she could see the stars, and memories began to surface of nights spent in Belize on *d'Riddem*. It seemed a lifetime ago, but now those memories were as clear as if they had happened yesterday. She had first gone to Belize with a man named Daniel. He was handsome, attentive, mysterious—a living fantasy—and she had been swept up into his world. *D'Riddem* had been his boat, a catamaran, and she remembered her first night on the trampoline, looking up at all the stars and marveling at how many more there seemed to be compared to the night sky at home. She remembered how the trampoline had creaked and bounced when Daniel had stepped onto it and joined her. The tropical night had been cooler than she had expected, and she remembered how the heat from the day had seemed to radiate from their bodies.

She shivered and pulled the blanket close. She tried to force those images from her head, but they refused to budge.

Jack had come for her just as Daniel had disappeared. In what may have been the only truly selfless thing he ever did, Daniel had given her *d'Riddem*. But more importantly, she and Jack had come to know Alphonse, who took care of the boat in their absence and his extended family, now friends for life. After many years, she and Jack had finally managed to get *d'Riddem* up to Rye Harbor.

Max tried to move her thoughts back to her earlier conversation with Courtney. Something about Courtney's story remained in a shadowy periphery, and it was bothering her. She sensed it, she felt it, and she even understood it, but she couldn't put it into words. Each time she felt that she had found those words, they dissolved back into the shadows.

Max rolled over onto her side and faced Jack. She leaned on her elbow, her head cradled in her raised right hand. As she studied his face, the dim light of stars softened his features, and she smiled. Ever so gently, she lifted her left arm and placed it on his chest. She needed to touch him, to connect. She could feel his heart beating slowly and steadily.

"Jack?" Max whispered.

"Hmph?" Jack jerked awake and turned his head to face her voice.

Startled, she pulled her left arm from him and stared into his face. "I'm sorry. I didn't mean to wake you."

That was a lie, of course. Through wide open eyes he stared at her, but it was obvious that he was not yet awake.

"Max? Wha . . . ?"

"Shhh," she touched his lips with her fingertips. "Go back to sleep."

Gently, she put her arm back over his chest and then placed her head on his shoulder. She could feel his heart beating, much faster than before. He shifted slightly, and she snuggled in while his fingers began to stroke her hair.

"What's the matter?" His voice was barely louder than a whisper.

When she remained silent, he asked again. "Hmmm?"

"I don't really know. Listening to Courtney tonight, I just kept getting this really bad feeling. It was like I know what's going to happen, but not really, and I can't do anything about it."

"All you can do is be a good friend. You know that things will work out; they always do. Courtney's a big girl."

"I know all that."

"So, close your eyes and try to go back to sleep."

His words echoed in her head.

"Don't you patronize me," she thought. She didn't want to go back to sleep. She wanted to talk about it. Only problem was, she couldn't put shape or form to it. What she knew and the clarity that had existed in her dreams was now gone, and it was obvious that he wanted to go back to sleep.

As his breathing once again became slow and steady, her mind continued to race. Slowly she lifted her arm from his chest, and ever so slowly she took her head from his shoulder and rolled away from him until she was able to slip out of the bed. Jack never moved.

CHAPTER 30

BETWEEN THE SUNLIGHT STREAMING IN THROUGH THE WINDOW and Cat pacing back and forth over his stomach, it was impossible for Jack to remain asleep. He pried his eyes open, looked over, and saw that he was alone in the bed.

"Good morning, Cat," he said. He scratched her head, and she responded with a whispered "Mrowh." Then she gave him a gentle head butt, settled down on his chest, and closed her eyes, totally content.

Jack, equally content, had all but fallen back asleep when Cat's moment of bliss ended. She stood, stretched, and, while purring loudly, began to pace on him again, this time with emphasis on his bladder. Any further chance of sleep was impossible, so he slid out from under Cat, sat up, spun sideways, and sat on the edge of the bed before standing.

Triumphant, Cat leapt off the bed. With a quick glance back to make sure that he was coming, she pranced toward the door with her tail straight up and led him out of the room.

Max was curled up on the couch, sleeping soundly. Cat was more interested in going out than having breakfast, so he pulled on some jeans, slipped into an old pair of running shoes, and tiptoed down the stairs with Cat leading the way. Opening the door, she dashed out. He followed.

The chill of the night still lingered, but the strong breezes of the past few days were gone, and he could feel the heat of the sun through his t-shirt. Cat, having dashed ahead, was standing between five and ten feet out on the lawn, perfectly still, save for her tail, which was rapidly swishing back and forth. Kitty footprints were visible in the dew-covered lawn, and he couldn't help but chuckle.

Her usual routine was to run out the door, move onto the lawn, flop down in the grass, and roll about. It was her way to celebrate the beginning of such a beautiful day. Obviously she hadn't been expecting the grass to be so wet.

While Cat considered her situation, Jack turned toward the sun. He closed his eyes, tilted his head back, and felt its warmth on his face. Stretching his arms upward while inhaling and exhaling slowly and deeply, he forced his mind to clear and enjoyed that moment for what it was. He knew that days this perfect would become more and more rare as each day's sunlit hours became more precious.

"Morning, Jack," a voice called out. He dropped his arms and could feel his face flush.

"Hey, Court."

"Listen, Jack, I'm sorry I was kind of a jerk at your workshop yesterday. I really wasn't paying enough attention."

"Court, don't be ridiculous. There's no reason for you to feel like that. I just thought you might find the boards interesting."

"They were, uh . . . are. Could I take another look at them?"

Jack wasn't expecting that. "Uh, sure. Now?"

"How about later? I have to get over to Ben's."

"Give me a call when you have time. I'm not planning on much today. Art said he'd come take a look at them, too."

"Okay. I'll call you in a bit."

CHAPTER 31

A FEW MINUTES LATER, MAX CAME DOWN AND JOINED HIM. She was wearing a thick green bathrobe, and he was instantly tempted to take her back upstairs and unwrap the sash. Unfortunately for him, she seemed to have other things on her mind.

"Can I see the boards?"

"Now?" He tried not to sound disappointed.

"Why not?"

"Sure. Just give me a minute here and I'll bring them out. The workshop's kind of a mess."

"When is it not?" she asked, and she rolled her eyes.

Ignoring her comment, he said, "Art's coming over later and so is Court. It'll be easier if I just bring them out."

As he brought them out and set them against the wall, she leaned sideways and tilted her head for a better view. In that position, her bathrobe gaped open at the top, revealing that she had little or nothing on underneath.

He set the last two boards down and tried to act as if he hadn't noticed.

"What do you think?"

"Interesting," said Max. She straightened, and as she did so, she pulled her bathrobe closed again.

"This how they go?" she asked.

He tipped his head and looked, "Not quite. Hold on, I've got an idea."

He disappeared back into the shop and returned with four two-by-fours that he leaned against the side of the building, creating two makeshift easels on which they could arrange the boards horizontally.

"There," said Max as she made one last adjustment to the order of the boards.

"Amazing, aren't they?" said Jack.

Max traced over the names with her finger as she read them aloud. "Frank McIntyre, H.C.V. McDonald, Billy McGuinnan, S.J. Haynes, Mattie Marden, Clem the champion Lobster catcher, Dave the man with the big hea . . . , Mike . . ."

She stopped and looked at Jack. "Some of these are too faded and I can't read them, but others seem familiar."

"From the dates that are by the names, these could be the grandfathers or great-grandfathers of some of the folks around here," said Jack. "But I'm not sure what this is all about." He was pointing at one of the corners where there was a series of numbers and what looked like a name that was partially worn away, then began tracing the letters with his finger. "J. .E. .S. ."

Max seemed more interested in the names and dates, then she said, "And you also found those boxes for Court?"

"I did. Took them over and put them in the cottage. Who knows, maybe there'll be something in them that might tell us more about these names and dates."

If she had noticed where his thoughts had been going about the bathrobe sash, she never let on.

* * *

A few hours later, Max left for her shift. Jack was standing outside with a cup of coffee, watching Cat stalking some unseen prey when Art came by. He offered to make him a cup, but his friend declined, saying that he was pressed for time.

"Come," said Jack and led Art toward where the boards were still sitting on the makeshift easels.

"So these are what you were telling me about?"

"Yup. I found them stored in a pile in the back of the shop."

"Any idea where they originally came from?"

"No, but I'm wondering if they might have come from the restaurant itself. Remember after Ben died, Courtney and her sister added on to the original building. I'm thinking these boards may have been part of that original building."

"Now that you mention it . . ." Art paused. "You might be right, Jack. You know that place wasn't always a restaurant, right? The original dining room used to be a kind of warehouse."

"Really?"

"Yeah. My grandmother told me about it once. Before it was Ben's, it was called the Moss Cottage. They used to harvest sea moss and dry it out on the flats at low tide. Then it was baled and sent to Canada for filtering beer. At least, that's what she said."

"Beer, huh?" said Jack.

"Yeah. Kind of a coincidence that now they serve beer at Ben's."

"Sure is," Jack agreed. Then he remembered why Art had stopped by, and he steered the conversation back to the boards. "So, you know any of these names?"

"Well, there's still a McDonald and a Haynes fishing out of the harbor. I'll have to ask them. The rest —I don't know, but I'll ask around."

"Any thoughts on this?" Jack pointed at that corner with the partially obscured letters and the seemingly random numbers.

"Part of another boat's name? I can't think of any beginning with Jes, and I don't recognize the numbers—I don't know," said Art. Then he checked his watch. "I've got to get going. Meantime, I'll ask around and I'll see if I can come up with some ideas about those numbers."

CHAPTER 32

"LUNCH MUST BE BUSY," COURTNEY THOUGHT. She reached for the ringing office phone, expecting that Max was calling from the bar downstairs for help.

"Good afternoon. Thank you for calling Ben's."

"And a good afternoon to you, Courtney."

As soon as she heard his gravely voice a chill ran down her spine and her hand began shaking at "Good." As much as she wanted to slam the receiver down, she couldn't move. It took a moment to find her breath. Her throat seemed to close, and all that she could hear was the beating of her heart in her ears. In that moment, a lifetime of thoughts seemed to flash through her head before she recovered enough to respond.

"You need to stop calling me. I can't help you."

"Oh, but I know that you can and will."

Her mouth started to open as if to respond, but instead, she clenched her teeth and dropped the phone's handset back into its cradle, ending the call. She closed her eyes, and it took several deep breaths before her hand stopped shaking. As her heart rate began to return to normal, she opened her eyes and let out a nervous chuckle. Whether it was from that simple act of hanging up on him or embarrassment at her reaction, she didn't know. But she did know that he thought she had something important, and she resolved to find out what it was. Maybe Jack would be able to help.

* * *

Courtney was just walking past her front porch on her way back to find Jack when Cat came skittering up.

"And how's Miss Cat, this beautiful day?" She bent over to scratch

Cat's head.

"Mrowh."

Cat head-butted Courtney's leg and began purring loudly while Courtney rubbed her ears.

The love-fest was interrupted when Courtney heard Jack call out her name. She walked over and joined him next to the two makeshift easels with the boards on display.

"I brought them out here so Max and Art could see them. I think they're pretty cool."

"You know Jack, I've been thinking, and I remember where they came from. When we put the addition on Ben's, we stripped the small dining room, and that's where they were. It used to be a storeroom, I think."

"That's kind of what Art suggested. I never really thought about the place being that old. Any of these names look familiar?"

"Not really."

"Have you had a chance to look through those boxes I brought over?"

"Just a quick look. I'm planning on digging through them more thoroughly as soon as I have time."

They continued to stare at the boards as they talked.

"You know what I find to be the most interesting?" Jack asked.

"No. What?"

"This corner."

Jack pointed at the faint letters and numbers he had pointed out to Art. "Everything else is clear and makes some sense—names, dates, pounds caught, that sort of stuff—but here, it looks like someone tried to paint over them."

She looked at where he was pointing, paused, then shrugged. Looking up at him, she said, "I'm sorry. I have no idea what it could be. But, these boards really are kind of neat. I should figure out some way to display them at Ben's."

"Well, if you figure something out or need any help, just let me know."

"I will. I've got to get going."

Courtney had turned and started to walk off when Jack called out to her, "Hey Court, that guy still calling you?"

She stopped and turned back toward Jack. That uneasy feeling returned again. She took a breath and tried to sound normal. "He is, but not as often."

"Has he told you exactly what he wants?"

"Not in so many words. But then, I usually just hang up on him."

"You'll keep me posted?"

"Of course. Gotta' go."

CHAPTER 33

"HI, AGAIN." THE VOICE CAME FROM THE END OF THE BAR.

When Max turned, she was surprised to see that the history buff had stopped by again.

"I'm sorry. I didn't see you come in."

"That's okay. You were busy, so I just slipped in."

"Something to drink?"

"Not today. I was just driving by, and I thought I might catch Courtney."

"Courtney?"

"Yes. She is the owner, isn't she?"

Max started to answer, but then she paused and looked at him more closely. If nothing else, years of tending bar, listening to every line and story imaginable, had honed her ability to tell truth from bullshit. Something about him and his reappearance didn't feel right.

He seemed to pick up on her reticence. He said, "I'm sorry. Maybe you don't remember me. I came in the other day. I asked about Ben . . . uh . . . Crouse, I think that was his name, and what you knew about this place back during World War II."

"I remember, but the answer is the same. I really don't know anything more now than I did then."

"Understood. I'm sorry. Well, like I said, no time for a drink. See ya."

He walked toward the door, and her register made a *chikka-chikka-chunk* sound as a new order was printed. As she began to make the drinks, she heard him call out her name.

"Hey, Max."

She looked up. He was standing by the entrance to the bar. The look of surprise on her face must have been funny, because he smiled and then added, "If you do see Court, tell her I said hi."

Max froze as a chill went down her spine. That was when it hit her: how did he know their names? Before she could ask, he disappeared around the corner and was gone.

She dashed out into the hallway, but it was too late. Instead of catching up with him, she nearly ran headlong into the boys—Leo, Ralph, and Paulie.

"Did you guys see anyone leaving just now?"

Leo and Paulie instantly shook their heads, but Ralph looked like he wanted to say something.

When he didn't speak up, she said, "Ralph?"

In a low voice that would have served him well for a confession, he said, "No, but I think I saw that guy who had been asking questions over at the harbor leaving in a car."

"You're sure?"

"Pretty sure."

Ralph didn't like being put on the spot and was beginning to get nervous and looked past Max's glare at his two friends who had just abandoned him for the bar.

Max could see his discomfort, and she still had that drink ticket in her hand.

"Come on, Ralph," she said. "Let me buy you a beer."

* * *

The bar was busy, and it took a while before Max had time for a few more words with Ralph. When she eventually caught his attention, she said, "Tell me about the guy you saw."

"Not much to tell. Leo and Paulie were ahead of me going up the steps when this car pulls out and nearly clips me. I had to kind of jump to get out of the way. And that's when I saw him. He was in the passenger seat and gave me a look as they drove past."

"Did you see the driver?"

He shook his head.

"What did the car look like?"

He shrugged and took another sip of his beer.

"Come on Ralph. Think."

"Looked expensive. Dark Blue, I think. Windows tinted. Unless it's a truck, they all look the same to me."

"Domestic? Foreign?"

He shrugged and finished his beer.

"Buy you another?" Max asked.

"Uh, sure," said Ralph, nervously glancing at his friends.

"On me," said Max. "Leo? Paulie? Another round?"

Both nodded yes and pushed their empty bottles toward Max.

"She's buying your beers?" Paulie asked Ralph. Like the rest of his "whispers," Paulie's voice managed to carry across the room.

"That's right!" Max said brightly. "Here you go." She placed a fresh bar napkin in front of each of them and then set down their beers. In the end, Max paid for all three of them, in exchange for a promise that they'd let her know if they saw the mysterious man again.

* * *

"Jack." Max touched his shoulder gently and gave it a slight shake.

"Wha . . . Max?" He sat up and began to swing his legs over the side of the bed. The light was on and he had to cover his eyes against the brightness.

Max giggled. "Jack. It's me. It's okay. I just got home. You awake?"

Now, grudgingly awake, he flopped back, his head landing on the pillow and his arm draped over his eyes, shielding them from the bright light. "I am now."

"I'm sorry. I didn't realize that you were asleep." She kissed his forehead.

"Well, I was. So, now that I'm awake, what?"

"That guy came in the bar again tonight."

"What guy?"

"The one I told you about. The one asking questions the other day. He didn't stay long, but when he left, it was as if he was a ghost. He just disappeared."

"And what does this have to do with the price of tea in China?"

"Nothing. I just think it's strange."

"Can't we talk about this in the morning?"

She didn't reply, and the room became incredibly quiet, which only served to awaken him more. The soft click of the light switch, and the ensuing darkness of the room, confirmed that she had indeed left the side of the bed.

CHAPTER 34

SHE COULD HEAR A RINGING SOUND. It was faint at first, but with each successive ring it became louder until finally Courtney became conscious enough to realize that it was her telephone. She sat up with a start and squinting in the bright light, groped around the bed until she found it. She didn't recognize the number, but she couldn't not answer.

"Hello?"

"Good morning, Sunshine." The voice was cheerful, with a carefree quality, and her heart began pounding as soon as she heard it.

"Edso?" All of a sudden she was wide awake, but she felt as if her voice barely squeaked out his name.

"The one and only. This isn't too early, is it?"

Regaining some composure, she managed to say in a more steady voice, "No. No, I've been up for hours."

That was a true statement. She had watched the sun rise after being up most of the night, but then she must have dozed off. She had spent most of the previous day going through the boxes that Jack had brought over.

"I was wondering, would you like to get together later?" he said. Even though his proposition was phrased as a question, something in his tone suggested that *no* would not be an acceptable answer.

"Maybe." She was intrigued. "What do you have in mind?"

"It's a surprise. Pick you up at say four?"

"What are we doing?"

"So, four o'clock it is."

"Wait, I didn't say yes."

"I think you just did."

She paused again. "What should I wear?"

"Your turn to surprise me."

"Come on, give me a hint."

He didn't answer immediately. Then he said, "There's never one sunrise the same or one sunset the same."

Courtney paused to take in what he had just said. Finally, she replied, "I'll see you at four."

"Four o'clock." Then he ended the call.

Court sat there staring at the phone in her hand until the screen faded to black. *"He didn't even say good bye."* As she slowly put the phone on the bed, she wondered, *"What the hell have I gotten myself into?"*

Forcing herself out of bed, she could only moan when she saw her reflection in the mirror on the bathroom wall. Fortunately, there was plenty of time for repairs before four.

* * *

Max was just opening the door to Ben's as Courtney walked up the steps.

"Hey, sleepy head."

"I'm sorry, Max. I didn't get much sleep last night."

Court's reply caught Max by surprise. She grinned as she began to imagine all sorts of lurid possibilities.

Court must have caught her grin. She said, "Stop. I know what you're thinking, and you can just get those thoughts right out of your head. I was home all night."

"I don't know what you mean," Max said, feigning shock that her friend would think that of her.

"I was going through those boxes that Jack brought over."

"And that kept you up all night?"

A car pulled into one of the parking spots by the front steps. The driver rolled down his window and called out, "This place open?"

Max turned and called back, "Just unlocked the door. Come on in!"

In the few seconds it took Max to answer his question, Courtney had already pulled the door open and was heading down the front hall-way.

Max caught up to her as she turned into the bar. "Court, slow down. You didn't tell me what was in those boxes that kept you up all night."

"Seems to be mostly old business records."

"And that kept you up all night?"

"I know. There were some old pictures, some deeds, legal documents, you know, the kind of old stuff that you might expect to find and . . ."

"And . . . ?"

"There were some old journals that Ben had kept."

"Journals?"

"I don't know what else to call them."

"What was in them?"

"Mostly notes on fishing."

"Logs. I think that's what you'd call them."

"Whatever. That's what kept me up all night. And now I have work to do. And then I have a date."

A million questions flew through Max's mind, but the register began its distinctive *chikka-chikka-chunk,* and Courtney disappeared up the stairs.

* * *

One of the things about the restaurant business in the fall was that while the lunches and dinners were still as insanely busy as they were in the summer, they ended more quickly. By two o'clock, things were quiet and Max convinced her friend and colleague, Patti, to watch the bar while she went up to talk to Courtney.

"Knock, knock," she said as she rapped on the partially closed office door, pushing it open in the process. Court was standing by the

98

window looking out over the harbor.

"You okay?"

"Can I ask you something?"

"Of course."

"I need some help deciding what to wear tonight."

That was not what Max had expected.

"Come again?"

"My date tonight. Edso is picking me up at four, and he was very secretive about what we were going to do tonight."

"The mystery man you can't find anything about."

Courtney nodded.

"What are you thinking?"

"I don't know. But there's something about him that I can't resist. We had lunch the other day, and he was a perfect gentleman. I like him."

"And yet you know nothing about him. How about that wife and twelve kids you imagined? Are you nuts? Didn't you learn your lesson with Russ?"

Ignoring that last comment, she said, "Max. Are you gonna' help me? I don't need you getting all preachy. I need to decide what I'm going to wear tonight."

Max knew that she wasn't going to talk her friend out of the date.

"What did he tell you about tonight?"

"Nothing other than he is picking me up at four and he is going to surprise me."

"No hints? Nothing?"

"When, I pressed him, all he said was, 'There's never one sunrise the same or one sunset the same.'"

"What? That's what he said?"

"Yeah."

"He so wants to get in your pants."

"Max!"

"Sorry. But my first reaction is that he intends for you to spend the night with him." Then, in a much lower voice she added, "Just like any good serial killer."

"What did you just say?"

"I said, *how romantic.*"

"You did not. You said something about a serial killer."

"Come on, Court. You gotta' admit it's a bit creepy." She stared at her friend.

"I suppose, but you haven't met him. Now, are you gonna' help me or not?"

"Fine."

CHAPTER 35

COURTNEY WALKED HOME WITH MAX'S VOICE still echoing in her head, but in spite of her friend's warnings and reminders, going out with Edso still felt right. As she opened her cottage door, it all hit her in a rush, and her hand began shaking. In less than an hour, a man she hardly knew and whom she had been unable to find any information about would be picking her up here for . . . For what? Suddenly a chill went down her spine as she realized that she had never told him where she lived.

Court took a deep breath, quickly stepped inside, and pushed the door shut. Then she leaned back against it as if that would hold at bay those disquieting thoughts. Light streamed in through her kitchen windows, and looking out she could see the barn, where she knew Jack was working in his shop. Just knowing that he was close by helped to ease her anxiety. She closed her eyes. It wasn't like she hadn't done this before.

A warm feeling washed over her as she remembered the last time. It had been last spring. Preparations for the upcoming summer season at Ben's had been exhausting, and she had needed to get away before hordes of tourists would arrive. Her solution had been a week in Jamaica at one of those all-inclusive resorts. That's where she had met Christopher. They met on her first night there, and when he suggested leaving the resort and finding a more "private" place to stay, she had said yes, so the next day, in a rented car, they left the security of the resort.

It had seemed an innocent adventure, like they were skipping school, when they drove out the gates. Even as they passed through small towns and villages it had been exciting. But as the road had gone further into the mountains, and there had been no more villages or houses to pass by, that initial exhilaration began to change to apprehension. They had ridden in silence, he watching the road and she, watching him. It wasn't until he had suddenly turned off the road and begun driving down what seemed no more than an overgrown path that she had finally questioned where they were going. She didn't remember exactly what his answer had been, but she remembered her reaction and it had been much like the way she felt when Edso asked her on this date.

The memories of that week of unrestrained pleasures in a spectacular Jamaican villa totally trumped any concerns that Max's reminder of Russ might have raised. She never did learn Christopher's last name, and they had returned to the resort just in time to check out and catch the tram to the airport.

Now, with Edso's arrival less than an hour away, and feeling more confident that it was the right thing to do, she headed for her closet to make the all-important decision of what to wear.

* * *

At five minutes before four she was standing in front of a full-length mirror for a final critique of her choices: a pair of linen, wide-legged slacks with a vertical pattern of wide, off-white stripes alternating with narrow bands of different shades of brown, and a nearly sheer silk white blouse. As she moved, the blouse shimmied in such a way as to reveal enough to tempt a potential partner without becoming a blatant advertisement. Knowing the night would be cool, she added a freckle brown cardigan sweater with leather knot buttons and a sash. She had brushed her auburn hair and then fluffed it with her fingers to create a slightly windblown, carefree look as it flowed freely over her shoulders. Simple hoop earrings, a thin, gold chain necklace, peep-toe heels, and a gold buckled belt completed the outfit. The final touch was the subtle shade of red on her lips—not too garish, but bold enough to make a statement.

She addressed the problem of whether she would return home or not by choosing a hobo bag. More casual than a clutch, it was large enough to carry overnight essentials.

She smiled in the mirror at what she saw. *"Well girl, if Max is right and he's a serial killer, you'll at least look great when they find you."*

A knock on the door downstairs brought her back to the present, and she giggled self-consciously at even having had such a thought. The fact was, she was excited, and she quickly headed down the stairs.

As she reached the door, she took a deep breath before reaching for the doorknob. Her hand was about to touch the knob when there was another knock. She pulled her hand back and took another deep breath to calm herself, not wanting to seem too eager.

Finally she opened the door and smiled.

"Hello," was all he said.

"Edso. I didn't expect you to be so prompt."

For a long second, he said nothing else as he faced her and she looked at him. He was wearing dark, aviator-style sunglasses, and when she couldn't see the look in his eyes, Max's warning flashed through her head again. But then he took off the sunglasses, and the smile in his deep blue eyes told her all she needed to know. Max was all wrong. He looked delicious, even better than when they had gone on their lunch date. He was wearing a linen blazer over a light-blue dress shirt, stone-washed jeans, and a pair of boat shoes.

"So, are you all ready?"

She nodded. "I am. You never told me where we were going or what we'd be doing. I hope I'm dressed okay."

"You're perfect. Let's go."

CHAPTER 36

"YOU THINK SHE'S GOING TO BE ALL RIGHT?" ASKED PATTI.

Max and Patti had just finished their shifts and were sitting at the bar having a glass of wine before heading home.

Max looked over at her friend and took a sip of wine. She swallowed slowly and nodded before saying in a low voice, "Yeah."

"But you're not convinced?"

"I hope this won't be like what happened when she hooked up with Russ."

"Me too."

"On the other hand we both know that happens when Court goes on vacation."

Patti nodded in agreement.

"She comes home all relaxed and glowing, never gives us any details . . ."

"Except that it's somewhere warm and romantic and men are involved."

"Right. The way she is when she gets back, we know she spent the whole time in bed."

"She is such a tramp."

Max could tell that the wine was beginning to get to Patti, and Courtney wasn't present to defend herself, so a little friendly bashing was clearly in order. Then a new voice joined in.

"Who's a tramp?"

"Jack. What're you doing here?"

"I knew you'd be getting out and I thought I'd stop by and see what you wanted to do about food tonight. So, who's the tramp?"

"Who do you think?"

"Are you two talking about Courtney?

Patti and Max lifted their glasses at the same time, clinked rims, and took a sip of wine.

"I knew it. Well, if it's of any interest, I just saw her leaving her cottage with some guy."

Simultaneously, both friends swallowed quickly and put their glasses down on the bar. In unison, they said, "What was he like?"

Max could tell by Jack's gleeful expression that he planned to torture them a bit further before sharing any information. Instead of answering, he said, "I need a beer," and signaled to the bartender,

"Jack! What was he like?" she repeated. "What did he look like? What kind of car was he driving? Come on, don't be a jerk."

The bartender put his beer on the bar. Jack reached between Max and Patti, picked up the pint, and took a sip.

"Jack Beale, you are being such a jerk. Tell us," demanded Max.

"Fine. Let's go sit out on the deck and I'll tell you everything."

* * *

"I had just finished up in the shop and was loading some trash in the truck when I saw this car pull up in front of Courtney's."

"What kind of car?"

"I think it was a BMW. Dark blue, tinted windows, one of the larger, more expensive ones."

"Dark blue? You're sure?"

"Max, I think I know what dark blue is."

"I'm sorry. Go on."

"Not much else to tell. I heard him get out, and a few minutes later I saw him opening the car door for Courtney, and then they left."

"A gentleman. What did he look like?"

"Never saw his face."

"What was he wearing? How did Court look?"

"I think he was wearing jeans and a light-colored jacket. Nothing special."

"And Court?"

Jack smiled. "She looked good."

"Good?"

"What is all this interest in how she looked?"

"Because I had a long talk with her about what to wear tonight on her date."

"Aha! So you knew she was going out. Is this with her mystery man?"

"Yes."

"And she won't tell you anything."

"Come on, Jack. You know she won't, and right now you're our best source."

"Okay. She looked great. Big baggy pants, baggy sweater, and a small suitcase."

"You are such a jerk!" She gave him a playful slap on the shoulder.

"Hey! She looked really nice."

"You're sure the car was dark blue?"

"Yes. Why?"

Max told him about the guy who had come into the bar, his departure, her encounter with the boys and their description of a dark colored car.

"And you think he might be Edso?"

"I don't know, but you have to admit it's quite a coincidence."

CHAPTER 37

"NICE CAR. AND A DRIVER. I'M IMPRESSED."

"Thanks. Did I tell you how nice you look tonight?"

"No, but thank you. My turn. What are we doing tonight?"

"You'll see soon enough."

They rode north on the boulevard along the coast in silence until the Pulpit Rock tower came into view. "Do you know what that tower was for?"

"Something to do with the war. It's abandoned as far as I know."

"You're right. It was built in 1943 as an observation tower, part of the coastal defense system."

His question had been innocent enough, but after the way he responded to her answer, something felt off to her. She looked over at him. If he was aware of her looking at him, he never let on.

She turned her head away and stared out her window, thinking about why she felt this sense of unease. Every now and then she was able to catch sight of the ocean as they passed by either a break in the line of houses or a low point in the rocks that separated the road from the ocean. The answer hit her at the same time that they turned off the road and into Odiorne Point State Park. She realized how much it had felt like she was back in school and he was her teacher, trying to draw out an even more detailed answer to his question. He was testing her, and she wasn't sure that she liked it. More to the point, why were they stopping here?

"This is it?" she thought as the car came to a stop.

As if he had read her mind, he held up a hand, smiled, and said, "No. This is not our destination. I just want to show you something."

He opened his door and said to the driver, "Wait here in the car," then quickly got out. She didn't move. She couldn't. Instead, she took a deep breath in an attempt to rein in the conflicting emotions that were sweeping through her. When she heard her door opening, she turned her head and looked up into his deep blue eyes as he looked down at her. Then he extended his hand to her. "Come."

Gone was the teacher voice. In a single word that was all at once warm and caring and yet commanding, she found herself powerless to resist. She took his hand, and without another word he helped her out of the car and then offered his arm to her for the walk across the parking lot toward the water.

She had to hold on to him for balance once they left the pavement. "You could have said something so I could have worn better shoes," she said as they began to walk across the grass.

"You'll be fine. I've got you." His voice was reassuring, and his arm was strong as she held on for balance. The sun was getting lower in the sky and the air was getting cooler by the minute, giving her another reason to hold on to him closely, and she couldn't help thinking about the possibilities that this night might present.

"Do you know anything about the history of Odiorne Point?" he asked as they neared the water.

The teacher voice was back. *"Again with a quiz,"* she thought as her bubble was popped. Pulling away slightly, she said, "I know that during World War II there were cannons here to protect the coast."

He smiled. His voice remained teacherly, but it did seem to soften as he said, "Basically. Prior to the war, this whole area was farmland and large estates. When the war broke out, everything from here to the sunken forest at Jenness Beach was taken over by the military. Can you imagine what it was like to have that happen? To live here, then?"

Courtney stopped, faced him, and locked her eyes on his face. "You never told me where you are from."

"No, I didn't."

"So where?"

He looked down at her and smiled briefly as he began to take a step. "Where what?"

Court held out her arms and stopped him. Looking hard into his eyes, she asked again. "You know what. Come on. Tell me. Where are you from? Not around here, I'm sure."

The look on his face softened. "You're right. I'm not from around here."

"So, where?"

He didn't answer for a long moment as he looked past her and out to the ocean. His expression changed, and she could tell that he had disappeared to some other place or time. Before she could ask again, he looked down at her and gently took her hands in his. Without a word, he stepped into her and gently pulled her arms around him until they were locked in an embrace. Only then did he release her hands and wrap his arms around her, pulling her closer still before whispering, "Later."

They remained like that for what seemed a very long time. Feeling how warm he was and listening to his heart beating in his chest, Court-ney decided that "Later" would be just fine.

Slowly, silently, they separated and continued walking arm in arm until they were standing at the water's edge. It seemed as if they were the only two remaining souls in the world. A lone gull swooped by over-head, crying out as if announcing their presence to the world. Echoing over the surface of the water, the sound of a single boat's engine could be heard as wavelets washed up against the rocks in a slow but steady *schoosh, schoosh, schoosh.* Whatever breeze there had been had died, add-ing to the stillness.

"*Zzzzzzz. Zzzzzz. Zzzzzzz.*" The perfection of that moment was abruptly ended by the arrival of first one, then seemingly hundreds of mosquitoes.

"Ah!" Court said as she slapped at the first one.

"Don't move," Edso said, just before slapping her on the forehead. "Hey!"

"Got 'em," he said. Then he licked the end of his finger and wiped it across her forehead.

"What're you doing?" she said, recoiling from his touch.

"Wiping the blood off. You didn't want me to leave it, did you?"

"I guess not." She turned and without waiting for him, began hurrying back toward the car, wobbling on her heels and flailing her arms like a scarecrow in a tornado.

Safe inside the car, he looked over at her. "I'm sorry."

"I forgive you, but now you owe me."

"Fair enough. Are you hungry?"

She nodded. "I am."

Ten minutes later they were being dropped off in front of Latitudes Waterfront, the more casual of the two restaurants at the Wentworth by the Sea hotel.

CHAPTER 38

"CAN I ASK YOU SOMETHING?"

"Of course."

"Do you remember when you asked me on this date and I asked you about what we'd be doing tonight?"

"Of course."

"You said, 'There's never one sunrise the same or one sunset the same.'"

"Yes, I remember."

"It's true, I'd never seen a sunset like the one tonight. It was magnificent."

They were the last diners in Latitudes Waterfront, and the views out over Little Harbor and the marina more than made up for its lack of formality.

"It was, wasn't it."

"Something's been bugging me, though. Did you make that quote up, or did you borrow it from someone?"

Edso looked at her, paused, then said, "I confess. I stole it. Carlos Santana said that. He's one of my favorite musicians."

Before he could say anything else, the waiter appeared at their table.

"May I suggest dessert this evening, or perhaps an after-dinner drink? Coffee?"

Edso looked up at the waiter and without even a glance at Courtney, he replied, "Not this evening. Just the check, please."

The waiter turned and walked off, offering no visible sign of disappointment at not having been able to add to the check or any indication of judgment toward what must have been obvious.

Looking back at Courtney, he said, "I'm sorry; you didn't want dessert or coffee, did you?"

"No, no, I'm fine," said Courtney.

As soon as the business of settling the check was finished, Edso looked into her eyes and said, "Come on, let's go."

Before she could speak, he leaned forward and touched his finger to her lips. "Shhh."

He stood and held his hand out to her.

She stared up at him for a moment, puzzled at herself. *"What is with you girl? He's doing it again. Stop being so compliant. This isn't* Fifty Shades of Rye Harbor.*"*

Remaining seated, and with growing anger toward herself, she said, "Where are we going? Tell me now."

"Please," he repeated. "It's a surprise."

"Why won't you tell me where we're going?"

"If I did, I'd have to kill you."

Max's warning flashed through her head, a chill went down her spine, and she stiffened. She glanced about for the waiter. Then she sat back stiffly, using body language to make it perfectly clear that she was not about to move.

He seemed to realize that he had made a mistake. "I'm sorry, Courtney." His voice softened and he said, "That came out wrong. I was just kidding. Please accept my apology."

Courtney continued to stare at him as he made his excuses.

"So where are we going?" she asked again.

"There," he said motioning toward the window.

She turned her head and looked out. The sun had set long ago. The night sky was nearly invisible due to the security lights for the walkways that led down to the docks. At the end of the docks, she could see a myriad of boats sitting peacefully.

"Where?"

"There," he said again, this time pointing.

She stared in the direction he was pointing. Tied to the dock was a large motor yacht, the kind featured on luxury television shows. The hull was dark, maybe blue or black, she couldn't tell, and above, there were stacked several decks, gleaming white with dark, tinted windows. Antennas and other electronic devices topped the yacht.

She stared. "That one?"

"Yes," he said. "Will you come with me now?"

Stunned, she stood. The bottle of wine they had enjoyed with dinner was beginning to take effect, and she took his hand and allowed him to lead her out of the restaurant. The evening was now quite cool, and a slight breeze was blowing in from off the water, making it seem even cooler. She shivered. Thankful that she had worn a sweater, she gave its sash a tug to cinch it closer in an attempt to ward off the chill, but the effort had little effect. She could feel her nipples growing hard.

"Would you like my jacket?" he asked when he saw her pulling her sweater close.

"I'm fine," she said. In fact, a pleasant warmth had begun to wash over her.

"Come." This time Edso's voice was softer, more guiding than commanding, as he put his arm around her and began walking her toward the ramp that led to the floats and the yacht.

"What the hell," she thought as she took his arm. She leaned into him slightly. *"The hell with Max."*

CHAPTER 39

"VORSPIEL?" SAID COURTNEY AS SHE LOOKED UP at the name board on the yacht. "What's that?"

"It's German. The boat belongs to my grandfather."

"What's it mean?"

Edso smiled at her, ignoring her question. "He's away on business, and this is where I've been staying. It's really quite comfortable."

Courtney looked at him. She thought, *"Comfortable?"* Then she added, "I'm sure it is."

"Come on," he said. He stepped off the dock and onto the swim platform off the stern of the boat. His tone had changed. He sounded more like a kid with a new toy that he wanted to show off than some kind of a psychopath intent on harm.

She smiled and accepted his hand for the long step onto the yacht. The swim platform was more like a patio. There were two curved stairways that led up from the platform, one on the port side and one on the starboard side. He led her up the starboard one and onto the main deck. Dumbstruck, Courtney froze. They were standing in what could best be described as the most luxurious back porch she had ever been on. She estimated that it was maybe fifteen feet deep and the full width of the vessel. There was a built-in couch between the two stairways up from the swim platform with a low coffee table in front. In addition, there were several groupings of upholstered deck chairs set on either side. Narrow, waist-high solid bulwarks with bright finished caps surrounded the porch then continued down the length of the yacht toward the bow, creating a narrow walkway alongside the main cabin. Ahead she could see chrome-framed glass doors that led to the inside, and there were even some potted plants on both sides of the door.

"Wait here, I'll be right back," he said. He walked toward the doors, unlocked one, and disappeared inside. Moments later, lights came on in the salon, followed by small lights recessed into the overhead in the patio area and down the walkways. If the yacht was impressive in the dark and shadows, the addition of light made her stunning.

"After-dinner drink?"

Startled, she turned toward his voice. She was so overwhelmed that she hadn't even heard him return to her side.

"This is where you live?"

"Sometimes. You didn't give me an answer. Drink?"

"Yes, yes that would be nice.

"Come with me."

He led her down the port walkway toward the front of the yacht until they reached the end, where he directed her up a stairway. As she stepped onto the upper deck, she could see that its layout was similar to the lower, main deck and that there was even another deck above. Looking aft she could see that dark, tinted windows lined the inboard side of the walkway, but the railing on the outboard side was more airy, having only the lower third solid and the remaining two thirds made up of glass panels set between white posts and topped with the same brightly finished wood cap. Instead of the small, single lights running down the center of the overhead as below, up here a ribbon of light emanating from a recessed niche that ran along the entire overhang gave off a soft glow, outlining the deck above.

"Go on," said Edso, his voice low and soothing as he joined her at the top of the stairs. The eagerness in his tone that she had noticed when they first stepped foot on the yacht was still there, but his clipped way of telling her what to do had also returned.

She turned and looked at him. He motioned her forward. The walkway wasn't as long as the one below, and when the wall of glass on her left ended, she stopped and stared. The deck above continued on, becoming a canopy covering perhaps half of a much larger deck area. That thin ribbon of light traced its outer edge as it crossed over the deck and then returned and disappeared up the other side of the yacht.

The deck below was stunningly elegant and intimate, but what she was now looking at was spectacular. This was an area made for socializing. A full bar, complete with bar stools, occupied the center of this covered area, and by each of the silver posts there was a large ceramic pot with a huge fern planted in it. Groupings of more upholstered deck chairs with small cocktail tables were strategically placed around the perimeter of the deck. On the other side of the bar, she could see that there was a stairway leading up to yet another deck.

He came up behind her, wrapped his arms around her, and whispered in her ear, "What do you think?"

"I don't know what to think? How . . ."

"I know. It's a little much. We don't have to understand it. We only have to enjoy it. Now, about that drink."

She turned within his embrace, put her arms around his waist, and leaned back slightly so she could look into his face. Their hips pressed together, and she couldn't be entirely sure if the warmth she was feeling was coming from her or him, but she liked it. "How about a Cosmo?"

"Coming right up."

She sat on one of the barstools. Then she watched as he went behind the bar and, without any searching or hesitations, made two.

Clinking rims, she said, "Nice job! You even used Nellie and Joe's. How did you know?"

His answer was a smile. Then he said, "Come, let's go inside. You look chilly."

He led her inside. As the door latched behind them, he turned the lights on. A ribbon of recessed lighting outlined the room, giving it the feel of some futuristic space ship. The room was furnished with overstuffed couches and chairs, arranged into conversational groupings with glass-topped coffee tables, several floor lamps, plants, and even some free-standing sculptures. Ahead, opposite where she stood, she could see that there was another room, created by a waist-high partition with glass panels above. It had a single glass entry door on the starboard side, and a stairway that led both up and down to port.

From the large windows that wrapped around that room, and the two raised, very comfortable-looking chairs facing forward in front of an impressive array of electronic screens, it was obvious that it was the helm from which the captain would drive the yacht.

"This is what you might call the family room. It's kind of casual," he said, breaking the silence.

"Casual?" she managed to squeak out.

"On the deck below, the space is much more formal—living room, dining room, master suite—and below that, guest suites, gym, etcetera. You want to see something really cool?" He was slipping back into excited-little-boy mode. "Come."

Courtney had hardly moved since coming inside, and she was so stunned at what she saw that she was hardly sipping her drink. She watched as he crossed the room, opened the door to the helm station, and motioned for her to join him before stepping inside. As she neared the doorway she could see him poring over a bank of switches. Then he flicked one, and the room turned red, just as she entered.

"The lights are red so you don't lose your night vision. Now watch this," he said as he flicked another switch. Instantly the glass panels and door that separated the helm from the guest area changed from clear to opaque. Edso was grinning from ear to ear.

"For privacy. So the crew won't disturb the guests, and the guests won't interfere with the running of the ship."

Courtney could only stare.

"Come on, let me show you the rest."

She remained in the doorway watching him, her thoughts frantically trying to keep up with what she was seeing.

"Doesn't a boat like this need a captain and crew?"

"Of course, but they're away on break for another few weeks. Since I'm staying here, my grandfather gave them some time off."

He motioned her to move back into the large "family room," then directed her toward the stairway.

"Down," he said, motioning for her to lead the way.

Reaching the next floor down, she abruptly stopped and stared. It was as he had said—a much more formal room. At the far end aft, she could see the glass wall and doorway they had faced when they first came aboard. Rich wood paneling and leather couches and chairs gave it the feel of how she would imagine a private men's club to be.

"Go on," he said softly. "It's okay."

She took two steps forward and stopped again, allowing him room enough to get off the stairs and stand next to her.

He said, "Incredible, isn't it?"

Court turned toward him. Still having a hard time finding words, she nodded.

"Next deck down aft is the crew's quarters and engine room. Then comes the galley, followed by the guest staterooms forward."

"What does your grandfather do?"

"Many things," he said, obviously avoiding a direct answer to the question.

"He must do them very well."

"He does." He paused and then added, "When he sets his mind to it, he usually gets what he wants."

She was about to say something else, but he didn't give her the opportunity.

"Come on," he said. He turned and began walking forward past an elegant dining table with seating for ten. At the end of the room on the port side was a passageway.

"Serving kitchen and pantry is down there. There's a dumbwaiter to bring the food up from the galley."

He crossed over to the starboard side where there was a door.

"Wait 'till you see this."

CHAPTER 40

BEFORE HE HAD TIME TO OPEN THE DOOR, Courtney took the last sip of her Cosmo.

"Just leave it on the table," he said. Then he slowly turned the knob, all the while watching her.

Slowly, deliberately, she put the glass down on the table. Keeping her eyes on him, she began walking around the table, her hand touching the back of each chair, in an effort not to stumble.

"What's in there?" she asked as she reached him.

Before he could answer, she wavered, and he released the knob so he could steady her. As soon as his hands touched her, she straightened, recovered her balance, and, blushing, said, "Thanks. I'm okay. Sorry. This is crazy."

"What's crazy?"

"This. You. Me. This boat. What the hell?"

"You okay?"

"I'm fine. What do you want to show me?"

She teetered again when he let go with one arm and reached for the door knob. She continued to hold on to his other arm. As he pushed the door open, he said, "This."

Her jaw dropped as Edso gently guided her into the room.

"What do you think?"

"Oh my God."

The room was like nothing she had ever seen before. Windows wrapped around, giving a full one-hundred-and-eighty-degree view overlooking the front of the yacht. A king-size bed dominated the space, but there was also a writing desk opposite and to one side, with a table and chair grouping on the other.

Courtney sat down on the edge of the bed and looked around,

wide-eyed and speechless.

Edso must have anticipated what she wanted to say because he said, "You get used to it. Here, check this out." He took her hand, coaxed her up, guided her around the bed, and opened another door. As the door opened, lights came on in the room, and white marble and glass and mirrors assaulted her eyes.

"You've got to be kidding me," she said as she walked in. It was a bathroom, but at the same time it was not a bathroom. She had seen luxury spas that weren't as well appointed. Yes, there was the obligatory throne and bidet. But then, there was a raised tub that looked large enough for four; a glass-enclosed shower with both an overhead and side jets; plush, navy-blue towels on warming towel rods; and properly monogrammed, matching robes, which hung on hooks on either side of twin vanities. A door labeled *Sauna* completed the room.

"Floor's even heated," he said.

"Can you excuse me for a minute?" she said, still in shock.

When she came out of the bathroom, he was sitting at the writing desk looking at some papers. He quickly shoved them into a drawer.

"So you live here, on this boat?"

He nodded.

"Alone?"

"Yes."

She shook her head and looked around again.

"It's not so bad," he said in an almost apologetic tone.

"Not so bad? Get out, it's incredible."

"So, I was thinking that we could go up top and sit in the hot tub and watch the stars. Up top," he repeated, pointing up. "You haven't seen the sky deck yet. There's a hot tub up there. It's quite nice."

She began to feel a rush of warmth wash over her. "That sounds lovely, but I didn't bring anything—"

He cut her off. "So?"

His smile confirmed what she already knew: a suit wouldn't be necessary. Motioning toward the bathroom, he said, "Grab one of the robes, and we'll go on up."

The door snicked closed behind her, and she stood a moment, looking around the room again. The lights seemed brighter than before. Court walked over to the vanity and stared into the mirror. From the moment she had met Edso, she had felt a strong physical attraction, and now things were about to play out in ways she had never imagined, at least not here.

Loosening the sash and buttons on her sweater, she slowly took the sweater off, carefully folded it, and placed it on the vanity. All the while she stared at her reflection in the mirror. The warm rush that had washed over her when he had suggested the hot tub was intensifying, and she watched the skin of her neck begin to flush slightly as the thin fabric of her blouse couldn't hide her growing excitement.

As stylish as her shoes were, and as good as they made her look and feel, that first moment when her feet were free of them always felt so good that it was almost orgasmic. Leaning against the vanity, she slipped off her shoes, first one and then the other. She braced herself for the shock of a cold floor, but as her bare flesh touched the warm, silky-smooth surface of the marble floor, her excitement increased. She sighed and closed her eyes.

Slacks and panties followed, and she folded and placed them on the vanity with her sweater. Now, nearly naked, she paused again. Looking into the mirror, she slowly began unbuttoning her blouse. As she did so, she imagined Edso standing there slowly working each button until it came free.

"Hey, Courtney, you all right in there?" His voice accompanied a soft knock on the door and quickly brought her to the present.

"Yes, yes. I'll be right out."

Blouse quickly folded and added to the stack, she took one last glance in the mirror and smiled before slipping into one of the blue robes.

She opened the door. He was wearing a similar robe, with a smile that probably matched the one on her face.

"Ready?" he asked.

She nodded.

He led her out of the master suite, past the dining table, and up the stairs. At the next deck he paused and said, "Go on up, I'll be right behind you."

Without a word, she continued up the stairs. At the top she stopped in front of a closed door and looked out its window at the sky deck. She could see that there were deck chairs and mats for lying in the sun scattered about the deck. At the far end she could see the hot tub glowing with a bluish light and steam rising off its surface.

"It's not too late to turn back," she thought as she placed her fingers on the door handle, but that didn't stop her. The door opened easily, and as it swung open, a small puff of the cool night air hit her, blowing up under her robe and against her bare neck, both at the same time. She shivered and pulled the robe closer, took a deep breath, and stepped out onto the sun deck. It felt like ice against her bare feet. Committed, she quick-stepped across the deck, finding relief only when she reached the mat next to the tub. It was warm, just like the marble floor in the bathroom. Next to the tub was a rack with towels and a hook for her robe.

The longer she stood there, the colder the night air felt, so she quickly took off her robe, flung it over the towel rack, and climbed into the tub.

"Feels good, doesn't it?"

Courtney's back had been turned toward the door to the sky deck as she climbed into the tub, so she hadn't seen or heard Edso come out. He was standing there in his blue robe, holding two wine glasses and a bottle of red wine.

"Edso! You've got to stop that."

"Stop what?" he said as he put the two glasses on the edge of the tub along with the wine bottle.

"Sneaking up on me."

He just grinned, took his robe off, tossed it on hers, and climbed into the tub. Courtney couldn't keep herself from staring, and in that moment she knew that it was going to be a special night.

CHAPTER 41

"NO. SHE'S IN THE SHOWER."

"Does she have it?"

"I don't know."

"What do you mean you don't know?"

"Exactly that. I don't know." Then he added, "Yet."

"Time is growing short."

"So you say."

"Listen, I have given you more than enough time—"

Edso cut him off. "You must be patient. This isn't 1942—"

"No! You listen. You may think there is time, but there isn't. We are so close. I know she knows. Now, finish it."

"I will finish it, but you have to let me do it my way."

"If your way is to screw it out of her—"

"Stop. I will get it done."

"I know you will. To help you focus, I'm removing some of your distractions. I've ordered the Captain and crew back today, and I've told them to leave immediately."

Click. The phone went dead.

"Jahwohl, you miserable old fuck," he mumbled under his breath. Still, as much as he disagreed with his grandfather's ways, he knew that the old man was right. He'd have to find another way.

* * *

Coffee. She smelled coffee, and she could feel the sun's warmth against her face. Her eyes were no longer tightly shut, but she kept them lightly closed against the brightness of the sun. Bits of the previous night began to take form in her mind: the hot tub, the heated marble floor, Edso's remarkable body, and the delicious red wine.

"Hey, Sleepyhead."

His voice intruded into her dreams, coaxing her closer to being awake.

"Coffee."

Draping her arm over her eyes, reluctantly she began to work them open. Her mouth was dry and her head was beginning to throb from the effort. "Edso?" she said as she finally peeked out from under her arm. The sun was blinding and she only got a brief glimpse of him standing next to the bed in a blue bathrobe. Then she rolled onto her side and pulled a pillow over her head.

She felt his hand touch her hip and rock it gently.

"Time to get up," he said softly.

Pulling her head from under the pillow, she rolled onto her back and, with a moan, forced herself up onto her elbows.

"Come on." He put the coffee on the nightstand, took her hands in his, and gently pulled her up to a seated position. She moaned again as she came upright, and he smiled as the covers slid down to her waist, exposing her still-naked body. Her only attempt at modesty was to raise her knees and wrap her arms around them as she looked at him.

"Here's your coffee," he said, offering the cup to her again.

She swung her legs over the edge of the bed but made no effort to cover her naked torso. Then she took the cup from him and took a sip.

"Thanks." It tasted as good as it smelled. "What now?"

"Now, you're going to rally, I have some things to attend to, and then, when you're ready, I'll make us breakfast."

"And after breakfast?"

He smiled. "We'll just have to see."

CHAPTER 42

AS SHE SHOWERED, MORE DETAILS OF THE PREVIOUS NIGHT began to creep into her memory. She remembered the wine, how good he felt, and how good it felt when he touched her. As the warm water ran over her, she imagined how nice it would be if he would suddenly open the door and join her. He didn't, so, slightly disappointed, she finished showering and got dressed. Stepping out of the bathroom, she was surprised to find that the room was now as it had been when she had first seen it: bed perfectly made, nothing out of place.

She walked over to one of the front windows and looked out. There was little activity on the docks. The summertime hustle and bustle was over, and the last gasps of the fall had not yet begun. Flags hung limp, and the surface of the water, while not mirror smooth, still looked like a sheet of glass. High, thin clouds had begun transforming the sky. For the past few days, the sky had seemed vast and limitless, but these clouds gave it a more closed and constrained feeling. A sailboat, clearly crewed by optimists, motored out of the harbor with sails up but hanging limp.

As she looked around the bedroom, she suddenly realized that this might be her only chance to find out a bit more about the man with whom she had just spent such a wonderful night. She walked over to the closet and opened the doors. It was perfect: nothing out of place, no empty hangers, no sign of previously worn clothes. She shook her head. *"No one is this neat,"* she thought as images of her own closet and bedroom flashed though her head.

As the closet door clicked shut, she turned and looked around the room again. That feeling that something wasn't quite right persisted in her mind. She moved over to the writing desk.

It was a simple desk, modern in design, made out of beautifully finished wood with a leather insert in the center of the top. As she walked around the desk, she let her fingertips slide along its surface. The finish was so fine and smooth that she closed her eyes, enjoying that sensual pleasure while in her mind she relived moments from the night before.

Then her stomach grumbled, snapping her out of her reverie. She sat down behind the desk, marveling at the simplicity and order. While her own desk was covered with papers, notes, junk mail, assorted pens, pencils, and paperclips, this desk had on its surface only a small, simple square of marble with a pen protruding from it. *"Who has a desk this neat?"*

The desk had two thin drawers, side by side, which were facing her. There were no visible handles, so she ran her fingertips under the front edge of each drawer, where she felt a shallow groove. With hardly any pressure, the drawer on the left slid open, surprising her with how effortlessly and silently it moved. Inside there was one of those yellow, legal pads of paper and several pens and pencils.

"Odd," she thought. It was almost like being in a hotel.

Then she remembered a trick she had read about years ago in a children's book featuring Nancy Drew. She removed the pad of paper and tilted it to the light to see if there were any impressions on the top sheet. There were. She tore the top sheet off, folded it, and put it in her bag so she could look at it more closely later.

She closed the left drawer and tried the same approach with the one on the right. However, it didn't move. She pushed back and examined it further. Like the left-hand drawer, there was no visible latch. Checking again with her fingertips, she felt along the groove for a second time. Puzzled, she stared at the drawer. Her thoughts drifted back to when he had first brought her into the room. When she had come out of the bathroom he had been sitting at the desk, and he had quickly put some papers away.

Her heart was beginning to pound as she began to imagine reasons why that drawer was locked—a wedding ring? Incriminating photos?

What? She began to run her hands over and under the desk, looking for some kind of latch and pausing every now and then to tug on the drawer.

"Hey, Sunshine."

She pulled her hands back and looked toward the door.

She could tell by the look on his face that he had seen her and he was not happy.

"Edso," she said, trying to sound nonchalant.

"Courtney." He paused before adding, "I came to see if you were ready for breakfast." The tension in his voice belied his true feelings.

"Yes . . . Yes, I'm starving."

He continued to stare at her as she quickly stood up. In an attempt to mask her embarrassment and discomfort, she blurted out, "I was just admiring this desk. It's so smooth."

As soon as she said those words, she could feel her face flush, and a little voice in her head chastised her. *"You idiot. You are so busted. Just don't say anything else."*

His face softened and all he said was, "Let's go eat."

CHAPTER 43

JACK WAS STARING OUT THE WINDOW of his apartment looking past Courtney's cottage out toward the harbor. He didn't hear Max come up from behind, but he smiled as she wrapped her arms around him and did that thing she did, tickling his navel with her fingertips.

"What're you looking at?" Her voice was slightly muffled as her face was pressed against his back.

"Nothing in particular. . . . I don't think Court came home from her date last night."

"Did you think she would?"

"I guess not," he said smiling.

Max eased her grip and slid around to his side, and as she did so, he turned to face her and put his arms around her, pulling her close. She snuggled in and held him tight, her head pressed against his chest as she listened to his heart beating. "Jack?"

"Mmm?"

"Even if you're not, I am."

"You am what?"

"Worried about Court. I mean, she hardly knows this guy. What if he's the one who's been calling her? You know, disguising his voice? I can't help but worry."

A few moments of silence passed before he said, "I know."

"I mean, last night when she went out, it was a total booty call."

"You might be right," said Jack. Then his gaze shifted slightly. "But in any case, she just got home."

Max immediately dropped her arms and turned to look out the window. In front of Courtney's cottage, Jack could see just the rear of a dark-blue car.

Max said, "It's him. Can you see them?"

His view was the same as hers. "No. Why? Do you think I have x-ray vision?

They stared at the car in silence for at least five minutes. Finally, the car backed up, turned, and drove off.

"Did you see him?" whispered Max.

Jack looked down at her. The windows of the car were tinted so dark that it was impossible to see anything or anyone inside. "What do you think?"

"I've got to go talk to her," said Max.

Jack grabbed her arm. "Give her a minute. She just got home."

"That's the point," said Max. Then she pulled away and sprinted toward the bedroom to get dressed.

As soon as she ran off, Cat came over to see what all the excitement was about.

"Mrowh," she said, alternately head-butting Jack's leg and looking up at him.

Jack picked her up and she snuggled into his arms, purring loudly as he continued to watch Courtney's cottage.

* * *

Jack decided to go for a run, and he was just tying his shoes when Max returned.

"So what did she have to say?" asked Jack.

"You are not going to believe this. He took her to Lattitudes at the Wentworth Marina for dinner, and she ended up spending the night with him—on a yacht!"

Jack knew that he was expected to ask for more details, but he decided to have some fun with her. After giving her a quick glance, he bent over and began stretching his legs in silence.

"Jack. Aren't you the least bit curious?"

He continued stretching.

"Jerk. I'll tell you anyway. You are not going to believe this."

"I'm sure I won't," he said standing back up.

"She spent the night on one of those huge yachts at the Wentworth. It's his grandfather's, and he's living on it. The captain and crew were gone, so they had the whole yacht to themselves. Hot tub under the stars, everything."

Finally, she stopped to catch her breath.

"So she had a good time."

"Yes, she had a good time."

"What was the name of the boat?"

"Yacht, Jack. It was a yacht."

"Okay. What was the name of the yacht?"

"I don't know. Began with a *V* and sounded foreign."

"That's helpful. I'm going for a run." He turned for the stairs.

"That's all? You're going for a run?"

He nodded. But as he put his foot on the first step down, he stopped and turned.

"After my run, how about I take you there for lunch and we check out this yacht? You're off today, right?"

Max's eyes lit up. "Go. Run."

She waved her hands as if shooing him away.

CHAPTER 44

JACK, LIKE MOST OF HIS RUNNING FRIENDS, felt that September and October were the best months in the year for running, and that day was no exception. The air seemed cleaner, spring's pollen and the heat and humidity of summer were past, and the cold of winter was a distant memory, even though it wasn't all that far off. He set off at an easy pace, loping past Ben's and heading across the bridge. By the time he reached the Boulevard his breathing was regular, he felt relaxed, and he was just beginning to break a sweat. Settling into a comfortable pace, less intense than racing but still honest, he turned right onto Route 1-A, heading north. As it curved around the harbor, he glanced across at Ben's and smiled, wondering what details Max would pry out of Courtney about her date last night.

Once past the harbor, Jack decided that he'd go as far as Odiorne Point. It would be a round trip of ten or so miles, a little more than his usual run, but he felt good and the extra mileage would be good for him. Even though he was running right along the coast, views of the ocean were limited by either beachside houses or the high stone berms that provided protection from storms, so whenever he came to one of the turnouts that allowed cars to leave the road, stop, and see the ocean, he found himself slowing so that he too could take in the view.

The high, thin, wispy clouds that had greeted the day continued to thicken, giving the day a soft gray feel. This atmospheric softening also had a mellowing effect on Jack's mood, and as he neared the halfway point in his run, he slowed to a stop at one of the turnouts near Odiorne Point. There had been little or no breeze while he ran, making it seem hotter than it was, and he wiped his face with his shirt as he walked from the road to where he could look out over the water. Both his heart rate and breathing slowed quickly, but sweat continued to pour over his body.

Standing near the water's edge, looking out over the entrance to Portsmouth Harbor, he was struck with how peaceful and calm, almost monochromatic, everything seemed. The brilliant blues of the ocean were muted by the overcast sky, which was still blue but now had gray overtones. The trees and grasses of the nearby marsh also felt more gray than green. A lack of breeze coupled with a slack tide left lobster trap buoys to lay flat on the now slate-gray surface of the water.

Far off, he could see a sailboat, sails furled, mast swaying from side to side, motoring back toward shore. He could also hear the slow, steady thrum of powerful engines from a boat that remained unseen but was definitely moving in his direction. Jack assumed that it was probably just a fishing boat approaching on its way out to sea, so he started to turn back to the road. Then it came into sight.

It was no fishing boat. He stopped and stared as a large yacht came into view. It took a while to fully reveal itself. Still sweating, once again he used his shirt to wipe the sweat from his eyes so he could see it more clearly. Even in the overcast and gray atmosphere, it sparkled. Its dark-blue hull was topped with a bright, white superstructure, three decks high, with tinted windows all the way around, giving it an air of mystery. When he squinted he could see a name board high on the second deck, near the front— *Vors . . . something*—glittering in gold leaf. As the yacht slid by, Jack remembered what Max had told him about Courtney's date.

It had to be the same yacht she had spent last evening on. Max had said the name sounded foreign, began with *V,* and was a single word.

"That's strange," he thought. *"Why are they leaving so soon, and where are they going?"*

The yacht slowly picked up speed, heading in the general direction of the Isles of Shoals. Her size continued to diminish as the distance between them increased. It was too late for Jack to get a good look at her transom to see the location from which she hailed. With his curiosity piqued, he finally turned away to resume his run.

CHAPTER 45

BY THE TIME JACK WAS ON THE OPPOSITE SIDE OF THE HARBOR, Max was on her way to Ben's. She wasn't scheduled to work, but she needed to pick up her check, and she was hoping to squeeze more details out of Courtney. She made her way up to Courtney's office and took a seat across from the desk.

"Hey, Court. How are you doing?"

"I need some coffee."

"Stay put. I'll go get us some." Max wasn't going to give Courtney the chance to escape.

Courtney surrendered and turned to stand at the window.

Here you go," said Max. She put the cup down on the desk. Courtney didn't even look up; she just continued to stare out over the harbor.

"You okay?" asked Max as she sat down beside her. "It sounded like you had a pretty good night."

"Yeah, I'm okay. Tired." She smiled, looking over at Max. "But, yeah, I'm okay."

Still, they had known each other for many years, and there was something in the tone of Court's voice that told Max she wasn't okay.

"You want to talk about it?"

Courtney sipped her coffee and stared out at the harbor. Then, without looking at Max, she said, "You know, Edso seems to be perfect. He's easy on the eyes, he's polite, gentlemanly, seems well off, good in bed . . . No, he's great in bed . . ." Her voice tailed off, and there was a hint of a smile on her face.

Max said nothing. She knew that Courtney needed to be allowed to say what she needed to say in her own way, at her own pace. There would be plenty of time later for questions.

"But . . ."

"But, what?" coaxed Max.

"I don't know. There's something that isn't right. I can't put my finger on it. It's like he's not really who he is." She paused again, groping for words. Then she looked straight at Max.

"Do you remember what it was like when Daniel first began pursuing you? He said all the right things. He was gorgeous. You were completely under his spell. But look how that turned out. You were totally played."

Max nodded, but before she could reply, Court kept on. "I feel that it's kind of like that. There is something about him that feels off. I've been trying to put my finger on it. Just when I feel like I've got it, I lose it. *Manipulated* is the best way to describe it. It's subtle. He has a way of making suggestions and leading me along like it was my idea and he's just following. Does that make any sense?"

"It does. But I didn't realize that about Daniel 'til it was too late. You, on the other hand, seem to be aware of what's going on."

"But what if I'm reading him all wrong? Maybe it's not that way."

"If your gut is telling you something, it's probably right. At the same time, if you like him—and I think you do—then keep the door open. Just make sure you keep trusting your feelings. Maybe you'll find out they're wrong."

After one last sip of coffee, Courtney looked at Max. In a stronger voice she said, "Thanks."

Then she returned her cup to the desk and walked toward the office door. "Listen, I've got to get this place open." Then, before Max could say anything else, she added, "Can we keep our conversation between just the two of us? Not Jack? Not Patti?"

Max nodded, but she was still very worried about her friend.

CHAPTER 46

"HOW WAS YOUR RUN?"

Jack was standing in front of his shop, looking at those boards again.

He looked up. "Run was good. Went all the way to Odiorne Point and back—somewhere around ten miles. How's Court?"

"She's fine."

From her tone, Jack had a feeling that there was more to Courtney's well-being than just "fine," but it didn't seem like he was going to get more from Max.

She asked, "We still going to lunch?"

"Absolutely, although I don't think we'll see Courtney's yacht."

"Why not?"

"I saw it leaving. At least, I'm pretty sure that's the one I saw. There can't be too many that big, blue, and shiny."

"What? Leaving?"

Jack could see how stunned she was. He nodded. "Weird, right? But I know some of the guys at the marina. While we're at lunch, I'll ask around. Maybe they'll be able to tell us something."

"God, I hope so. Courtney didn't say that he was leaving. *At all.* How soon can we go?"

"In a minute. I just wanted to look at these boards again. I had some thoughts while I was running."

"Well, hurry up." She turned away. "I'll be upstairs."

Ten minutes later, Jack walked up the stairs.

"What's so interesting about those boards, anyway?"

He started to open his mouth, but she cut him off before he could answer. "Come on, hurry up. I'm getting hungry."

"Okay, but I need a shower. I'll be quick; then we can go."

* * *

"Hey Max, the restaurant doesn't look too busy. How 'bout we walk down to the floats and check out the boats before lunch?"

"As long as we don't take too long. I'm hungry."

"Deal."

As they reached the bottom of the ramp that led to the first set of floats, a voice rang out, "Jack! Jack Beale!"

Jack looked around, at first unsure of where the voice came from. Then he spotted its source. Standing in a relatively small, cuddy cabin boat that was outfitted for fishing was someone he hadn't seen much recently. He had a hose in hand and was waving in their direction.

"Over there," said Jack. "Come on."

Behind him, Max asked, "Who's that?"

"Guy named Ken. I met him a few years ago. He winters in Florida and summers up here. Mostly fishes. You'll like him."

By the time they reached Ken's boat, he had shut off the hose and was waiting on the dock. There was nothing subtle about him. Younger than Jack, he was of average height, short cropped hair, obviously in prime physical condition, and his eyes sparkled with a confident exuberance.

"Hey man, how you been?" he said as he hastily wiped his wet hand on his shorts before extending it to Jack.

"Ken, it's good to see you," Jack said, He shook his hand and was instantly pulled into a bro-hug.

"Who's this pretty little thing?" Ken said, staring over Jacks shoulder at Max.

He hoped that Max hadn't heard what Ken said, and as they separated he turned toward Max. By her forced smile, Jack could see that she had heard Ken's question, so, in an effort to get past it, he quickly said, "Ken, this is Max. Remember, I told you about her."

Ken looked at her, obviously puzzling over who she was, then he broke into a big smile, "Max! Jack told me all about you. It's so nice to finally meet you." He held out his hand to her and pulled her in for a hug as well.

"Okay, Ken. That's enough," said Jack, rescuing Max from his too-tight, too-long hug.

"Oh, sorry man," said Ken as he released Max. Turning from her, he directed his attention back to Jack. "So what brings you down here?"

"Max had the day off, so we thought we'd have lunch. You want to join us."

As soon as he extended the invitation, he knew that he had made a mistake.

Ken, having just experienced Max's frosty reaction to his hug, said, "Thanks, but no, I've got to get the boat cleaned up. Fishin's pretty much done for the season. Time to put her away and head back to sunny Florida."

"A bit early, isn't it, this year?"

"A bit. But I have my own pretty little thing down there waiting for me. I stay away too long, she might get jumpy. I'd hate to lose her.

Matter of fact, she's a redhead just like Max here. Natural, if you know what I mean." He winked with a lecherous grin.

That last statement from Ken made Jack cringe and he glanced quickly over at Max. He could practically see steam coming out of Max's ears.

She said, "Jack, I'm going to walk up to the restaurant while you two catch up. I'll see you there."

Before either he or Ken could say anything in reply, she walked off.

"I hope it wasn't anything I said."

"Don't worry about it, Ken. New boat?"

"Yeah. Sort of. Pretty sweet. Handles well, good on fuel. But more to the point, how long you been with her?" he said as he looked around Jack.

Jack turned and watched her climbing the ramp and understood exactly what he was looking at. "A while. We live together."

"Good for you. Smart. Like me. Best of both worlds. Like having a friend with a boat, you get to go boating all you want without any of the expense."

Jack flashed him a look. "Not exactly."

He didn't want to get into a discussion on relationships with Ken, so he quickly changed the subject.

"So tell me. You know anything about a big blue yacht that was here recently?"

"Sure. Why?"

"I was out for a run this morning and I saw one leaving. I think a friend of mine might have met the owner. I didn't get a good look, but the boat's name was *V*-something?"

"Yeah. That's her. Names *Vorspiel*."

"Sounds German."

"It is." He grinned, "You know what it means?"

"*Vorspiel*? No, why?"

"Means foreplay."

"What?"

"You heard me. Means foreplay. There's got to be a good story about that, don't 'cha think? Crazy name for a boat. Sure like to know the story there."

Trying to suppress a grin, Jack thought to himself, *"I wonder if Courtney knows that?"*

Ken continued, "You know, I got a strange feeling about that boat."

"What do you mean?"

"Most people who have boats like that pretty much keep to themselves. You know, they don't hang out with us commoners, and this one was no different, but usually the crews are pretty friendly. Not this one. Hardly ever saw 'em, didn't talk to anyone, 'cept once, right after she arrived."

"What happened?"

"Couple weeks back, I had just come in from fishing, and she was here. Came in while I was out, bust of a day. Waste of bait and fuel. I had just tied up when one of the crew walked by. He said something about my boat,—hail port or somethin'. Don't remember, doesn't really matter. Anyhow, we got to talkin'. Turns out, his home is in Florida too, and we actually live near each other. One thing led to another, and he told me that they were here to meet the owner. He was flying up in a few weeks. In the meantime, his grandson would be staying on the boat. Now here's where his story became a bit weird. The crew were all to leave the boat, even the captain. That had never happened before. Not only were they ordered off the boat with no reason given, they had to remain available. The entire crew was unhappy about this, and had been ordered not to talk about it, but it was obvious he needed to talk to someone and I happened to be there. And the more we talked, the more nervous he became."

"Did you ever see them?"

"Who?"

"The owner or his grandson."

"Not the old man. I did see the grandson, or at least I presumed him to be the grandson, a few times, from a distance. Never talked to him. I think he was entertaining a lady last night."

Jack nodded. *"Had to be Courtney,"* he thought, as a grin started to come over him.

"Did I say something funny?"

"No. It's just that I think his woman friend may have been a friend of ours."

"She okay?"

Surprised by that question, Jack stared into Ken's eyes. "She is. Why'd you ask that?"

"No reason."

"Don't bullshit me. Give."

"Nothing really. Just a vibe I got from that one conversation I had."

Jack remained quiet for a moment, before asking, "Did he say anything else about the owner or his grandson? Why they were here? Anything?"

"Not really. He did say that the owner was European. Given the boat's name, probably German. Told me they hardly ever saw him, even when he was on board. Only the Captain and the first mate ever really had contact with him. The joke amongst the crew was that he was probably some old ex-Nazi, you know, total movie stereotype."

"Did he ever show up?"

"Don't know."

"Can you tell me anything else about the grandson who was staying on her?"

"Not much. He'd come and go. Kept to himself. Like I already told you, this morning he leaves with a real good lookin' gal. Kind of in a hurry if you ask me. Both looked a bit ragged, if you know what I mean." He grinned and winked as he said that.

Jack gave him a look.

"Sorry. I guess he was takin' full advantage of the yacht. But after a bit, he returned, and suddenly the crew showed up, he got off, and the boat left. Gone."

"Did the owner ever show up?"

"If he did, I never saw him."

Ken's story left more questions than it answered, but with what Jack knew of Courtney's date, it was more than enough.

Listen, Ken, Max is probably wondering where the hell I am." Then without thinking he added, "You sure you won't join us?"

As soon as the words left his mouth, he realized what he had done. There was a momentary silence as he hoped that Ken would decline again.

"Nah. But thanks. Hey, here. Take my phone number. Give me a call if you ever make it down to the Sunshine State."

"Thanks. Here's mine. It was good seeing you, man. Thanks for the info, and have a safe trip back down to Florida. Keep in touch."

Ken reached out and shook Jack's hand while pulling him in for another bro-hug.

"You take care of that little filly. Looks like you've got a keeper."

CHAPTER 47

MAX WAS WAITING IN THE RESTAURANT WHEN JACK GOT THERE. She was sitting by one of the windows and already had a glass of wine. On his way to the table, he ordered a beer.

As he sat, she looked up at him. "You were wrong. I didn't like him."

Jack wasn't ready for that. "Ken?"

"Yeah, Ken. So, what's his story?"

"What do you mean?"

"You know exactly what I mean."

"I admit, he's a bit much, but he's really okay." Trying to deflect her upset, he added, "Gave me the story on the yacht."

She didn't bite. "A bit much? 'Ya think?"

"Come on, Max, he's harmless. Anyway, he's heading back to Florida soon. You'll never see him again."

Then, trying again, he added, "He told me that the boat's name, *Vorspiel*, means foreplay in German."

"What?"

Before Jack could say anything else, the waiter appeared with his beer and asked if they were ready to order.

Before Jack could respond, Max said, "Could you give us a few more minutes?"

Jack was relieved to hear that her tone had softened.

The waiter retreated, and Max looked at Jack.

"Foreplay?"

"Yeah. Crazy isn't it?"

"Do you think Court knows?"

He could tell she was trying to hold back a grin. He shrugged, now smiling too.

"Don't know."

Ken was forgotten, the lunch was delicious, and they consumed it amid much laughter and speculation over the yacht's name. Still, no matter what, their conversation kept returning to Courtney and the mystery that was Edso.

* * *

It was late afternoon by the time Max and Jack left the marina. Throughout the day, the cloud cover had continued to thicken. There would be no sunset like the previous night's, but merely an ever-increasing gloom that would gradually turn to darkness.

Little was said on the ride home. It wasn't until they reached the harbor that Max broke the silence.

"Jack, I've been thinking about Court and Edso. I'm worried. What if he turns out like Daniel? At least I had you to save me; she doesn't really have anyone."

"She has us."

"I know, but it isn't the same."

"I beg to differ."

"Promise?"

"I promise."

As Jack stopped his truck in front of their apartment, Max looked over at him. "I'm going to see if Court is home. She was pretty tired, so she probably didn't stay too long at Ben's."

* * *

Finding the door to Courtney's cottage unlocked, Max opened the door just enough to stick her head in and called out, "Court? You here?"

"Upstairs," came the muffled answer.

Max closed the door behind her and began climbing up the stairs. Narrow and steep, they led to a small hallway, off of which were three doors. The first, on her left, was for a large walk-in closet and was closed. Ahead was the bathroom, its door ajar. A few steps down the hall, on the right, was the door to Courtney's bedroom, and Max could see that it was open. She looked in. Her friend was sitting on the bed, staring intently at what looked to be a journal of some sort. Scattered around her was a collection of loose papers and a stack of several more journals. Max couldn't tell if Courtney even realized that she was being watched. Knocking softly on the doorframe, she said, "Hey. You okay?"

Her question was greeted with silence. Then, without looking up, Courtney held up one hand and lifted her index finger. "Just a minute."

Max remained in the doorway, watching her friend. Finally, after a few moments, Courtney stopped reading and looked up at Max.

"What's so interesting?" asked Max.

"I'm not sure." Courtney's voice was low.

"What do you mean you're not sure? You're reading it."

Instead of giving a response, Courtney looked back down at the notebook.

Puzzled, Max said, "I'll be downstairs."

"Sure. Fine. Give me a minute."

Max shrugged and retreated down the stairs. It wasn't a minute. A solid five minutes passed, and Max was considering going back upstairs to see what was taking Courtney so long when the phone began ringing. She moved to the bottom of the stairs, intending to call up to Courtney to see if she wanted her to answer it, but the phone stopped ringing before she could say anything. Curious, Max moved several steps up the stairs. Hardly daring to breathe, she listened, straining her ears to hear who was calling. She knew it was none of her business, but she couldn't resist the little voice in her head that told her that she had to know.

"Max, I know you're there."

Startled, she quickly retreated down off the stairs, stealth no longer a priority. She could hear Courtney moving toward the stairs, and Max had barely cleared the last step and ducked around the corner when she began descending.

"What?" called back Max, feigning innocence.

She listened as Courtney slowly walked down the stairs. As she stepped off the final step and turned into the room, Max turned.

As soon as she saw her friend's face, she knew something had happened. "Are you all right?"

Silently, Courtney nodded.

"No, you're not. What's going on? Was that Edso on the phone? Was it something you read? What?"

Courtney remained silent. She just stood there, a blank expression on her face, holding the notebook she had been reading in one hand.

"Yes."

"Yes, what?"

"It was him."

"Him who? Edso?"

"No. Not Edso. My anonymous caller. I hung up on him." Before Max could reply, she added, "Max, I need you to look at something."

"What?"

"This." She held up the notebook. "It was in those boxes Jack had saved and brought over. There's a bunch of these notebooks. Seems Ben kept a daily record of his fishing. Mostly pretty boring stuff, except this one."

"What's in it?"

"You'll have to read it for yourself." She held out the notebook to Max. "While you read it, I'm going to go outside for a minute. I need some fresh air to clear my head."

Max sat down at the small table in front of the windows that looked out over the backyard. She glanced out. Cat was chasing a bug or something in the grass, and she could see that the shop door was open and Jack was standing outside, staring at those boards again. She began reading.

18 August 1942. 8pm. Wind SE calm No moon.
Good patrol, No sightings.

* * *

31 August 1942, 8 pm, NW force 3, Seas Flat,
Cloud cover reminded me of last rum run.
Saw one Navy patrol, avoided them. Uneventful.

* * *

29 September 1942 8pm. Wind NNE force 4, rising
Seas building, Heavy cloud cover.

* * *

Max didn't hear the door open. She hardly noticed the soft gust of cool air that blew into the room or the two sets of footsteps that followed. It was the sound of the door being pushed shut that finally brought her back into the present. She looked up. Courtney and Jack were standing there, staring at her.

"So, what do you think?" asked Courtney.

Max said nothing for a few moments. "I don't know exactly what to think. You didn't know about this?"

"No. He never spoke about what went on during the war. It was long before I was born, and I never had any reason to even think about it."

"Do you mind if I ask what you two are talking about?"

Both Max and Courtney turned and looked at Jack.

Courtney spoke first. "Those boxes that you had saved and brought over here, I've been going through them. Mostly nothing, until that." She pointed at the notebook in Max's hand.

CHAPTER 48

WHILE JACK SCANNED THE JOURNAL, Max and Courtney retreated outside to the front porch.

"Jack and I had lunch at the marina today."

"You did?"

"Yeah, we wanted to check out this yacht you were on."

"And?"

"It wasn't there."

"Wasn't there?"

"Gone. Jack ran down toward Odiorne this morning and saw it leaving."

"What time was that?"

"Late morning, noonish."

"He didn't say anything about leaving."

Max couldn't be sure, but she thought she could see Courtney's eyes beginning to water.

"Maybe only the boat left," said Max, trying to soften this revelation.

"He would've said something, wouldn't he?"

"You'd think."

"I guess."

Max stood silently next to her friend.

Court said, "You know, while I was in the shower, he completely cleaned up the room, and I mean *cleaned*. When I came out, it was as if we hadn't even spent the night there."

She paused, looked at Max, and continued. "There was this writing desk in the room. I saw him there, looking at some papers, but then he shoved them in a drawer, almost as if I had caught him doing something he shouldn't have. Anyway, this morning, after my shower, I went and checked out the desk. There were two drawers. I found a pad of paper in one, but the second drawer was locked. I was trying to open it when he walked in. I know he saw me."

"So he caught you snooping?"

Rather than answering, Courtney jumped up.

"What?" asked Max.

"The paper. I tore the top page off the pad."

She returned a moment later with a folded piece of yellow paper in hand. "I almost forgot that I had this."

"So what happened?"

"He didn't say anything, but I could tell from his face that he wasn't happy. Then, breakfast seemed a little too quick, and he brought me home."

"But he never said anything?"

"No. But now that you tell me he's gone, I'm really wondering."

"I didn't say he was gone. I said the boat was gone."

"Yacht."

"Okay, yacht."

"He's gone. I know it."

Before Max could say anything else, Jack walked out onto the porch.

"This is amazing," he said, holding the notebook in his hand.

"What's amazing?" asked Courtney.

Jack held out the notebook. "This. You're Uncle Ben was a real badass. Didn't you read it?"

"I guess he was."

"The paper?" asked Max.

"Oh, yeah. I took this when I was on the boat. Max, can you grab a pencil?"

Now, it was Jack's turn to be confused. "So?"

Max handed her a pencil and she began to run the pencil lightly over the indentations on the paper.

Courtney stared silently at the paper.

"What do you suppose it means?" whispered Max looking over her shoulder.

"Can I see?" asked Jack.

He looked at the paper — *Courtney, Ben's Place, the key is . . .* —

"Are there other notebooks?"

"There's a whole bunch."

"Can I see them?" asked Jack.

"Sure."

CHAPTER 49

HIS NECK WAS STIFF. All he wanted was to sleep, but the woman whispering in his ear wouldn't let him. He couldn't see her. She was behind him, always behind, and he couldn't move.

"Jack," she whispered again. This time he could feel her lips brush softly against his ear. He struggled to open his eyes. The room was dark save for the light that shone in his eyes. There was a weight, something heavy on his lap.

"Jack," the voice whispered again. This time he felt something touch his cheek, and it was so soft and delicate that it made every nerve where it touched tingle.

He tried to speak, but no words came out.

"Tell me. Tell me what I want to know, and I'll set you free."

He couldn't tell her. As much as he wanted to, he couldn't. Her hand slid down his chest, her touch ever more electrifying. Waves of pleasure shot through him, and he could feel that warm pressure beginning to build just below his waist.

With a jerk, he suddenly sat up, his eyes open, his sleep-clouded brain a step behind what his eyes were seeing.

"Jack, come to bed. It's late."

He grinned sheepishly as he swung his legs off the couch and the journal he had been reading fell on the floor, landing on top of the others there. "What time is it?"

"Nearly one."

The room was dimly lit, the only light coming from the lamp at the end of the couch, bright enough for reading, it still left most of the room in the shadows.

He looked up at Max. "I was having the strangest dream."

She was standing in front of him wearing one of his old t-shirts that he had won at some long-forgotten race. The way it draped over her body, accentuated by the interplay of light and shadow, was intoxicating, and his dream began to take life.

She held out a hand to him and said again, "Come."

Her hand was warm, and as he stood, he shivered. "Aren't you cold?"

"I wasn't, but now that you mention it—"

Jack didn't let her finish her sentence. Still holding her hand, he gently pulled her toward him. She stepped into him, wrapping her arms around his waist and pressing tightly against him.

Returning the embrace, he ran one hand down over her back, feeling the smooth contours of her body under the t-shirt and noting that it was all she had on. The room was cool, in contrast to the warmth of her body.

"What were you dreaming about?" she whispered.

"I'm not exactly sure. I think I was being interrogated. I'm pretty sure there was this woman there—"

Max cut him off. "A woman?"

As the tone in Max's voice changed, Jack knew exactly what she was thinking: *Sylvie.*

"No. Relax, Max. It wasn't her," he said, perhaps a bit too quickly, in an attempt to reassure her that it was not the case. He had met Sylvie years before during a race. Shortly thereafter it had become obvious that she had a thing for Jack, much to Max's dismay. Her appearances seemed random, always mysterious and if not for the fact that she had saved his life at least once, Max would have hated her even more.

"Then who?" The tone remained, and she stepped back and stared at him.

In an attempt to explain, he tried to remember the dream. "It was a dream . . . I don't know. It was like I was in some old forties movie. Uniforms, thick German accents . . . I'm not even sure she was doing the questioning, or even if she was there. It was quite bizarre."

Max turned and began walking toward the bedroom. Unsure of what exactly to expect, he bent down, picked up the journal from the floor, and paused for one more look.

* * *

It was dark, very dark. The overcast sky blocked out any light from the stars and moon, making the room seem even darker as he made his way across toward the bed. Reaching the side of the bed, he paused and listened to her breathing. He could tell that she was not asleep. As he reached out and touched the edge of the bed, he heard her move and before he could climb into the bed, a warm hand touched his stomach. He wasn't wearing a shirt and despite its warmth, that touch sent a chill through him.

"Come here," she whispered. Her hand slid down his torso, further intensifying his reaction to her touch. "Lose them," she added, as she ran her fingertip along the waistband of his shorts.

He closed his eyes and his breathing became more rapid, barely keeping pace with his pounding heart. In his mind's eye he could picture her lying on the bed, propped up on one elbow, her arm outstretched as it teased him.

He pushed his shorts down and climbed up onto the bed. As he did so, he felt her move. "Lie down, roll over and don't move," she commanded in a low voice. Stretched out face down on the bed, he felt her climb onto his back, straddling him as if riding a horse, and began to rub his shoulders. As he relaxed, he could feel the warmth building between her legs and it took great effort not to roll over.

After a few minutes, she leaned forward, her breasts pressing into his back and whispered in his ear, "So, tell me about this dream you were having."

He so wanted to roll over, but she remained lying on top of him, her legs straddling his back, forcing him to remain face down. As interrogations go, he was enjoying it so he remained face down and played along.

"I don't know. It's all a muddled mess. You know how dreams are, they make perfect sense until you try to remember and re-tell them. It was today, then back in 1943, here and somewhere else, Court was in it, that yacht and . . ." He paused and sucked in his breath as she slowly began working her hands underneath him.

"Go on."

He tried to remain focused, but it was becoming increasingly hard. "I don't know. The more I think about it, the less I remember and the less sense it makes, but I can't shake the feeling that the answer is staring me in the fa . a . a . ace."

That was when her hands found him.

Jack shifted and let out a soft moan. Max pulled her hands out from under him and sat up, lifting her hips just enough for him to roll over. She took his hands in hers and stretched forward, pushing his hands above his head, her hair falling in his face and then slowly adjusted her hips, melting onto him until they became one.

* * *

Since his interrogation, that deep restful sleep that usually followed their love making eluded Jack. All he could do was lie there, next to Max, listening to her deep and steady breathing, as images of those boards and what he had read in Ben's journals cycled endlessly in his mind.

In the dark, time moved slowly, and he was convinced that he hadn't slept, and yet each time he'd glance over at the clock, he'd discover that time had indeed passed. It wasn't until the sun began to break the horizon that he finally did sleep.

It may have been the smells of breakfast cooking, or maybe the fact that he reached out for Max and she wasn't there, or that it was something else, but whatever the reason, Jack woke with a start and sat up. Cat jumped up on to the bed and bumped him, looking for attention.

"Mrowh."

"Good morning, Cat."

She purred and continued to bump him as he scratched her head while he tried to retrieve his dreams. He knew that if he stayed there any longer, he could easily fall back asleep.

"I'm sorry, Cat, but I have to get up," he said as he gently pushed her aside.

"Mrowh," she said while looking at him with an expression that could only be described as disbelief that he would dare leave her.

CHAPTER 50

"GOOD MORNING, SUNSHINE."

"Hey, sleepy head."

"What's cookin' good lookin'?" He grinned as he came over to get a cup of coffee.

"Well, I'm making a Belizean breakfast — eggs with guacamole and salsa and refried beans, toast with guava jelly."

"No fry jacks?"

"Sorry. Toast was easier. Coffee?"

"Thanks. So what's the occasion?"

It was rare that Max cooked breakfast, at least an elaborate one like she was now making.

"Nothing. It's just gloomy outside and. . . I don't know, it kind of reminded me of that stormy day when we were in Belize, and, well, last night was . . ." She paused and turned to the eggs she had cooking in the pan.

"Last night was what?" he asked as he came up behind her and whispered in her ear.

"Breakfast is nearly ready. Go get your plate."

He backed away, smiling as images of his interrogation flashed through his head.

"You didn't sleep very well, did you?" she asked as she slid two eggs onto his plate and then spooned guacamole and salsa over them.

"Not really. I can't shake the feeling that those boards and that journal are connected in some way, but I'm just not seeing it."

"Maybe you're thinking too much."

"Probably. This is delicious. I may have to find some special way to thank you."

"Sorry, I have to get to work. No time."

* * *

By the time Max was dressed and ready to head for Ben's, Jack had cleaned up the mess from breakfast, and she found him standing by the window looking out over the harbor.

"What're you thinking about?"

"The journal." He turned and motioned toward the couch where it lay. "Courtney going to be in today?"

"I would expect so. Why?"

"There're some things in here that I want to ask her about."

"I can't imagine that she'll be much help, but I'll let her know you'll be looking for her."

Max stopped as she was about to head down the stairs, looked back and said, "You know, what you really need to do is to find some old person from around here who might remember more about what it was like back then."

Before Jack could respond, she turned and disappeared down the stairs.

"Mrowh," Cat said as she jumped up onto the couch, and sat down on the open journal.

"Mrowh," she said as she stared at him, blinking her eyes.

Scratching Cat's head, Jack sat down and gently pulled the journal out from under her, opening it. Cat, for her part, resettled herself next to him in such a way that he could easily scratch her head while reading. With eyes closed and purring loudly, she was in a state of total contentment as Jack began to re-read the first journal Courtney had shown him.

He quickly realized that this journal raised more questions than it answered, so he began going through all of Ben's journals again. The earlier ones contained mostly notes on trap locations, yields, and set times. Jack thought the later journals were more interesting, since they contained information about the building of the jetties in the late

1930's, the dredging of the harbor in the early 1940's, and other tidbits of information about what life was like back then. He made a mental note to show them to Art the next time his friend started bitching about how hard it was to make a living fishing. To Jack's eye, it didn't seem to be dramatically different from the present—at least where the end result was concerned—and he was glad that it wasn't the life he had chosen.

While he pored through the later journals, he realized that some of the names Ben mentioned seemed more and more familiar. After a bit, he finally realized why: their names were on the boards. With the journal in hand, he headed for the stairs to go to the shop and take another look. After a loud "Mrowh" of protest, Cat slowly followed him out.

As he stood in front of the boards, he alternately flipped back and forth through the pages of the journals to compare names and dates to those on the boards. He was right. Many of the names and dates matched. Before he could give that fact much thought, he felt Cat rub up against his leg.

"Mrowh," she said, looking up at him when he looked down at her, acknowledging her presence. Butting her head against his legs and winding around and through them, she made herself impossible to ignore.

Bending down, Jack scratched her head. "Are you telling me you want to go back in?"

She left little doubt that this was what she wanted, because she abruptly pranced over toward the door and looked back at him. "Mrowh."

As if on cue, the breeze, which had been nearly nonexistent, suddenly picked up. It came directly off the water and sent a chill though Jack.

"You know something I don't?" he said to Cat as he looked up at the thickened clouds. It seemed even darker now than when he had first come out.

* * *

"Knock, knock," said Max as she rapped on the doorframe. Court was holding the phone to her ear, listening intently, but as soon as she looked up and saw Max, she abruptly said, "I'll see you shortly," and hung up.

"Who was that?" asked Max as she walked in.

"No one," said Court. "What's up?"

By her tone, Max could tell that she had not expected to be disturbed.

"Nothing. Jack said he might be over later to talk to you. He has some questions about those journals."

"I've got a busy day ahead. If he can catch me, I might be able to give him a few minutes. I'm not sure how helpful I can be."

Max could tell that she really didn't want to talk. She shrugged. "Just thought I'd give you the heads up."

As she turned to leave, she stopped and looked back, worried for her friend.

"If you need to talk, I'll be down setting up the bar."

CHAPTER 51

"HEY, MAX." JACK LOOKED AROUND. The bar was empty, and no one was out sitting on the deck. "Where is everyone?"

Max shrugged. "I think it's the weather. And Courtney's gone, too. I told her you had some questions, but she left about an hour ago. Said she has a lot to do. Want something while you wait?"

"Nah, I'm good. When she gets back, tell her I stopped by."

"I'll tell her."

Before leaving, he stepped behind the bar, gave her a quick kiss good-bye, and whispered in her ear.

She blushed slightly. With a smile, she said, "Where are you going, anyway?"

Jack smiled back. "There's someone I need to see."

* * *

Jack drove north along the boulevard. Traffic was light. The weather was gloomy enough to make people stay home, but not bad enough to call out the looky-loos who always wanted to see and feel Mother Nature's fury during a stormy high tide. Some nuts would even risk their lives by climbing out onto the rocks to see how close to the waves they could get.

While not bad enough yet to draw crowds, the weather conditions were definitely deteriorating. The wind was steadily picking up, and whenever Jack was able to get a glimpse of the ocean, he could see that the swell was building and that whitecaps dotted its surface. Each time he passed stretches of salt marsh, he could see waves of wind as it brushed over the grass like an unseen hairbrush repeatedly trying to tame some unruly mane.

The closer to Odiorne Point he came, the slower he drove. He alternated checking his mirror to make sure that he wasn't impeding traffic with looking for the beginning of her drive. Gladys' cottage was set well back from the road, seemingly in the middle of the salt marsh, and it was impossible to see from the boulevard. Although he had never been there, he knew that her drive was marked by a solitary granite gatepost at the end of one of the many stone walls that were common all over the coast.

In another lifetime, the salt marshes had been regularly harvested for their salt hay, and her drive had once provided access deep into the marsh. Now that salt hay was no longer harvested, the marshes were slowly reverting to a wilder state. The canals that had been dug to provide water flow from the ocean were slowly filling in, and small islands of higher ground were being created. Overgrown with scrub brush and small trees, a whole new ecosystem was developing.

Even knowing about that granite post, Jack nearly drove past the drive. He had to brake and turn quickly, thankful that no one was behind him. After a few truck lengths, the boulevard was no longer visible. Nearly a quarter of a mile in, her cottage finally came into sight. It was tiny, and even from a distance he could tell that it needed a new coat of paint. The roofline sagged a bit and the walls were no longer square, but it exuded a certain charm, and Jack made a mental note to see if she needed help with any repairs.

Before the engine shut off, Gladys walked out the front door to see who was visiting.

"She hasn't changed a bit," thought Jack as he opened his door.

Short and wiry, her long silver hair pulled into a braid that ran down the center of her back, she wore khaki slacks and a baggy white shirt. Today, her standard boots, which were suitable for hiking about in the marshes, had been replaced with a pair of rubber gardening shoes. The only other things missing from her usual appearance were the too-large binoculars that were always slung around her neck and the large straw hat she always wore. She raised her hand over her eyes as she squinted to see the new arrival.

"Jack Beale? Is that you?" she called out as he walked toward her.

He was surprised how clearly he could hear her, considering how noisy the wind in the trees and in the marsh surrounding them was.

Before he could even say hello, she said, "What are you doing out here? Tell me inside. Come. I'll put some tea on." Then she turned and motioned for him to follow.

Jack held onto the door to prevent the wind from slamming it shut, and suddenly all became quiet and cozy. He didn't see her, but he could hear her rustling about in what had to be the kitchen. Her cottage was both neat and tidy and completely cluttered, all at the same time. Other than where a window or a door broke up a wall, there were either framed illustrations or paintings of birds and bookshelves filled with more books about birds than he had realized existed. Interspersed on the shelves were mementos and smaller framed photographs that told the story of a life in Rye Harbor and its birds.

He was taking it all in when he heard her say, "Tea will be ready in a few minutes. Why don't you come in the kitchen and tell me why you're here? I don't get many visitors, so I can only guess that you want something, but I can't imagine what. Please, come."

He followed her voice and stepped into a small, seriously outdated kitchen, but then, what wasn't outdated in her cottage? Her back was to the door, and she was standing at a counter next to the stove where a large, steaming kettle had just begun to whistle. Using a kitchen towel she had deftly folded into a small, thick square, she picked up the kettle of boiling water, which promptly went silent, and began filling an old-fashioned teapot. Jack was impressed with how easily she did that, considering her stature and the size of the kettle. As she poured, the water hissed as it hit the sides of the kettle.

Still with her back to him and the door, she said, "So, Jack, are you still seeing that little redhead? What was her name? Yes, Max. That's right, Max. How is she?"

"Yes, Max and I are still together. She's fine. Thank you for asking."

Gladys turned. In her hands she held a tray with the teapot, two cups on saucers, and a small plate with two cookies. Her eyes had a twinkle about them that was full of life, but Jack could also see that she was delighted to have a guest.

"Now, let's go in the other room and sit down and have our tea. I just got back the other day from Florida, and my, it's good to be home. Nothing but tourists and old people there, although the birds are pretty swell. Now, I can tell that you have something you want to ask me, but first, you have to tell me all about what you have been up to since that incident with that horrible man. That really was awful, too bad about your boat. I understand that you have a new one. Please sit down."

Gladys never spoke in single sentences, and her rapid-fire stream of questions and statements was sometimes a bit hard to follow, so Jack just smiled and nodded his head and took his seat.

She stopped talking as she handed him his cup of tea, but all he was able to say was, "Thank you," before she started talking again.

"Cookie?" She held the plate out to him. "I made them yesterday. Gingersnaps. Ginger's really good for you. Grew it in a pot right in my kitchen. I'm sure you know that ginger is good for seasickness. Of course you do, you're a sailor."

"Yes. Thank you." He took the offered cookie, but before he could say anything else she began again.

"I love birds. But, you know that. They're starting to leave now. They always know when the seasons change. Do you like birds?"

She took a sip of her tea then, and when she set the cup back down, she paused to appraise Jack. As she studied him, her eyes seemed to pierce right through him.

"Why are you here?" she finally said, before she sat back and continued to stare at him.

Her sudden change took Jack by surprise, and he too paused.

"I'm looking for some information."

She remained motionless.

"Courtney, Ben's niece who now owns Ben's, has been getting mysterious phone calls. The caller insists that she has something important from the past, but he won't say exactly what it is. Now those calls are becoming more insistent, almost threatening. She began looking around and found some old boxes stored away upstairs in Ben's and has been going through them. So far it looks like they are mostly old business records. You may not know, but way back, when I first arrived here, I needed a place to live. She offered the old barn behind her cottage to me. All I had to do was turn the second floor into an apartment. In the process I found, stashed in the barn, some boxes of old records. More interestingly there were some old boards with names painted on them, as well as dates mostly from the thirties and forties. Apparantly they came from the original part of Ben's, before she put on the addition."

Jack noticed a slight shift in her posture as he mentioned the writing on the boards. She was paying much closer attention to him now.

He went on. "So, long story short, those boxes contained notebooks filled with information about fishing: locations, yields, and the like. But the last one was written during the war, and it doesn't say much about fishing. Instead, it seems that Ben and the other fishermen would patrol the coast watching for U-boats. Most of the entries were detailed and uneventful, save one. It had no details."

Gladys was now sitting forward on her chair looking intently at Jack. "And what does this have to do with me?"

He looked at her. "I, um, we want to know what it was like here during the war. We want to try to understand exactly what Ben was writing about. No offense, but you've been here forever; you know Rye Harbor probably better than anyone else alive, and I'm guessing that you were a young girl during the forties. I thought that you might remember some of these things and help us find answers."

"So in other words, I'm old and still alive, unlike most of my contemporaries."

Jack looked down, slightly embarrassed.

"That's okay. You're right. You're welcome to stay for supper. I have some stew that I made as soon as I got home. It's always best after a couple of days."

"Thank you, but I should get going."

She went on as if she hadn't heard him. "It will give me a chance to tell you about the submarine."

CHAPTER 52

"AFTER THE WAR BROKE OUT IN EUROPE, there was real fear all along the coast. We weren't in the war yet, but I think everyone knew it was inevitable. The military closed the coast road, blackouts were in effect and coast watching patrols were organized. Several coast watching stations were set up in town, and one was on Straw's Point. Patrols were organized that would walk the coast both day and night watching for enemy activity. Since most of their shipping targets were further south, the real fear here was of enemy agents landing on the coast.

I heard tell that sometimes on dark, calm nights the engines of German U-boats could be heard just off shore as they recharged their batteries, and that just heightened those fears. Then it happened. One day a raft was found washed up on shore just south of Little Boar's Head."

"Do you remember when that was?"

"Not really, but it was about this time of year. It was on the morning after a bad storm. The raft was torn apart, probably from getting pounded on the rocks, and I overheard that weapons were found in it."

"Was a body ever recovered?"

"I don't know, the whole thing was hushed up pretty quickly."

A second pot of tea later, Jack sank back into his chair. "And you're sure about all this?"

"As sure as I can be. It all happened so many years ago and I haven't thought about any of this for a very long time."

He glanced at his watch.

"Crap," he mumbled under his breath. "It's later than I thought. I don't mean to run off, but it's sounding like it's getting nasty out, and I'm sure Max will be wondering where I am."

Gladys stood, picked up the tea tray, and began walking toward the kitchen.

* * *

Rain was coming. He could smell it. The wind buffeted his truck, and in the dark it seemed even more fierce. He could hear the continuous roar of the ocean, driven by that wind, as it slammed over and over against the rocky shore. In places the road was only wet, but occasionally spray from waves hitting the rocks made it necessary to use his wipers. His imagination drifted back in time, and as he thought of Gladys's stories, he could picture Ben out on the ocean on a night just like this.

As he rounded the harbor, the first drops of rain hit his windshield, and by the time he made the turn to Ben's, and home, it had become a full-on deluge. Even with his wipers set to fast, he could barely see the road ahead. Out of habit, he turned into Ben's even though the restaurant was dark and the parking lot empty. Straight ahead, he could see an occasional wave come over the rocks that protected the parking lot. Ben's provided enough of a wind break that the rain, as hard as it was falling, didn't seem quite as bad. Pulling up near the rocks, with his headlights shining out over the harbor, he could see Art's boat *Sea Witch* riding steadily on her mooring. He knew that further out, where *d'Riddem* was moored, the harbor would be considerably rougher, but there wasn't anything he could do about that.

CHAPTER 53

"WHERE HAVE YOU BEEN?" said Max as Jack made his way up the stairs. He shook the raindrops from his hair. In just the few steps from his truck to the door, he had gotten soaked.

"I'm sorry. Time got away from me. I went to visit Gladys. You know, the bird watcher."

Max looked at him. "Gladys? Why?"

"She's lived here all her life, and I thought she might be able to answer some questions I have about what it was like back during the war."

"And did she?"

"Yes, and no. Let me make some coffee and I'll tell you all about it."

* * *

They were sitting on the couch facing each other. As the story unfolded, Max became more and more quiet, totally focused on his words. Then she inhaled and whispered, "So Gladys confirmed that Ben had an encounter with a German U-boat."

"Not in so many words."

"But Ben and some of the other fishermen patrolled the coast on dark nights."

"True. She also said the Navy was as much a danger to them as any potential enemy threat, so they were very secretive about what they were doing."

"So she's not really sure?"

"No. Remember, she was a young girl, and no one really talked about it."

"Until they found that raft."

"Yes. Until they found that raft."

"So, what do you suppose really happened?"

"I don't know."

CHAPTER 54

COURTNEY MADE THE FINAL TURN into the Great Bay Marina. His call that morning had been a surprise, and now she wasn't sure what to expect. Their night together on *Vorspiel* had been memorable to say the least, but its abrupt ending still bothered her. Then there was the mystery of the departure of the yacht. More than once on the drive over she had asked herself why she was meeting him. There was no rational reason, but then, lust was never rational.

As she drove through the gates to the marina, she began to have real doubts. The rain was pelting down now, and the graveyard of broken boats looked eerie. While it was true, they had spent one incredible night together, the fact remained that she knew precious little about him. As the marina proper came into sight, the few security lights, each with its own small cone of light, made her feel like she was entering into a scene of some B grade movie. Driving slowly with gravel crunching under her tires, she headed toward the unlit corner of the lot where he asked her to meet him. She scanned the lot, and other than a couple of cars parked near the ramp that led down to the boats, the dimly lit gravel lot where she had agreed to meet him seemed deserted.

In her imagination she began to picture him walking out of the shadows, leaning into the wind with his shoulders hunched against the storm. With his hands shoved deep into the pockets of his trench coat, it's collar pulled up, and his fedora tipped down, his face would be hidden in shadow, leaving only the red bud of a cigarette visible.

Her thoughts were broken by the sound of waves of rain hammering her windshield. She shivered and asked herself once again what she was doing there. As the sounds of the wind whistling through the marina drowned out the sound of her idling engine, she looked out the window, one part of her hoping he would show up and another hoping he would not. Slowly, tentatively, she reached for the ignition key and turned it. With the engine silent, the storm's intensity seemed to increase. It almost felt like she had just terminated her last lifeline.

The rain fell harder, and soon the sound of it drumming against her car was all she could hear. Her thoughts returned to Edso. *"Who is he? What was it that made him so compelling to her, besides his physical abilities?"*

More questions were forming than answers when the passenger door was pulled open and he leaned in.

"Courtney. Thank you for coming."

"Edso—"

Before she could finish her question, he slid into the passenger seat. "Nasty night."

She looked over at him. His hair was wet, water droplets were running down his face, and the shoulders of his jacket were soaked.

"What are we doing here?"

"I needed to see you, and I owe you an apology."

She looked at him, not saying a word. *"Even soaked like a wet rat he looks delicious,"* she thought, her defenses weakening.

"I'm sorry about the way things on the boat ended. While you were in the shower, I got an unexpected call from my grandfather. He had heard that you were on board, and he wanted to meet you."

"So, what's the big deal?"

"I couldn't let that happen. Not then."

"Why not? Were you ashamed of me?"

"It's complicated."

"So un-complicate it. Tell me." She was beginning to lose patience.

"Understand, I just did what I had to do."

This was not what she wanted to hear.

"Okay. You did what you had to do. I get it." She stared at him, thinking, *"Tell me, you son of a bitch."*

"Okay, but you have to hear me out."

"Fair enough."

She watched him try to wipe off the water that was dripping down his face. She said, "There's a towel in the back."

He twisted around and retrieved the towel, and she watched as he wiped his face then rubbed his hair in an attempt to stop it from dripping. Satisfied, he stopped rubbing, lowered the towel, and looked at her.

"My grandfather . . . Let's just say he's something of an amateur historian, and he's looking for something He thinks that what he's looking for is in this area and that you are the key to finding it."

"Me? Did you know that someone has been calling me asking me just that?"

"Who?"

"I don't know. He won't identify himself. Was it him?"

"I don't think so."

"You don't think so!"

"I don't. That's not the way he does things."

She continued to stare at him, thinking, "*So why didn't he just ask me?*"

"I know what you're thinking: Why didn't he just ask you?"

She nodded.

"I wish there were a simple answer."

"Seems simple enough to me."

Edso let out a loud sigh.

"It's not. He has his quirks and at times can be unpredictable—almost volatile—and he's definitely impatient. I was afraid that if he met you and you weren't able or willing to tell him what he wanted, well . . . I was worried about what he might do."

"What he might do! Tell him what he wanted? What the hell are you talking about?"

Ignoring her outburst, he went on. "He asked me for my help, and I've been helping him."

"Stop. So you were just using me."

"No! That's what he wanted, but—"

"You son of a bitch—"

"No. Court, hear me out."

For a moment, it became eerily quiet in her car. She even stopped noticing the rain on the roof.

"Before I ever met you, he knew all about you. He asked me to get close to you, to do whatever it took to find out what he wanted to know."

"So this was all a sham."

"No. That's not what I'm saying."

"Sounds like it to me. I think you need to leave. Please get out of my car."

He didn't move.

"Courtney, truly. I like you, and I know him."

Court stared at him, mouth open, hardly daring to believe what he had just said to her.

"I wanted to warn you without him knowing. That's why I'm here tonight."

"Get out of my car."

He didn't move.

"Get out!"

"Court, let me explain." He reached out and took hold of her arm. Surprised, she pulled back, but he held on, refusing to let go.

"Stop. You're hurting me."

Even in the near darkness of the car, she could see that something in his face had changed and that, despite his words, he intended to find out the answer to his grandfather's questions.

"I'm sorry, Court. Believe me, I do like you, very much, and I wish it didn't have to be this way. However, I think he's right. I think you do have what he's looking for, and I intend to get it before he does. It's the only way."

Trying to control her panic, she continued to stare at him. She thought, *"The only way?"*

She decided to stall for time.

"So tell me what it is you're looking for, because I really have no idea. Just tell me, and I'll help you get it." She hoped that her voice didn't sound too desperate.

"Will you?"

She could tell he didn't believe her.

"Yes. Whatever it is, I'm pretty sure that I can still live without it." She fought to steady her voice, not wanting to give him any advantage.

He eased his grip, but he did not release her arm.

"I want to believe you. I really do, but we'll just have to wait and see about that."

She took a deep breath. "Look, Edso, I understand, but if I'm going to help you, you have to tell me what you're looking for."

"In 1942 . . ."

As soon as he said that, a chill went through her as she remembered Ben's journals.

"Nineteen forty-two?" she said.

"In 1942, there was an incident that your Uncle Ben was involved in. It resulted in a disappearance and probably a death."

"I have no idea what you're talking about. My uncle Ben was a fisherman."

"I know. But did you know that during the war we believe that he was part of a group who would patrol the coast looking for German submarines."

She lied. "I did not. What's that have to do with anything?"

"There was a night, not unlike tonight. The war was in full swing. Up and down the eastern seaboard, German U-boats were preying on allied shipping, often within sight of the coast. On that night, instead of looking for targets, a German sub crept in close to the coast near here, intending to land an agent. That man was never heard from again,

174

and he was presumed to have drowned. That agent was my great-grand-father's best friend. I was named after him. Records confirm that at about that time, a German rubber raft washed up onto the shore south of Rye Harbor."

Unwilling to reveal the validity of what he was telling her, she made herself giggle, as if she was mocking him.

"You're kidding, right? If anything like that had ever happened around here, I'm sure I would have heard about it, especially if it concerned Uncle Ben. But I've never heard this. Sounds more like an old movie."

His hand squeezed her arm a bit tighter.

"It's not. I'm telling you this because I don't want to see you harmed."

"You have a funny way of showing your concern."

"Court, you don't seem to be getting the gravity of your position."

Anger washed over her. "Oh, I get it all right. You're nothing more than a deceitful, spoiled little prick. You've been told a story and, I don't know why, but for some reason you believe it and you used me—"

She didn't finish her sentence as he raised his other hand as if to hit her, then stopped. She stared at him, knowing that a line had been crossed that couldn't be uncrossed.

His face softened immediately. "I'm so sorry. Court, I really am trying to help you."

"I need to go home. Please get out of my car!"

She was able to control the quiver in her voice, but the tears flowed as soon as he stepped out and shut the door.

AFTER COURTNEY DROVE OFF, Edso stood there watching until her tail-lights had disappeared from sight. He was angry at himself for being such a fool. He had let his emotions cloud his judgment. Maybe his grandfather's way was right. He had taken a chance, convinced that what he and Courtney had shared together, that one night, would be enough to sway her, even though deep inside he knew it was unlikely. But he had allowed his feelings to cloud his judgment. If his grandfather found out about what he had done, Courtney would be in more danger than before. And now he . . . no—she—would have to pay the price. His grandfather would see to that.

Edso looked toward the docks. After their lunch, he had returned to the marina to see if they knew of any boats available for charter. As it happened, Rusty overheard the conversation, caught up to him when he walked outside and offered *Christine* to him, for a price.

* * *

He was soaked and beginning to shiver as he walked to the docks. As dark as it was, it was easier to see where he was going if he stayed in the shadows because the well-intentioned security lights created blind spots as their light reflected off of the wind-driven rain. In the parking lot there had been a steady whooshing of the wind through the surrounding trees, punctuated by the steady tinking from some wayward halyard slapping against a mast. As he neared the docks, what had seemed a steady whooshing sound from the wind, changed. It became more complex and layered as it blew through and around all the different kinds and shapes of boats tied to the floats, each one producing it's own set of subtle whines and whistles. Adding to those overtones, now he could feel as much as hear the percussive thuds and clanks as boats alternately tugged and slammed against the floats. Those, in turn, would make a dull thud as they bashed against the pilings that held everything in place.

The ramp down was wet and slippery, forcing him to hold onto the railing with both hands. At its end, he began negotiating his way down the floats. More slippery than the ramp and buffeted by the wind and driving rain, they rose and fell, shook and shuddered and his thoughts flashed back to a time as a young boy when his grandfather had taken him to a carnival, and they went through the fun house together, only this time he wasn't afraid.

Tied at the far end of the floats, straining against her lines to break free, was *Christine*. Compared to *Vorspiel*, she was tiny and spartan, but her trawler design inspired a look of invincibility. She was well found and had weathered far worse storms than this in her lifetime, and more importantly, was unknown to his grandfather. As he fumbled for his keys to the cabin door, he swore softly under his breath. He had to try to find another way to fix this without hurting Courtney, and at the same time, he just couldn't let his grandfather down. Not now, not after all these years, when they were so close to success.

He pulled the cabin door open and slipped inside. He had to lean against the door to keep the wind from slamming it shut. As soon as it was securely closed, much of the noise from the storm ceased and even though she tugged and jerked against her lines, she was far more stable than being outside on the floats.

A puddle began to form at his feet. Rather than tracking water all through the boat, he peeled off his clothes and dropped them there by the door. Now, naked and wet he began to shiver more violently and wished that Courtney were there to help fight the chill. He rapidly-moved forward and down the stairs to the stateroom where he quickly toweled off and put on dry clothes.

With chattering teeth, he moved aft, past the head to the galley and put a kettle of water on for coffee. Knowing it would be a few minutes, he went back up the stairs to the salon to retrieved his wet clothes. By the time he had them wrung out and hanging in the head to dry, the water was ready. As he pressed the plunger down on the french press, the smell of hot coffee filled the galley. He took a large mug out of the cupboard and filled it with the steaming brew. Cupping it in his hands, he felt its warmth and inhaled its aromas before gingerly taking his first sip. Swallowing, he could feel that first sip as it traveled the entire way down from his mouth to his stomach. Feeling better, he returned to the salon.

He purposely left the lights off in the salon so as to be able to see out. He couldn't help but notice how much colder and foreboding it seemed in the dark, in sharp contrast to the warm cozy feeling below where he had left the lights on. The sound of the rain slashing against the glass and the steady moan of the wind sent a shiver through him as he moved forward and stepped up to the helm. There, there were two seats, side by side, and in front of them was an impressive array of electronics and the controls for driving the boat.

After first placing his coffee in a holder on the instrument console, he hiked himself up into the seat on the right. He switched on the radio and a faint green glow from its screen filled the helm station. Switching the channel to one of the NOAA weather reports, he listened intently. The storm was relatively fast moving and by morning would be mostly past.

Radio off, coffee in hand, he sat there, looking out into the storm and began to consider his options. Earlier he had made a mistake, a combination of overestimating his charm and underestimating her independence. He didn't think it was insurmountable, but it definitely was a setback. A bigger problem was going to be his grandfather.

Edso and his grandfather shared similar pasts. Both grew up without their parents, each raised by a grandfather, but that's where the similarities ended. Edso's parents were killed in a automobile accident in the high alps when he was a young boy. His grandfather, as his only living relative, took him in and raised him as his own. He was sent to the best schools and, when he was old enough, his grandfather took him along as he conducted his business all over the world. Edso watched and learned as his grandfather amassed wealth beyond imagining. They developed a unique relationship that was as much father and son as it was business partners. He loved his grandfather, and even though his grandfather was never one to openly express his emotions, Edso always knew he was loved.

Over the years, there were times when Edso would ask his grandfather about his own father and mother, and when he did, his grandfather's reaction was always the same. He would become very quiet and turn his head away just enough so Edso wouldn't be able to see his face clearly, his jaw muscles would tense and then, slowly, he'd turn back to face him, and would say, "Someday, just not today."

It wasn't until recently that that someday arrived. And now he was helping his grandfather in what some might consider a quixotic quest. *"But what if it didn't exist?"* he thought as a particularly heavy gust of wind hit, causing the trawler to heel over. Jerked back to the present, he could hear the moans and creaks as the lines that held her to the dock fought the wind. For a moment it was a draw, then the wind eased and the lines held. It was time to go to sleep.

CHAPTER 56

COURTNEY GLANCED BACK ONLY ONCE AS SHE DROVE OUT OF THE MARINA. Even though she couldn't see him, she could feel him standing there, watching as she drove off.

It was a long, slow ride home. Straining to see through the combination of her tears and the driving rain, she replayed everything that had happened from the first time she met Edso until she left the marina. Instead of any clarity she was left with only questions: *What are they looking for? What happened on that night in 1942 to her uncle? Who is Edso, really?*

At the end of her drive, just as she turned to park in front of her cottage, her headlights swept across the front of Jack's place, and for a split second they lit the boards still standing in front of his shop. In that moment her fatigue vanished as she remembered that Jack wanted to talk to her. Recently, he had become obsessed with the journal and those boards. Tomorrow, she would seek him out first thing.

* * *

"She's home," said Max the next morning as she looked out the window over at Courtney's cottage. Even though the sun was up, the low, thick clouds filtered its light into a monochromatic, grey.

Jack joined her at the window. "Looks like the rain stopped. Bet the sky will be clear by sunset."

"Are you going to talk to her?"

"It's still a bit early, but yes. Later, I will."

He turned away from the window, picked up Ben's journal, and sat down on the couch. He began flipping back and forth through its pages, checking his notes, reassuring himself that his theory made sense.

A loud knocking on the door sent Cat scurrying off the couch where she had settled to help Jack review his theories.

"Coming," he called out, Jack knew that whomever was at the door probably wouldn't hear him, but that wasn't the point. He was acknowledging to himself that he knew someone was there. Glancing at his watch as he stood, he was surprised at how late it was.

Max, peering out the window as he moved toward the stairs, said, "It's Courtney."

That quickened his step.

As soon as Jack unlocked the door, Courtney walked in without even giving him time to say hi.

"Jack, we've got to talk."

"And good morning to you," he said, as she hurried up the stairs.

Before closing the door, he looked outside and inhaled deeply, taking in that rich, salty, seaweedy, post storm ocean smell.

"Jack, you coming?" Courtney called down, ending the moment.

"On the way."

"Jack, we've got to talk. I have an idea what this is all about. Where's that journal?"

He pointed toward the couch.

She walked over to it, sat down, and began flipping through pages, obviously looking for something.

"Here." She stabbed her finger on a page.

"What's that?"

"This," she said. She turned the journal toward him. It was that partial entry.

29 September 1942.

"What about it?" asked Jack.

"Something happened that night. I'm sure it's the reason behind all those calls I've been getting.

CHAPTER 57

EDSO, WAKING UP ON THE CHARTERED TRAWLER, was startled by a chorus of gulls shattering the silence. Not fully awake, he lay in his berth, eyes open, and struggled to separate his dreams from reality. A soft light filled the cabin. Then a lone gull cried out, as if it were a cantor in some silent church, followed by the others, who provided the response. The storm was over, and he realized that he had not been awakened so much by the gulls as by the silence that surrounded them.

He stopped in the galley to put water on for coffee before walking up the stairs into the salon. Outside he could see that the clouds were beginning to thin and break. Wet leaves not only littered the docks but also were plastered on the windows of the trawler. In the water, trapped in the nooks and corners where float met float, and between boat and float, small branches had accumulated, along with great gobs of seaweed and a wide assortment of other flotsam.

Hearing the water boiling, he went below to get his coffee, and by the time he returned to the salon, rays of sun were poking through the clouds. He was still filled with regret about Courtney. Closing his eyes, it was easy to remember her feel and touch from their night together on *Vorspiel.* But that memory was short-lived as his thoughts drifted to her departure last night. Had he said too much, or did he not tell her enough? Regardless, she was upset, and he never should have grabbed her. Still, he remained convinced that she had what his grandfather wanted, and he was still confident that he would be able to get it. His main concerns were his grandfather's impatience and the thought of what could happen if he was not successful.

Those thoughts were interrupted by the ringtone on his phone.

"And good morning to you," he said, knowing who was calling and making no attempt to hide his true feelings.

There was a pause on the line. "Yes, you as well. Do you have it?"

Edso paused before responding. "I will."

"Time is growing short. I'm heading back to the marina. See you soon."

The line went dead, and Edso looked at the phone in his hand. "Shit."

* * *

Edso's departure from Great Bay was quick and efficient. He needed to get to the Wentworth Marina before his grandfather. He couldn't let the old man go after Courtney.

The trip down the Piscataqua was relatively quick as he rode the outgoing tide. Lacking its usual blue-green hue, the river had a flatter look that seemed almost muddy. He overtook small branches, blown from trees along the river bank, patches of seaweed that had been set afloat by the storm, and even an old plastic chair with one leg snapped off. As he passed under the I-95 bridge, he looked up and couldn't help but feel really small. Noting the speed with which the sky was clearing, he guessed that the sunset most likely would be spectacular, and he smiled for a moment as he remembered the sunset he and Courtney had watched together.

Passing between the jetties into Little Harbor, he noted that *Vorspiel* had not yet arrived, and he breathed a sigh of relief. Edso moved the trawler up against the fuel dock, and he was securing his last dock line when he heard a familiar voice call out. He looked up and saw the dockmaster walking toward him.

"Edso, I didn't expect to see you. *Vorspiel's* returning some time tonight. I'm hanging out until she arrives. I would have thought you'd be on her."

"Hey Jeremy. Is she?" He acted surprised.

"Yeah, called this morning."

"Really? Where's she coming from? My grandfather on board?" He knew the answer to that last question, but he decided to play dumb.

"Don't know, and I didn't ask. The captain just said that they'd be arriving sometime tonight."

"That's so my grandfather. Says he's coming, gives no time, makes people wait for him," thought Edso.

"Hope he doesn't keep you waiting all night."

"Me too. Thanks." Jeremy looked over the trawler and added, "Nice boat."

"Chartered her. I'm planning on cruising down Maine. She's comfortable, handles well. Very seakindly."

"What brings you back here?"

"Came to visit a friend."

Jeremy smiled. "Anyone I know?"

Edso shook his head. "Listen, any chance you got a slip for me? Maybe somewhere down this row?" He motioned down dock A.

Jeremy paused a moment. "How long?"

"Not sure right now. Couple days at least."

"Sure. About halfway down. You need fuel?"

"I think I'm okay."

"Let's get you moved then."

As the last dock line was made secure and the trawler was sitting placidly in her new home, Edso said, "Hey, you guys still provide a courtesy car?"

"We do, but it's out. Give me an hour and I'll get you some wheels. Just stop by the office."

"Thanks." His stomach grumbled. "Oh, one more thing. Best place for a bite to eat, not too fancy."

"The Green Bean Dockside right here in the marina. Great sandwiches and soups. They'll deliver to the boat. Number's in here."

Jeremy took a brochure out of his back pocket and handed it to Edso.

"Thanks again."

Edso watched as Jeremy walked down the dock. The slip that he was in was perfect. He could easily see the entrance to Little Harbor, but it was nestled far enough down the dock that even if his grandfather knew he was there, he would be hard to see.

A quick phone call and lunch was on its way. He had just enough time for a shower, a change of clothes, and a quick beer on board before it arrived.

As he finished his sandwich and soup, the afternoon slipped by quickly. True to the forecast, the sky continued to clear. Edso thought of Courtney again with both longing and regret. There was no doubt now that the sunset would be beautiful.

CHAPTER 58

MAX OFFERED TO MAKE COFFEE, leaving Courtney and Jack alone. As soon as they heard her move into the kitchen, they both spoke at the same time, their words becoming an unintelligible jumble.

They both stopped.

"You first," each said at the same time. That broke the tension. Jack motioned toward her to speak first.

"This has to be what it's all about." Again she pointed at the journal. "Edso told me as much."

"What is *what* all about?"

"This." She held out the book to Jack, pointing to the September 29 entry. "Edso told me a story about his great-grandfather. In 1942 he was second in command on a U-boat that was on a secret mission to land an agent here in the United States on that night. He was killed before the war ended. That agent was his great-grandfather's best friend, but he was never heard from again. Ever since, Edso's grandfather has been looking for answers about his father's friend's disappearance in the hope that it would help restore his father's reputation as well, and Edso is helping him. Your turn."

"I saw Gladys last night."

"The bird-watching lady?"

"The same."

"Why?"

"I read through all Ben's journals and I had questions. She's about the only person I know who was around here back then, so I went to talk to her."

"What did she tell you?"

"It took a while—you know how she rambles—but over several hours, a few pots of tea, and some killer stew, she told me a story about how Ben was the only one to actually encounter a U-boat."

"He did?"

Jack could tell that this was news to Courtney.

"Apparently. He would never talk about it so it was all rumor and whispers, but she remembered that it happened on a night like last night."

"That night. September 29th?" she said, pointing at the journal.

"She couldn't remember the exact date, but she did say it was about this time of year, so I am assuming so. The only thing she could say with any certainty was that a German raft washed up on shore just south of Little Boar's Head. She never saw it, because the Navy came and quickly took it away, but she heard there were weapons in it."

"So if he never talked about it, maybe that's why there isn't more to this entry."

Max returned with the coffee and handed them each a cup.

"Quite a story!" she said. "So, what are you going to do?"

Jack said, "What do you mean by *do?*"

"I don't know," Max said. "Contact the authorities?"

"Who would you contact?" Courtney asked.

Max said, "The Navy? The FBI?"

Jack broke in. "Listen. This is something that may or may not have happened a very long time ago. No one is going to be interested. All we have is a journal with a date and a notation of the weather on that day and some stories from a crazy old lady."

"You're wrong," Courtney said. "Don't forget Edso. He's interested—*very*. And so is his grandfather."

Jack knew she was right. Then, before he could say anything else, she went on.

"What about those boards outside that you keep staring at?"

"Well, here's the thing. You've seen them. Most of what's painted on them is boat names, a few dates, and some catch weights. But as I read his journals, I realized that some of what was painted on the boards matched up with what was in the journals."

Max said, "And those boards came from Ben's? Remind me—what was in that building before he set up the restaurant?"

"You weren't here when we added the new dining room at Ben's. We wrapped around the old dining room and in doing so, that room was stripped out and openings cut in to open it up to the new room. I remember that those boards were from some of those cut-outs. I had them saved thinking that someday I would use them for decoration. Obviously I never did and forgot about them."

"So before Ben's was a restaurant, what was that room?"

"It was a storeroom, or something like that, that he used for his fishing gear."

Jack said nothing as he thought about what she had just said.

"What are you thinking?" Max asked.

"I'm not sure. Come down with me." With that, he began walking toward the stairs.

The clouds were beginning to break up and small patches of sky were appearing, but everything was still wet.

"Look here. See these names—here, here, and here. I found them mentioned in one of his journals."

Max and Courtney looked where he was pointing. Then he continued.

"But over here, in the corner, where it's kind of painted over, there are some things that I'm still trying to figure out. These letters, see. He traced them with his finger. J.E.S. and these numbers."

Court leaned in for a closer look. "I don't know, Jack. Do you suppose they continued onto another section of wall? One that wasn't cut out?"

"It's possible."

She shot him a look.

"Court, no. I would never expect . . ."

"Good. Now that we're clear, I have to get over to Ben's. Good luck." Then, turning to Max, she asked, "You in today?"

"Yes, I'll be right along," said Max.

CHAPTER 59

"DAMN IT, BEN," COURTNEY MUTTERED TO HERSELF.

She was standing in one of the second-floor rooms above the dining room, from which those boards were cut out. Surrounding her on the floor were the contents of several of the boxes that she had found tucked away in a closet up here—business records, old newspapers from the early fifties, and several old and faded photos of Rye Harbor, both before and after the jetties were built. There was one striking image of a fishing schooner under full sail that someone had written across the bottom of the picture "Schooner *Jessica* returning from the Grand Bank, circa 1930." When she realized that it was a photo of the model in the bar she looked at it a bit more closely. On the back was a note that she was lost during the hurricane of 1938. She made a mental note that she should get it framed and displayed next to the model. There was also an assortment of desk junk—paper clips, a typewriter ribbon, pencils, pens and several old mugs, including one that looked like it had never been washed.

"I know it's here," she mumbled under her breath.

As she looked over the piles of stuff, a scene kept playing in her thoughts—a day when Ben had pulled her aside and said some strange things and that memory was haunting her.

By late afternoon, she had just begun to repack the contents of the boxes when her phone rang. She considered not answering it, but in the end, she couldn't help herself.

It was Edso.

"Hello, Court. . . . Please don't hang up."

She didn't, but at the same time, she said nothing.

"Look, I'm sorry about last night. I dumped all this stuff on you and then I lost my temper. It was inexcusable, and it won't happen again. Can we meet?"

"I don't think we have anything to talk about."

"No. Wait. Look, I know how you must feel—"

"You don't know anything about how I feel."

"Then let me come talk to you."

There was a long silence before she answered. "I'll be at Ben's until closing tonight."

Then she hung up and went back to work.

CHAPTER 60

JACK WAS SITTING AT THE BAR, a half finished beer in front of him, when Courtney came down.

"Max here?" she asked, as she walked behind the bar, came around front, and sat next to him.

"Just went to the kitchen. You okay? Max said you've been upstairs all afternoon. She made it very clear you didn't want to be disturbed. Did you find what you were looking for?"

"No. In fact, I'm not even sure what I'm looking for. But years ago, Ben started to tell me about something he had or maybe something he had done and now it's really bugging me."

"What was it?"

"I need a glass of wine. You want another beer?"

"Sure."

Drinks poured, she sat back down and looked at Jack. "This morning when we were looking at those boards, something popped into my head—I don't know why, but I remembered something Ben had said to me once."

"And that was?"

Courtney became silent and stared at the glass of wine in her hand. He said something like, "It was wrong, he didn't care and that someday it would be mine."

"Well, he did leave you this place."

"I know, but I just feel that that's not what it is. I remember back after he died, I was going through old papers and stuff and found some things that didn't make much sense. But now, with what's been going on, I think they might hold the answers."

"I'm assuming that you didn't have any success finding them."

"None."

"Do you remember what they were about?"

"Not really. I just have this feeling that they're important."

"Hey Court," it was Max. "Everything OK?"

"Yeah, fine."

She gave Court a look that said she wasn't buying it.

Jack looked at Court and said, "Let's try this. Do you remember anything else about when he said that to you?"

Court closed her eyes and tipped her head back and began speaking in a very deliberate tone, telling him the story. "It was shortly before Ben died. Late one fall, when Kara and I were working here, I found him sitting out on the dock by himself. He wasn't his usual gruff self. He seemed subdued and asked me to sit down with him. He started rambling on about how things had changed once the breakwaters were built. There was a storm coming in that night, and he said something like it was going to be like "that night". She used air quotes for emphasis. Before I could ask him what night, Kara called me to help with something. As I got up, he grabbed my arm and that's when he said that he knew it was wrong, but he didn't care. He said that what was left would be mine."

"And you had no idea what he was talking about."

She shook her head. "I guess at the time I just thought he meant Ben's. We got interrupted, and he never said anything else. But after all of these recent events, I don't know. I guess I thought I'd find something in one of those boxes upstairs.

Max, who had been listening intently, said, "Maybe he found some treasure or something and kept it. You haven't found any old treasure maps, have you?"

"Don't be silly. I'm sure that if he had found some buried treasure, we would have heard about it."

Suddenly Jack said, "That's got to be it."

"What?" said Max and Court together.

"September 29. What if it's true and Ben found that raft first, kept whatever was in it, and didn't tell anyone. Remember—Gladys said that a raft washed up south of Little Boar's Head."

Max smiled. "See? Like a treasure."

"Oh my god. You're right. That has to be the night Edso was telling me about. So now what?"

"I don't know. We have to find it first," said Jack.

CHAPTER 61

"HEY, COURT," SAID MAX, as she plopped down the case of beer she had just brought in from out back. "Everything is set for the rest of Angela's shift. You need anything else before we leave?"

"I don't think so. You and Jack go on and get out of here."

Then, turning to Jack, she said, "Thanks. Maybe tomorrow I'll find it."

"Let's hope. Get some rest. Good-night."

Courtney watched as they walked out of the bar, and it wasn't until she heard the clingling of the bells that hung on the front door that she knew they were actually gone. She took a deep breath to calm her pounding heart. She hadn't realized how anxious she had been that Edso might show up while her friends were still there. She finished her glass of wine and after making sure that all was set in the restaurant, she went back upstairs.

She returned to that small room where she had been before Jack had showed up With the door pushed shut, she leaned back against it looked and at the pile of boxes that sat in the middle of the room. "OK Ben, let's try this again," she said under her breath.

Ben's words kept cycling through her memory *"I know it was wrong, but I didn't care. What's left will be yours some day."*

"What did you do and what did you leave me?" she said to the empty room.

She began going through the boxes she had looked at earlier again. It wasn't until the phone rang for the second or third time that she noticed it. *"Come on Angela, get the phone."*

When it continued to ring, she finally got up from her task and picked up the phone. Her hello went unanswered. A chill went down her spine and she could feel her heart pounding. "Hello?" she repeated.

The line remained silent and then she heard a click and the line went dead. Until she went to hang up the phone, she hadn't realized how much her hands were shaking.

It took a few minutes and some deep calming breaths before she was able to resume her search. Shaken, she decided that she wouldn't wait for Edso, but would leave at the same time as Angela.

The knock on the door made her jump. "Court, I'm all set. Do you want me to wait for you?" It was Angela.

"Could you? Give me a minute and I'll be right down." That minute was more like ten.

As she reached the bottom of the stairs she could hear voices. First Angela's then Edso's. Her heart began to pound. She had hoped to escape before he arrived.

"Courtney, look who's here," said Angela when she saw her. "Just after I talked to you he came in and introduced himself. He wanted to surprise you. I've been entertaining him until you got down."

"Hello, Court."

"E-Edso. What a surprise."

Sensing some tension, she asked, "Court, you want me to stay?"

"No. Go on and get out of here. I'll be fine. Thank you."

* * *

"Thank you for waiting," he said.

She said nothing. Instead, she poured herself a glass of wine and took a sip, all the while eyeing him. He looked as good as she remembered in those jumbled memories that she had from their night together.

"What do you want, Edso?" she asked, trying to remain distant.

"I want to help you."

"Bullshit. That's not what you said the other night. You and your grandfather want something from me. I don't know what it is, and I'm pretty sure I don't have it."

"I'm sorry."

"Stop. Don't waste any more of my time with your apologies. You—or maybe *Granddad*—has been harassing me for months with anonymous phone calls. Then you conveniently bumped into me at The Pic. You used your grandfather's yacht to seduce me, and then you got all secretive and demanding. I'm sick of it, and I want you to go away."

Edso stood and looked at her. "Fine, I'll go—if you really want me to. But know this: my grandfather won't stop until he has satisfaction. As far as he's concerned, your uncle stole from him, I'm not joking around, Courtney. Your only chance of coming out of this in one piece is with me."

She stared at him in silence. As much as she wanted to discount his words, she could tell he was speaking the truth, and she was scared.

"He stole something from your grandfather. How can that be?"

"I'll try to explain. Remember I told you about how his father was second in command on a U-boat, and that one of their missions was to land an agent off the coast here. His father tried to delay the mission because of the weather, but the Captain insisted on proceeding. The mission failed and the agent disappeared with a sizeable fortune in cash and gold. To avoid taking responsibility, the captain implicated my grandfather's father as having been an accomplice in the agent's disappearance. Before he could clear his name and reputation, he was killed in the war."

"So how does my uncle fit into this story."

"We believe that it was he who killed that agent and stole the gold and cash."

"You've got to be kidding."

"No, I'm not. My grandfather blames your uncle for his father's death and he thinks that by recovering what he presumes your uncle stole, he'll be able to prove that he was a hero of the Reich, not a traitor."

"Edso. Listen to yourself. That makes no sense."

"Maybe to a sane person, but to my grandfather it is the truth."

"So, what exactly are you doing here, and what do you want?"

"I told you. I'm here to help you."

"Help me how?"

"Help you by keeping you safe and protecting you from my grandfather until I/we can show him that he is wrong."

"I don't need protecting."

"You do. You don't know him like I know him. He has been on a lifelong quest filled with anger and revenge. Now he feels that the end is in sight, and he won't be denied. I'm sorry to sound so dramatic, but I don't know any other way to put it. He's absolutely ruthless. Over the years, I've seen him crush anyone who got in his way: business rivals, enemies, even friends. The result is always the same, and now you are in his sights."

"And I'm supposed to just believe you."

"I think you have to. There's too much at stake right now. I really do care about you, Courtney. You have to trust me. "

Again, silence filled the bar. Finally, she said, "It's time to go."

"Go," she repeated. Then she put her hand on the light switch and motioned for him to go out the door.

The deadbolt snicked as she turned the key. He was waiting for her at the top of the stairs, and she turned and walked toward him, stopping only when she was close enough to feel the heat of his body. In a small, soft voice she said, "So, how are you going to protect me?"

CHAPTER 62

"WELL, WELL, WELL. WHAT HAVE WE HERE?"

Ken was sitting quietly in his boat, waiting for *Vorspiel* to arrive, when he first saw them. He recognized Edso before realizing that his companion was the woman from a few nights before. But this time, instead of flirting and grabbing his hand, she was following behind him like a cowed dog. When he reached the bottom of the stairs he didn't even pause for her to catch up, but rather strode down the boardwalk heading toward the far end of the marina.

Ken's curiosity was piqued, so he continued to watch them carefully. When they were about to move out of his sight, he climbed off his boat and quietly followed.

Reaching the end, Edso opened the gate for Dock A and they passed through. In order to remain out of sight, Ken did the same, only he went through the gate that led to Dock B which ran parallel to Dock A. This way he could use all the boats tied in their slips for cover but still see exactly where they were going.

About halfway down the B dock, he stopped when he saw the lights and then the unmistakable shape of a very large yacht coming into the harbor. Glancing across at the other dock, he saw Edso also stop and look at the arriving vessel before quickly ushering his companion onto a small trawler.

"Interesting," he thought.

However, he didn't have time to dwell on the couple further, because his real interest was just arriving and he needed to get back to his boat.

* * *

"I'm sorry that the accommodations won't be quite as luxurious as on *Vorspiel*," he said as he stopped on the dock in front of a boat.

She took a quick look. It wasn't anything like *Vorspiel*. Small and blocky, what it lacked in flash and sexiness it more than made up for with a solid, practical, workmanlike appearance.

"Yours?"

"I chartered it."

He motioned for her to climb aboard. As she stepped from the dock to the boat, she heard a low thrumming sound and the faint crackle of people talking on radios. To her right, near the harbor's entrance, she saw the enormous yacht, and a chill went down her spine.

She turned to Edso and said, "It's them, isn't it?"

"Yes." His reply was terse as he brushed past her and unlocked the door. "Come inside, it's chilly out here."

He was holding the door open for her. She slid past him and stopped inside the main salon. He followed, and she couldn't help but notice that he made no attempt to turn on any lights.

"So now what?" she whispered.

"You don't have to whisper, no one will hear us," he said, but his own voice was soft.

"Are you going to turn on some lights?"

"Not planning to."

She could hear the smile in his tone, and as her mind flashed back to their one night together, she blushed, thankful that the cabin was dark.

"Okay, I'm here. Now, what's this about protecting me?"

She didn't move as he stepped toward her, and for a split second she could feel the heat radiating off his body.

Another step and he gently took her hand. His hand was warm, and it made her shiver.

"You're safe here . . . with me."

CHAPTER 63

HOLDING HER HAND, EDSO LED COURTNEY down the steps and into the stateroom. He still did not switch on any lights, and she had to rely on the small amount of light that came in through the portlight on either side of the stateroom and through the overhead hatch. In the low light, shadows barely existed and touch was needed to fill in what the eyes could not see.

He pulled her close now, and as their bodies came together, a wave of warmth flooded over her. She could feel her heart racing and her legs weakening.

Then, releasing her hand, he slowly, gently, cupped her face in his hands. First his breath moved to her cheek, just brushing past her lips. Then, ever so lightly, his lips touched hers. That first tentative kiss could not have had a more intense reaction had it been a high-voltage line. Every part of her became hypersensitive, and all at the same time she wanted it to stop even as she wanted more. Her lips parted as did his, and they kissed deeply, driven by an urgency that could not be stopped.

Breathing heavily, he pulled back from her, and as his fingertips began to loosen the buttons on her shirt, she sucked in her breath as another wave of current passed through her. She reached down and fumbled with the buckle on his belt, all the while staring up into his eyes. Taking turns, clothing began to drop on the floor until there was none left to drop.

Now it was her turn to take his hand, and she guided him to the bed. The sheets were cold, which caused them each to suck in a deep breath followed by a small giggle. Ever so slowly, they each touched the other. They drew circles with fingertips on bare flesh, kissed and nibbled, and continued to pleasure each other until there was nothing left to kiss or nibble, and then they became one.

200

Courtney sat up with a start. It took her a moment to remember where she was, and when she did, she blushed. What had awakened her, she did not know, but as she sat up, she realized that Edso was not beside her. She patted the bedcovers just to make sure.

"Edso," she said softly.

There was no answer. Her imagination began to take over her thoughts. She climbed out of the bed and groped around on the floor for something to put on. The first thing her hand touched was his T-shirt.

"He couldn't have gone far without his shirt," she thought, and without thinking further, pulled it on. She could still smell him in the fabric, and that made her wish that he was there.

Just as he had not turned on any lights when they boarded the boat, she did not turn on any as she looked for him. Her eyes were fully adjusted to the near dark now, and she could see surprisingly well.

After leaving the stateroom, she looked in the galley before making her way toward the stairs. There was no sign of him, and as her imagination fully kicked in, she started to panic. Slowly she moved up the stairs, testing each one before putting her full weight on it, trying hard not to make a sound. She stopped as soon as she was able to see into the main cabin, but, as below, there was no sign of him there. Neither was he all the way forward in the helm station.

"Edso, this isn't funny," she thought, trying to fight off the fear that had taken hold.

As she finally stepped off the stairs and into the main cabin, she was able to see outside. Other than the small lights on the pedestals between each pair of slips, all was dark. She could see, far on the other side of the marina, the glow of lights that had to be *Vorspiel*.

"Did he go see his grandfather?"

After the way he had been acting, she didn't think this seemed likely, but he was definitely gone as evidenced by the fact that other than his T-shirt, all his clothes were gone. With every passing minute, she became increasingly apprehensive, and it didn't take much for her to convince herself to leave. She went back downstairs, gathered her clothes off the floor, and started putting them on. All the while she was dressing, questions flashed through her head: What would he do if he returned now and found her getting ready to leave? What if she got off the boat, but he found her before she got out of the marina? Was he really going to protect her from his grandfather?

By the time she was dressed, her panic had escalated, and she decided that she should call Jack. Her heart seemed to stop when she couldn't locate her purse, but she finally found it under a chair in the main cabin. She breathed a sigh of relief.

"*Probably got kicked there when we were . . .*" She could feel herself starting to blush again when she thought about their recent tryst, but she didn't finish the thought.

"*Where's my phone?*"

She had been groping about in her pocketbook for the phone and it wasn't there. She began crawling about on the floor, praying that it had fallen out when the bag got kicked under that chair. The relief she felt when her hand touched it was as intense as any orgasm she had had with Edso. It was time to go.

CHAPTER 64

RELIEVED AT HAVING FOUND HER PHONE, and just wanting to get away, she did not try calling right away. She'd do that when she got to the hotel. There she could call Jack once she was safe. She left the trawler quickly, carefully closing its door behind her, and walked down the dock as swiftly as silence would allow. Had this been a month earlier, there would have been people around, but now, the marina was filled with dark and silent boats. Every time a halyard slapped against a mast, every clink and clank that the docks made as they moved with the tide, caused her heart to race. She made it to the end of the dock and passed through the gate, being careful not to let it clang shut. She was now fully committed to her escape.

Each of the docks had its own locked gate, so until she made it off the boardwalk, her options for escape were limited. She hurried past the darkened cafe and the empty dockmaster's office, only slowing as she reached the gate for the third dock. She could now see the lights on the top decks of *Vorspiel*, as well as the stairs that would take her from the docks to the safety of the hotel.

Then she heard men's voices. She stopped and ducked behind a large planter, hoping that she wouldn't be seen if they came in her direction. She held her breath and listened.

The voices were muffled and seemed to be some distance away, but with her heartbeat pounding in her ears, she couldn't be sure. Suddenly the men stopped speaking, and she heard footsteps hurrying in her direction. She froze and listened. When she was sure they had passed by, she lifted her head to try to get a look at who it was.

"Edso?" She couldn't be absolutely sure that it was him, but deep inside, she knew. She didn't know where he had been, but she could guess. She felt sick. Why had she allowed herself to fall for him again?

But none of that really mattered at this particular moment. All she knew was that she needed to get to the hotel—*now.*

She stood and began walking as quickly and as quietly as she could, trying to be as invisible as possible in the open spaces of the boardwalk. Then, just as she was about to go up the stairs, she heard the static and click of a two-way radio being keyed. That was all she heard before darkness overcame her.

* * *

"What the hell?"

Ken, made it back to his boat before *Vorspiel* docked. From inside his cabin he watched, and the quiet efficiency with which she was quickly tied to the dock was impressive, but it was what happened next that had him wondering. As soon as all was secure, several members of the crew hurried off the yacht and spread out over the docks. This odd behavior at such a late hour had initially grabbed his attention, but now that he could see they were clearly armed and taking defensive positions, he was captivated. *"What were they protecting?"*

It wasn't long before a lone man approached one of the guards. Undeterred, he gave the guard a nod and walked right past him, heading for the yacht. Reaching the yacht he stopped, and looked behind and around, before quickly stepping on board. As he did so, the guard raised a radio to his mouth and said something.

"What are you up to?" thought Ken when he recognized Edso.

Much earlier in the night, Ken had been surprised to see him leaving the marina, but he was even more surprised when he returned with the same woman he had spent the night with the last time *Vorspiel* was here. Only this time it clearly wasn't a date, but he did remember that she was Jack's friend.

Edso wasn't on the yacht for very long when he left as quickly as he had arrived. As Ken watched him run off toward the far end of the marina, there was a great deal of commotion, with several guards running about and talking on their radios. Then it ended as quickly as it had begun, and he saw two of the guards carrying a limp form onto *Vorspiel.* Trailing behind them was a man he recognized as Edso.

CHAPTER 65

"COURTNEY." SHE FELT A HAND ON HER SHOULDER, gently shaking her. Her head hurt. All she wanted to do was sleep, but the voice was insistent. Slowly she pried her eyes open, but the sunlight streaming in the room forced her to squint them closed.

"Courtney. Look at me."

She recognized the voice. "Edso?"

"Yes, it's me."

Her eyes snapped open and panic filled her mind when she saw him sitting there, staring into her face. She sat up quickly, pulling away from him. Her head began to spin, and she grabbed it with both hands while fighting off tears.

"Easy. It's all right. You're safe." He reached out to touch her shoulder, but she slapped his hand away.

"Get away from me," she screamed. "Where am I? Who were those men? Someone drugs me and you say I'm *safe?*"

He remained silent, but when she looked around, she realized where she was. She was on *Vorspiel,* in the same bed as that first night she had spent with him.

"How long have I been here?"

"Only a few hours."

"Bullshit! It was midnight when I left your boat. Look outside. The sun has been up for a while. It's been more than a few hours."

"I'm so sorry. It wasn't supposed to be this way." His voice was soft and seemed to beg forgiveness.

"What the hell do you mean?"

"I just wanted to talk to him first. You were asleep. Then, while I was here, you tried to escape."

"Escape! I woke up and you were gone! Which part of that gives you the right to assault me and drag me here?"

"Courtney, listen. It was my grandfather who had you brought here. I had nothing to do with that."

"Forgive me if I think you had everything to do with that."

"I didn't. I swear."

"Tell you what. Since you're so not involved in this, how about you just take me home."

"I can't do that. They're my grandfather's men. He was a little over-enthusiastic in his instructions . . ."

She cut him off. "Overenthusiastic! Are you on drugs?"

He looked at her silently, knowing that nothing he could say would change her mind. "It's not that simple. My grandfather needs to speak with you. I will speak with him again in a moment and see what he wants to do."

CHAPTER 66

"SO. IS SHE GOING TO COOPERATE?" Edso's grandfather asked.

"They didn't have to knock her out."

"You didn't answer my question."

"I don't know."

"You don't know? What do you mean, you don't know?"

"Just that. You need to leave her alone for a bit and let me work on her."

"No."

"Look Grandfather, this isn't 1942. We're not in Germany. Things are different."

"You think I don't know that?"

"Sometimes I wonder."

His voice softened. "Edso, you know I don't have a lot of time."

"I know." Then under his breath, he added, "So you've told me countless times."

"Edso."

The force with which he said his grandson's name implied all the correction necessary.

"Now, tell me what you have learned."

"First, I'm positive that she does not know if she has the gold."

"But you're sure she has it."

"Yes. Of that I'm sure. I also have a feeling that her uncle kept it a secret from everyone. So what happened to it, I don't know. It could still be intact or there is none left. We won't know until we find it."

"It's not how much is left. I have more than any man should have. What I need is proof of what happened so that I can prove my father a hero of the fatherland. That is what's important."

* * *

An hour after sunrise, Ken was sitting out in the cockpit of his boat, sipping a coffee when he saw Jeremy, the dockmaster, walking back from the direction of *Vorspiel*. Ken quickly left his boat and, with coffee in hand, headed up to the boardwalk, intending to intercept Jeremy.

His timing was perfect, and he was just closing the gate to his dock as Jeremy approached.

"Mornin' Jeremy. Beautiful day."

"Oh, hey Ken. It is."

His voice seemed strained.

"You okay?"

"Yeah, fine."

Ken gave him a look that said he wasn't buying it. "Buy you a coffee?"

"No need, but I was just on the way to the cafe by my office to get a cup. Come join me.

As they walked, Jeremy began talking, as much to himself as to Ken. "You know, I was just over on *Vorspiel* to welcome them back."

"I saw."

"I don't know what's up with them, but they were real A-holes this morning. I stayed here quite late last night waiting for them to arrive. Finally I gave up and went home around ten. Of course, they showed up after. Not a big deal, right? They were expected, so the space was there for them on the dock, and they know the drill. But when I went over just now to welcome them back, this one goon—and I mean goon—came out and started giving me a rash of shit for stepping on board. Like I had never done that before," he added sarcastically.

"So what was the guy's problem?"

"No idea, but I wasn't going to stick around to find out."

"How long they gonna' be around this time?"

"I don't know. Couple days, maybe a week or two."

Ken had his mug topped up at the café, and they walked to Jeremy's office. He took a chair next to Jeremy's desk.

"So tell me, what's the deal with that boat?" Ken asked. "The name is strange enough."

"Ya think? Who would name their boat *Foreplay?*"

"I know. Really."

And with that, they both had a good laugh.

"German, right?"

"Yeah. Guy who owns her is this old German guy—Otto Jäger. I've only met him once. If you were to go to central casting and ask for a Nazi officer, he would be the guy. He's the complete stereotype. I've even heard the crew refer to him that way, although the guy I ran into this morning would have been perfect in the Hitler Youth."

Then he looked uncomfortable. "Sorry," the dockmaster said. "I shouldn't be talking about them that way."

"It's okay. After the way they treated you this morning, you're allowed."

"Don't tell my boss. It's not allowed. We're meant to be very discrete."

Ken nodded. After an awkward silence, their conversation turned to safe topics like fishing and the weather, but Ken had a feeling that Jeremy had more to say about *Vorspiel*.

"You know," said Jeremy, "late yesterday afternoon, something kind of strange happened."

"What?"

"Off the record, right?"

"Off the record. Of course."

"You know the grandson?"

"No."

"Name's Edso. Well, yesterday, he arrives here on this little trawler, mid-afternoon. Acted like he didn't know his grandfather was coming, but it felt like a lie. Anyway, he asked for a slip as far from *Vorspiel's* slip as possible. I had a feeling he didn't want his grandfather to know he was there."

"So where'd you put him?"

"On dock A, over by the breakwater, about halfway down. Boat's name is *Christine*."

"*Christine?*"

Jeremy shrugged. "Said he chartered the boat and was planning on cruising down Maine before it gets too cold."

After a minute, he added, "Brought a lady friend down to the boat later. I didn't get a real good look at her, but I think she was the gal he had entertained on *Vorspiel* before she last sailed.

Keeping his thoughts to himself, Ken knew that this was right and Jeremy confirmed what Ken already knew about Otto and Edso.

CHAPTER 67

JACK WAS TAKING ANOTHER LOOK AT THOSE BOARDS when Max came outside.

"Jack, I just got a call from Angela over at Ben's. She seemed pretty upset. Apparently, Courtney's car is there, but there are no signs of Court. Angela said that when she was leaving last night, a guy pulled into the parking lot. She thinks Courtney went off with him."

"Edso?" Jack asked.

"Maybe. Look, I'm going over there. Stay put in case she comes home. I'll call you if I find out anything else."

* * *

Max wasn't gone more than five minutes when the phone rang.

"Jack? Hey, it's Ken."

"Ken, what's up? I thought you had gone back to Florida."

"Trip got delayed. Look, there's something going on over here at the marina that you might be interested in."

A few minutes later, Jack was in his truck on the way over to Ben's to get Max.

* * *

"What do you mean you think she's been kidnapped?" asked Max. Jack could see the panic in her eyes.

"Ken just called me from the marina."

"Ken? That obnoxious guy who called me a little filly?"

"The same."

"What did he want?"

"Said he saw Courtney being carried onto *Vorspiel*."

"Carried?"

He recounted what Ken had told him as best he could.

It took Max a few moments to process this.

"He's sure it was her?"

"Yes."

"Edso kidnapped her?"

"That part's not clear. He's there, but according to Ken, it was some of the crew who grabbed her."

"We've got to call Tom."

"Look, Max, normally I would agree with you, but let's check it out before we involve the police. We know where she is now. Maybe Ken got it wrong."

Standing beside him, Max clenched her jaw as she considered his proposal. Then she said, "All right, but if he makes any more chauvinistic comments, I might just smack him."

"Fair enough."

* * *

Little else was said during the fifteen-minute ride to the marina. When they arrived, Ken was waiting up in the parking lot for them.

Jack got out first.

"Ken," he said walking around the car.

"Jack."

Max joined him.

"You remember Max?"

He smiled and nodded in her direction. Then he looked at Jack and said, "Come." He immediately turned and began walking down toward the docks. As he reached the bottom of the stairs, he stopped, giving Jack and Max a chance to catch up.

Looking over at *Vorspiel,* Ken said, "Nothin' going on there. Haven't seen any activity since what went down last night."

There was no sign of life on the big blue yacht.

"Follow me," said Ken. "We'll go down to my boat. That way we can watch her without being too obvious."

They walked past the gate for dock E where *Vorspiel* was tied. At the next gate, Ken stopped to punch in the combination code. He opened the gate and said, "It'll lock when it shuts." Then he proceeded down the ramp. Jack ushered Max through, and they followed.

His boat was about halfway down the line of slips on the easterly side of Dock D. She had been backed into her slip so her cockpit faced the dock, allowing for a reasonably good view of *Vorspiel,* while being partly obscured by the boats on the opposite side of the dock. Ken nimbly stepped aboard and turned to help his guests aboard. Max arrived first, and before moving to board, she stopped and stared down at the stern of the boat.

"Everything okay?" asked Ken.

She looked up.

"Yes, yes, everything's fine." With that she stepped over the stern and into the boat, rebuffing Ken's efforts to help.

Jack had seen her pause, so he too looked at the stern before boarding. Immediately he knew why she had stopped. The name of the boat was *Sylvie.*

"Welcome aboard," said Ken.

CHAPTER 68

"SO, NOW WHAT?" ASKED JACK.

Max was standing by the stern looking over at *Vorspiel*. It wasn't easy to see her lowest deck, but the view of her top decks was clear.

"Tell me about your friend," said Ken.

"Not much to tell. She owns Ben's Place down by Rye Harbor. Not sure of all the details on how she met Edso—"

Max turned and interrupted. "They met in the Pic."

"The Pic?" asked Ken.

"Pic N' Pay. Local grocery store, changed hands and name a few years back, but locals still call it the Pic." Then she turned back to watching *Vorspiel*.

Jack went on. "He asked her out, she accepted, and they ended up there." He motioned toward *Vorspiel*.

Again, Max turned and spoke. "You almost got it right. They went to lunch first, out at Lexie's, over at the Great Bay Marina. Then he asked her out to dinner, and after dinner he took her to the yacht. She spent the night, but in the morning he abruptly took her home, and then he disappeared." She then returned to looking at *Vorspiel*.

"What she said," said Jack. Then he said, "Now, about your phone call. What do you suppose was going on last night?"

Ken looked at him. "I was talking to the dockmaster this morning. He said he went over to *Vorspiel* this morning to welcome them back and got a real rash of shit from some of the crew and needed to vent. Also, told me that Edso had arrived the day before on a small trawler. It's in a slip on the other side of the marina. You know it's his grandfather who owns that yacht. Anyways, he arrives by himself, asks to have a slip far from his grandfather's boat, almost as if he didn't want him to know he was there. Then later, after dark, he brings her back to his boat, not *Vorspiel,* your friend. Some time after that I saw the crew carrying her to the yacht. I've been watching the yacht since then, but I haven't seen any activity."

"Shouldn't we call the police?" asked Max.

"I don't think that would be a good idea," said Ken.

"And why not?" snapped Max. "Jack told me we'd come check it out, and now we have. Seems like Courtney needs help."

Ken silently gazed at the yacht, as if considering his answer.

Finally, he said, "Jack, can we speak?"

"Of course."

"I'm sorry. I didn't make myself clear. I'd like to speak to you alone."

"What!" Max cried out.

"Look, Ken, anything you have to say to me, you can say to Max."

Max flashed him a look that said, *"Thank you."*

Ken looked at the yacht again, obviously wrestling with what he was going to say.

"Fine. We've come to the conclusion that your friend Courtney has something that they want."

Jack saw Max's jaw drop. Equally surprised, he looked hard at Ken.

"How do you know that?"

"I can't tell you."

"Wh—" Max started to protest, but Ken held his hand up and shook his head.

"Like I said, she has something that he wants."

"Who? Edso?"

"No, it's his grandfather, but Edso is helping him."

"And he's been using Courtney?"

Ken nodded.

"I warned her," said Max, shaking her head and mumbling under her breath. "I've told her time and time again not to jump into bed so fast. They always want something besides her."

"Max. Stop. Let Ken go on."

She gave Jack the evil eye and sat back, mouth closed, and signaled with her arm for Ken to go on.

"During World War II, Edso's great grandfather's best friend was in the intelligence service. When a secret mission he was on failed, in an effort to cover their asses, his superiors floated stories that he had deserted and had stolen a small fortune. His great grandfather was also implicated and he died in the war without ever being able to clear his name."

"So, what was this mission?"

"The details are lost to time, but from what we've been able to put together, they planned to land him in the United States with the mission to disrupt the war effort."

"Son of a bitch," said Jack in a hushed tone. Then, staring at Ken, he asked, "Who's *we?*"

Ken ignored Jack's question.

"And what does it matter?" Max asked. "That was a very long time ago."

"I'm getting to that," Ken said. "Remember, he had a small fortune with him, in cash and in gold. The facts support that he was killed, probably drowned while trying to get ashore. We know his raft was found along with some weapons, but no documents, money, or gold were ever found."

"And they think Courtney has it?" said Jack.

"That's how it seems."

"Jack, tell him about the journals you found," said Max.

Jack said, "As best we can tell, Ben and other fishermen took turns going out at night to patrol the coast. The Navy wasn't okay with that, of course. We've found some old records that Ben kept, and with some stories we heard, it seems possible that he found that raft. If he did, maybe he really did keep whatever was on it."

"You haven't actually found anything, though," said Ken.

"Correct."

Max added, "There is one entry that just contains a date and notes on the weather. Jack thinks it could be important."

"What's the date?" asked Ken.

Jack said, "September 29, 1942."

CHAPTER 69

"THE DATE IS ABOUT RIGHT," SAID KEN. "What you're saying is certainly plausible. It certainly jives with what we know."

"And now Courtney's in there," said Max, motioning toward the yacht.

Jack looked at Max and Ken. "Any ideas?"

"Why don't we just go over and ask if Courtney's there?" said Max.

"I don't think that would be a good idea, Max," said Ken. "Those guys are actually armed."

Jack saw the color drain from Max's face.

Ken said, "I'll tell you what. How about you two stay here and watch the boat. I'm going to go talk to Jeremy again."

"Who's Jeremy?" asked Max.

"He's the dockmaster here. Maybe he can help us."

"Help us do what?" Max asked.

He looked at Max for a moment, then the tone of his voice shifted into a command.

"Keep an eye on the yacht and stay put. I'll be right back."

As soon as he was out of earshot, Max turned toward Jack. The blood had returned to her cheeks and she looked angry.

"Stay put! Where does he get off talking like that? And what's up with the name of this boat?"

"Max, let it go. I'm sure he didn't mean anything by it. And the boat name must be a coincidence. Let's just focus on Courtney right now."

She picked up a pair of binoculars that Ken had left on the seat. As she studied the yacht, she said, "Jack, what if there is some hidden treasure that Courtney doesn't know about? What if she's being tortured? What if they come after us because we're her friends?"

"Max, you're getting ahead of yourself."

She lowered the binoculars and turned to Jack. "Did you notice how Ken ignored your question? Who's *we?* Maybe he's no better than they are. Maybe he also wants the money."

Jack said nothing while he considered her question.

"You know," Max continued, "I had a bad feeling about him from the start. You know what I think. I think we have to be careful with what we say and do, at least until we find out a bit more about your 'friend' Ken."

"Well, you're right about the last part. He's actually more an acquaintance."

"Jack!" He could tell she was losing patience. "Think about it! Don't you find it kind of strange that he called *you* after watching Courtney get kidnapped? Why didn't *he* call the police?"

Jack shrugged.

She raised the binoculars to her eyes again and studied the yacht.

"Do you think she's okay?" asked Max.

"Yes . . . Yes, I do." He didn't add what he was thinking: *"For now."*

* * *

"Hey, Jeremy."

Looking up from what he was working on, Jeremy seemed surprised when Ken walked into his office.

"Hey, Ken. What's up?"

"Listen, remember before when we talked? There was something I didn't tell you."

"And what would that be? Something wrong with your boat?"

"No, nothing like that. Last night, after *Vorspiel* came in, there was some commotion out on the docks. It woke me up."

"What kind of commotion?"

"Well, I think that a woman was kidnapped and taken on board. I think Edso is on board too. But there's been no sign of life aside from your encounter with the goons since."

Jeremy began to reach for his phone.

"Stop. Who're you going to call?"

"First, *Vorspiel*, to see what's going on, then maybe the police."

"Please don't."

"And why not?"

"Just don't. Please."

Jeremy put down the phone. "And what would you have me do, now that you've brought this up?"

"I'd like to take a look in Edso's boat. The one he came in on yesterday. *Christine*."

"I could lose my job."

"That's why you don't know what I'm going to do. However, if Edso shows up, I need you to keep him occupied until I return. Dock A, right?"

Ken took the dockmaster's silence as agreement and left the office.

A few minutes later, he was stepping onto *Christine*. The boat had been left unlocked, and he quickly slipped inside. Nothing seemed out of place in either the main cabin or the helm station. He went below, and other than the unmade bed and a pile of still-wet clothes, nothing seemed out of place. He rifled through drawers and opened lockers, but there was nothing suspicious. Satisfied, he left as quickly as he had come.

Stopping back at Jeremy's office, he poked his head in the door and said, "Thanks."

"Find what you were looking for?"

"Nope."

"What about the girl?"

"Let me worry about her. If I need any help, I'll let you know. I do understand your position, and the less you know, the better."

CHAPTER 70

EDSO WALKED INTO THE MASTER SUITE. "COURT?"

There was no answer, but he did see that the breakfast tray he had brought her was on the desk, contents mostly eaten, and that's when he heard the shower running. Suddenly he had a flashback to their first night together. But as much as he wanted to walk in and join her, after last night, he didn't think that he'd receive a very warm reception.

He sat down at the desk and, sliding his fingers under the drawer on the right, felt for the hidden catch. Then, without a sound, the drawer slid open. Inside was nothing but a single, plain, manila envelope held closed with a short piece of string that wound around two small pressboard disks. He unwound the string, opened the envelope, and pulled out a single sheet of paper. Yellowed with age, it was all in German and bore the crest of the Third Reich and had *Top Secret* stamped across the top in faded, red ink. It was a simple document: a statement of orders and a list of materials that would be necessary to carry out those orders. He knew its contents by heart, but before he could read it again, he heard a click. Looking toward the bathroom door, he saw its handle beginning to turn. He was just slipping the paper back into the envelope as the bathroom door opened. Quickly he dropped it in the drawer and as he stood up, pushed the drawer shut.

Courtney stepped into the cabin and froze the instant she saw him. She was dressed, but her hair was still wet, and she was holding a towel against it. As she lowered the towel, her face darkened, and she said, "What are you doing here?" The hostility in her voice was unmistakable.

He stepped from behind the desk, hoping she didn't notice, and smiled as if everything was all right.

"You were in the shower. I came to check on you. My grandfather wants to see you."

She continued to stare at him.

"Are you going to tell me what's going on?"

"All in due time. Come."

"No."

He reached out for her, intending to steer her toward the door, but she turned too quickly and went back into the bathroom. He followed.

"I have to brush my hair," she said. She stepped in front of the mirror and picked up a brush.

Edso moved close behind, reached around, and gently took the brush out of her hand. Then he slowly began to run it through her hair.

"Why am I here?" she asked again.

"I told you. You have something that my grandfather wants, and he's determined to get it."

"But you're not going to tell me what it is."

"Correct."

He stopped brushing her hair. Reaching around her, he placed the brush on the table. He could feel the warmth of her body and that fresh, just-showered smell, and he wanted her.

She turned to face him while pushing him away at the same time. The look on her face told him that it was not a possibility.

"Why not?" she demanded.

He didn't respond. Instead, he stepped back, taking hold of her arm.

"You ask too many questions. Now, come along. We need to go."

She didn't resist, but he didn't release his grip, either.

* * *

As they walked into the formal salon, Edso finally released his grip on her elbow. She stopped and rubbed it while staring at the man before her. He was not at all what she had expected. He was an imposing fig-ure, even though he was at best five and a half feet tall. He was obviously fit, with close-cropped silver hair and eyes that were the intense blue of arctic ice and just as cold. He commanded the room, exuding the strength and vitality of someone half his age, and there was no doubt that he was someone who was used to being in charge and getting what he wanted.

"Courtney, I'd like you to meet my grandfather, Herr Otto Jäger."

A chill went through her. *"Jäger.?" Edso had told her his name was Harding."*

After a curt "Fraulein," which he said with an imperceptible nod, he turned his back to her and said, "Do you understand why you are here?"

Inhaling deeply, she stood as straight as she could and tried not to let her voice betray her fear.

"No. I don't. Would you care to explain?"

"My grandson didn't tell you?"

"He tried, but I want to hear it from you."

Otto began to pace back and forth, speaking slowly and deliberately.

"Let me explain. First, a little history lesson. In 1942, we were winning the war. Our U-boats were operating right off your coast, sinking thousands of tons of shipping all up and down the Eastern seaboard, much within sight of land. My father was on one such submarine. He was second in command and part of their mission was to put a man ashore near here. That man's mission was a simple one: using the resources that he had with him, and in concert with other agents, he was to disrupt your war effort by adding to the fears that our U-boats had already created."

He paused as if to let that sink in.

Courtney, with sarcasm dripping from her voice, said, "And how did that all turn out?"

Edso stepped closer to her. In a low voice he said, "I don't think you want to antagonize him."

Otto ignored her comment. "That agent was my father's best friend, Edso was named after him. He disappeared that night, and he was never seen or heard from again. We know that his raft was found, but neither his body nor much of what he had with him was ever recovered. He was discredited as stories were circulated that he had defected and because my father had tried to delay the mission that night, his carreer suffered as well. My father was killed before the end of the war. His disgrace became my disgrace, and I intend to rectify that."

He stopped and stared silently at her.

"And you think that somehow I have the answers."

"I do."

"Well, I don't. I wasn't even born until the war was long over."

"I grant that you are too young to have taken part personally in this event, but I believe that it was your uncle who was responsible. After he died, you inherited his estate . . . and what I seek: proof that my father and his friend both died as heroes of the Reich."

Courtney couldn't believe what she was hearing.

Then Otto spoke directly to Edso. "Take your little friend back to the suite. Talk to her, and make sure she understands the seriousness of her situation. Then come back and talk to me."

The old man left, and Edso quickly turned back to face Courtney.

"You know, he expects an answer."

Then he took her by the elbow again and escorted her out.

CHAPTER 71

"SO?" JACK WAS THE FIRST TO SPEAK when ken returned to the boat.

"I got Jeremy to let me take a look at *Christine*. Nice little trawler. Said Edso chartered it."

"Find anything?"

"No."

"Nothing?"

"Nothing. Other than a messed-up bed and some wet clothes in the head, there wasn't much of anything on board."

"What did you expect to find?"

"I don't know."

"Hey, guys," said Max.

"See something?" asked Jack.

"I think I just saw Court."

"Where?" Ken took the glasses from her.

"The windows just below the name boards."

Ken looked hard at that spot but saw nothing. "You sure?"

"Not a hundred percent, but I'm pretty sure I saw someone looking out."

He lowered the glasses. "Those windows are for the master suite. If that's where she is, she's quite comfortable."

Before he could say anything else, Max said, "Look."

Two men were standing underneath the canopy that covered the second deck. Ken immediately lifted the glasses to his eyes again.

"Otto and Edso. You sons of bitches," Ken whispered to himself.

"What?" asked Max.

"Nothing," said Ken, continuing to watch them.

"No, I heard you say something. Who's Otto?"

Ken lowered the binoculars as the men moved inside. "Edso's

grandfather. He owns *Vorspiel*."

Max said, "What else aren't you telling us?"

Then Jack joined in. "Really, Ken. We need to know the whole story."

Ken considered his options and shrugged. "Okay, fine. Come inside."

They moved into the small cabin. It was close, but there was room for the three of them.

Ken turned and faced them. "We've been following the old man and his grandson for quite some time now because of his involvement with neo-Nazi groups. He's not someone to cross."

"Who's *we*?" Jack asked again. "And what does it have to do with Courtney?"

Ken looked at him, raised his hand, and said, "Let me finish."

"Go on."

"It's complicated. What I didn't tell you before was that Otto's father, Jurgen Jäger, was the second officer of that U-boat that we believe Ben Crouse encountered on September 29, 1942. The sub's mission was to land an agent off the New Hampshire coast. We think Jurgen had suggested waiting for better conditions, but the captain wasn't swayed, and despite the weather, the captain decided to attempt the landing. The attempt failed as the raft was swept away, and the agent, Jurgen's best friend, was lost. That man's name was also Edso. The captain refused to take responsibility for his bad decision and instead created the story that Edso had defected."

He paused to let them digest what he'd said. Then he continued.

"After that mission, Jurgen returned to Germany and met his son, Otto, for the first time. Then he was sent back into battle, and he was killed during the war. Otto was raised by his mother, a bitter and vengeful person who preached hatred to him 'til the end of her days. Between her stories of Otto's father and the glories of the Kriegsmarine, it's no wonder he's as vengeful as he is."

Max said, "And how does Courtney's Edso fit in?"

Ken said, "Edso's parents died in a car crash when he was five. His grandfather raised him in an environment of fear and shame. Otto thinks getting revenge for the first Edso's death will buy them power and glory again."

"And Courtney?"

"They think she has the proof or knows something that will help their cause."

"That's ridiculous," insisted Max.

Ken shrugged. "Maybe. We don't know if she does."

"Okay," Jack said. "So, Otto and Edso are neo-Nazis, and they think Courtney has something. But you still haven't said who *you* are working for."

Ken paused for a long moment.

"I'd rather not say."

"You'd rather not say?"

"Look, it's for the best. Trust me."

Jack shook his head. "That's not good enough. Look, Ken, remember, you're the one who called me about Courtney. From that, I'm assuming that you want our help. So what's it going to be? You can tell us what we want to know and we'll stay and help you, or we'll leave and you'll be on your own. Not only that, but we *will* call Tom."

"Jack, you and Max are certainly free to leave, but if you do, understand that if you get the authorities involved, I will disappear, and then the odds are very good that your friend will be dead. I'm your only hope in saving her, and I'm only doing it as a personal favor to a friend."

"A friend?" said Max.

Ken saw her face fall as she began to connect the dots.

"Oh no," she said, shaking her head. "Not—"

"Sylvie."

CHAPTER 72

COURTNEY LISTENED TO THE DOOR CLICK SHUT as Edso left the suite to report back to his grandfather.

"That son of a bitch," she muttered under her breath. "I've got to get out of here."

Certain that time was limited, she began to assess her situation. First, she went to the cabin door and put her ear to it. She could hear voices outside, but not what was being said.

She began pacing about the cabin, considering her options. She went to the window and peered out. She knew that the windows were heavily tinted, so anyone outside would have a hard time seeing her inside. If only she could get out and slip past the guard. Surely they wouldn't attack her again in broad daylight; there would be too many people about.

Turning from the window, she looked around the room. The first thing she noticed was that her breakfast tray was gone. Then she looked in all the closets, cabinets, and drawers. Most had been emptied out since her last visit to the suite.

She looked at the desk again, recalling Edso's reaction to finding her at the desk after that first night they were together on the boat. This morning, she had seen him sitting behind it when she came out of the shower. He had tried to act like he was just waiting for her, but she was sure she had seen him put something in it.

"*What is in that desk?*"

She sat down and slid the left-hand drawer open. Just as before, it contained only a pad of yellow paper and several pencils. The drawer on the right-hand side still would not open. She ran her fingers across its face, then underneath, still feeling nothing but smooth wood. She expanded her search and ran her hand down one of the legs and heard a small click. The drawer released, and she pulled it open. Inside there was a single, large envelope, which she removed and opened. What was printed on the yellowed paper had to be in German and the symbols were unmistakable.

She folded the document and put it in her pocket. Then she replaced the envelope and closed the drawer. If she was able to escape, at least she would have something.

* * *

"Tell me you have good news," said Otto Jager.

Edso shook his head. "She insists that she knows nothing of what you're looking for."

"She must. Perhaps I should talk to her alone. Persuade her."

That was what Edso was afraid of. "I don't think it would be such a good idea to do that here."

"Perhaps you're right. Out at sea would be better."

The sound of a clearing throat interrupted their conversation.

It was Gerhard, his chief of security. "I'm sorry to interrupt you, *mein herr*, but there are some people watching us."

"When you have a yacht like this, people always look."

"I know, but this is different. Two men and a woman, on the next pier. They've been watching us for hours."

"Where? Show me."

"Come inside. They will not be able to see us through the tinted windows."

Gerhard handed Otto a pair of binoculars and pointed down at the docks.

"There, that small boat, *Sylvie*."

Otto looked down and studied the boat. "Looks like they're inside. Here, Edso, you take a look."

Edso took the glasses and focused them on the small fishing boat.

"Well?" asked Otto. He tapped his foot impatiently.

"I think I recognize the woman. She works for Courtney."

He handed the binoculars to Gerhard, who then took a look.

"Sir, I recognize one of the men. I see him almost every time we're here, and I think I've seen him elsewhere. He must be following us."

Otto turned to Edso. "I think it's time for us to leave."

"Yes. But what about Courtney?"

"What about her? If she chooses not to give us what we want, well, the ocean is a very large place."

"I'm sorry Grandfather but I don't think that would be wise in this case."

"Edso. Do not argue with me. I know what you have done with her. She has some formidable skills and I'm sure that you found her satisfying."

He looked at his grandfather, dumbfounded by what he had just heard. "What do you know about our time together?"

"I know everything. If I were younger, I might partake myself, but now, I'm just happy to watch."

"Are you telling me that you have been watching us?"

"Not at all. But, Gerhard here, has been filming everything, and he did show me some very interesting moments. I must say, of all the women you have entertained on this boat, she is far and away the most creative and enthusiastic. And I must say, you have made me proud. You are truly the product of a pure and superior bloodline."

Edso felt his face reddening and a knot began forming in his stomach. A quick glance over at Gerhard nearly made him vomit when he saw the twisted grin on his face.

"Are you telling me what I think you are telling me?"

His grandfather gave him a look that confirmed his worst fears. "You have been filming me without my knowledge," he said, his question becoming a statement.

With a nonchalant shrug of his shoulders, his grandfather said, "Edso, dear boy, I don't know why you are so surprised. You know what our mission is. You know that I will do anything to succeed and honor our fathers who came before us and the fatherland that has been taken from us. Besides, when your little friend sees her performance, I think she'll become quite cooperative."

"*You son of a bitch*," thought Edso. "When do you plan to confront her?"

"Edso, I'm surprised at you. I don't plan on confronting her. Confrontation is such a harsh and ugly word. No, getting her to cooperate, I am going to leave that up to you."

Then, turning to Gerhard, he said, "Would you please queue up the tape from his night here with her? Have it play in the master suite. I'd like my grandson to see what a splendid performer he is."

Edso knew that to protest would only anger his grandfather.

"Now, both of you, go."

As Edso and Gerhard reached the door, Gerhard turned to him and said, "You do know that what I did was not personal, it was for the cause."

Edso yanked the door open.

As he stepped through, Gerhard said in a low taunting voice, "You know, she was most entertaining to watch. One of the best you've ever had. I'd even consider doing her myself."

Spinning around, his fist found Gerhard's face and blood spurted from his nose. Gerhard was knocked back into the room as Edso glowered at him, his fists clenched at his side. Regaining his balance, Gerhard drew his arm across his face, wiping the blood that was dripping from his nose on his sleeve. In much the same way the alpha in a wolf pack would stare at a challenger, his eyes narrowed to slits and the muscles in his neck and shoulders began to tense up. He fixed his eyes on Edso, then his expression began to change. The corners of his mouth began to turn up, his eyes, no longer slits, seemed to glow red as if reflecting the fires of hell. He daubed at the blood, still dripping from his nose and then leapt toward Edso.

Edso was able to partially shut the door, slowing Gerhard's counter-attack, and Otto, at first frozen by his surprise at what Edso had done, grabbed a heavy Alpine walking stick and ended the melee with one swing to the back of Gerhard's head. He crumpled and now it was Otto's turn to glare at Edso.

"I think you had better go, right now, and get what I want from her."

* * *

Courtney was standing by the window looking out when she heard the door latch click. She turned as the door swung open and Edso walked in. His shirt was splattered with blood, he was breathing hard and rubbing his one hand with the other. She had never seen him look so agitated. As he stepped into the cabin, he pushed the door so that it shut behind.

"Eds—"

She started to say his name, but he cut her off. Striding across the room, he stopped when he reached her and said, "Listen to me! There isn't much time. I need to have what my grandfather wants. Your options are very limited."

"But I don't—"

He cut her off again. "Look, Courtney. I don't think that you want to know what he plans to do. You need to trust me."

CHAPTER 73

AFTER HEARING THE NEWS ABOUT SYLVIE, Max quickly left the cabin and went out to the deck for some fresh air. Seconds later, she stuck her head back in.

"Uh, guys. Something's going on over there."

Ken stepped out into the cockpit, grabbed the binoculars, and focused on *Vorspiel.*

"Shit."

"What do you see?" asked Jack.

"Looks like all three are taking turns looking at us with binoculars."

"Three?" said Jack. "Who's the third guy?"

"Gerhard," said Ken. "He's a real piece of work. If he's not a diagnosed sociopath, and he may be, he's as close to it as it comes. He does most of Otto's dirty work."

"And you know this how?" asked Jack.

"I told you. We've been watching them for a long time."

"So now what?" asked Max. "Now that they know we're watching them."

"Things are about to get a whole lot more interesting," said Ken. "They just went back inside. I bet he's preparing to leave."

"Leave!" Max shrieked. "But what about Courtney?"

"Max, I don't know, but my best guess would be that she is rapidly becoming expendable. If he gets what he wants from her, all bets are off. If not, you can bet that her life is going to become a living hell."

"We've got to save her," Max said.

Ken said nothing; he just kept his eyes on *Vorspiel.*

"Jack, talk to him," Max begged. "Make a plan. Do something. Anything!"

Jack looked over at Ken. "You've got an idea, don't you?"

"Maybe."

* * *

Courtney was weighing her options now that it didn't seem like she'd have a chance to escape. She turned to Edso and said, "If I decide to trust you, what does that get me?"

"Your life"

Before Courtney could say anything else, the television in the cabin came to life.

She turned toward the screen.

"Don't watch," said Edso.

"Why?"

Before he could offer a reason, Courtney walked over and stood in front of the screen. The picture was dark, but not so dark that you couldn't see exactly who was doing what to whom.

Edso had followed her over in front of the screen.

As they watched the two lovers on the screen, all she could say was, "Oh my God," over and over. If the bedroom scenes weren't bad enough, there had been cameras in the bathroom as well.

"You have to know that he will hold this over you forever. Even if you give him what he wants, he'll always find ways to get more."

A numbness began to creep over her. She turned to face him and said, "What did you mean when you said I had to trust you? It's because of you that this . . . this even exists."

"Court, I know that there is no reason for you to believe me, let alone trust me, but I did not know that he was capable of going to this extreme. He's got us both under his thumb. If you disappear, I'm sure that I will be the chief suspect. He'll make sure of that. He'll stop at nothing to get what he wants."

"I'm finding this all so hard to believe."

"That may be, but I know him. He lives in the past. To him, the

Third Reich will still rise again and rule the world. That is his reality. You know that it will never happen, and so do I. This may be my only chance to stop him, and I need your help."

CHAPTER 74

"GRANDFATHER, YOU WERE RIGHT, AS ALWAYS. She saw sense and has finally agreed to give you what you want. She has some old notebooks that belonged to her uncle. There were some passages she did not fully understand, but I explained what happened on that night, and now she does. I would suggest that I take her back there now on my boat. I'll retrieve the documents and the gold and then rendezvous with you near the Isles of Shoals."

His grandfather looked relieved. "Edso, of late, you have given me some cause for concern about your dedication to our mission. It gave me no pleasure to kidnap your lady friend, but it was necessary. Sometimes a great cause requires that we do things that are less than honorable. Such was this. I trust that you understand."

"Yes, Grandfather. Perhaps I could take Gerhard with us in case I run into any trouble."

"Edso, you are a good boy. I will trust you to do this as you have described. And yes, take Gerhard with you. You will leave tonight, but first, let's have a nice dinner together."

His grandfather raised his right arm in the Nazi salute, and Edso followed suit.

Then Otto said, "Now, you go. You have a guest to prepare for our dinner, and I have a dinner to prepare for our guest."

* * *

As Edso left his uncle, he passed Gerhard in the corridor.

Stopping, he offered his hand to Gerhard.

"She's agreed. You'll be coming with us tonight when we go to retrieve what we came for."

Edso hoped that Gerhard didn't notice the sweat on his palm or that his hand was trembling. It didn't appear that he did. All he got from Gerhard was a grunt and a dirty look.

When he reached the door to the suite, he knocked twice and then twice again. Courtney opened the door and stepped back to let him in. He locked the door and said, "Dinner will be served in two hours."

* * *

Edso checked his watch. It was time to go to dinner.

"I don't think I can do this," said Courtney.

"You can, and you must, if we are to get out of this alive. You'll be fine. He will be courteous, probably charming, and most likely he will talk about music, art, and the sea. He thinks that he is some kind of a renaissance man."

The look on her face told him that she wasn't convinced.

"Remember, my grandfather doesn't think that he has done anything wrong, and he assumes that you feel the same."

"But he had his men kidnap me . . ."

"Listen to me. He is a twisted individual. His reality is not like that of any normal person. To him, if something is done as a means to an end—a tool, if you will, that will help him achieve his goal—that's different."

"So I have to sit there with him and pretend that he's not some kind of a narcissistic psychopath?"

Edso nodded.

"I'm afraid so. I can almost guarantee that you will never have any inkling that he ever planned to hurt you."

"Promise?"

"Promise."

There was a knock on the door.

The color went out of her face, and she said, "I have to go to the bathroom."

Edso opened the door partway and looked out. He breathed a sigh of relief when he saw that it wasn't Gerhard who had come for them.

Without giving the crewman a chance to look in, he said, "She's almost ready. We'll be right up."

"I'll wait. I'm to escort you."

"Suit yourself."

CHAPTER 75

"I SEE HER," SAID MAX, AS SHE UNTANGLED HERSELF from the blanket and knocked on the door to the cabin of Ken's boat. She had been watching for signs of movement on *Vorspiel,* and now that the sun had set, the yacht's tinted windows, which had worked so well in protecting the privacy of its occupants during the day, were ineffectual.

In fact, Max had been able to see the crew preparing dinner, and she had briefly dreamed about the pleasures of dining on a yacht. Then she remembered that if Otto had his way it could be Courtney's last supper, and her simple tomato, hummus, and cheese sandwich had suddenly seemed quite good.

Jack and Ken were inside the small cabin exploring ideas for how to get Courtney away from *Vorspiel.* According to Ken—and to Max's delight—Sylvie was away on another case and they would remain on their own. Now, in response to Max's knock, they turned out the lights. Even though Otto and company knew they were there, they still wanted to remain as inconspicuous as possible.

"Last supper?" said Ken as he lowered the binoculars.

"That's an awful thing to say," said Max, even though she'd just had the same thought herself.

"Sorry, but it looks too perfect. Here." He handed the binoculars to Jack.

Jack took a long look. "You're right. They all seem too normal considering what we know."

"My guess is that they'll leave in the middle of the night. Whether they get what they want or not, I would put good money on the fact that *Vorspiel* will disappear."

An awkward silence filled the cockpit.

"So, what are we going to do about it?" asked Max.

Ken and Jack answered together. "We're working on that."

* * *

"Gerhard says that they are still watching us," said Otto in German, as coffee was served. The dinner was elegant and delicious, so much so that Courtney found herself thinking that when she got back, she'd see if Chef could duplicate some of the dishes. They'd be perfect for wedding dinners or other special occasions.

"Well, then, let's give it a little time before we leave," said Edso.

Otto agreed and then he excused himself from the table.

"You okay?" asked Edso.

Courtney nodded.

"Dinner was good."

Again, she nodded.

The sound of Otto's voice startled her as he reentered the room.

"Gerhard and the crew are going to begin getting the boat ready for our departure. As they do so, he will slip away and meet you on your boat."

Edso stood up. "We'll go get ready."

* * *

Jack and Ken were not interested in watching the dinner party, so they went back inside while Max watched and continued to fantasize about their menu. The dinner took a full two hours. Max watched as Otto finally left the table but then returned. After his return, Edso and Courtney stood and disappeared from sight, and Otto stepped out onto the aft deck and began barking orders to some of the crew.

Max knocked on the cabin door again. "Something's happening," she whispered as soon as the door cracked open.

The men joined her on the deck, and together they watched as the crew of *Vorspiel* took up positions on the dock and on the deck. Soon they could hear her engines fire up.

"They're leaving," said Max.

"Not yet, but it won't be long," said Ken.

Then they saw Edso and Courtney walk out onto the back deck, where they joined Otto.

"There they are," said Max.

As Max watched from afar, Courtney and the two men stood and talked for a few minutes. Then Edso shook Otto's hand. Next he took Courtney's hand in his own and led her down the steps, onto the swim platform, and off the boat.

"Maybe we won't have to do too much," said Jack.

"Don't believe it. Something's going on."

They watched as Edso and Courtney climbed the ramp up to the boardwalk and began walking away from the stairs that led to the hotel.

"They're going to his boat," said Ken.

"That's good, right?" said Max.

"Why? What are they doing?" Jack asked.

Before they could discuss this new development, the crew of *Vorspiel* began to release the dock lines, and the yacht began edging away from the dock.

CHAPTER 76

"THEY'RE LEAVING," SAID MAX, stating the obvious, with a bit of excitement in her voice.

Ken ignored her and began quietly talking to himself. "There's no way he's just letting her go. Whatever he wants from her has to be at Ben's. *Vorspiel* can't get into Rye Harbor, so they've got to be taking Edso's boat there."

"What did you say?" asked Jack.

"That's the only possible reason Edso and Courtney were allowed to leave."

"Ken, what are you talking about?"

Ken ignored Jack's question.

"Okay, here's what we'll do. You and Max take your car and drive along the coast back to Ben's. That way you'll be able to keep track of Edso, who must be heading there on *Christine*. Call me when they arrive."

"Ken. Slow down. What are we doing?"

Ken repeated his instructions.

"But they are still here."

At that exact moment, they heard another engine starting.

"Max, could you go down to the end of the dock and see which boat is leaving?"

Ken's question was clearly a command. She started to protest, but Jack said, "Max, we need to know if the boat that just started is Edso's. Do it for Courtney. Please."

"Fine."

When she returned, she said, "A boat was leaving."

Ken said, "What did it look like?"

"I don't know. It was too far away, and it's dark. I couldn't see who was on it—just the shapes of people. I'm sure there were three of them, though."

"Three? You're sure?" said Ken.

"Positive."

He remained silent for a few moments. Then he said, "Shit. Maybe Otto doesn't trust Edso either. Now we don't know if they're with Otto, or Gerhard, or someone else."

He glanced at the harbor, looked at his watch, and said, "You two had better get going."

"You're sure about this?" asked Jack.

"Yes."

"What're you going to do?"

"I'm going to take my boat, follow *Vorspiel,* and try to figure out where she is going. The Isles would be my bet. When you call me, I'll head for Rye Harbor and meet you there."

CHAPTER 77

IT TOOK JACK AND MAX ABOUT FIFTEEN MINUTES to get past Odiorne Point and to the first road turnout where they would be able to see the ocean. Jack turned off his lights before pulling in, preferring to remain in the dark.

Climbing out of his truck, they walked up to where they could see the ocean.

"You see them?" asked Jack.

"Yeah, I got 'em." She pointed to the south. They had gotten further than Jack had thought they would.

"He's really pushing it. Let's go."

As they followed Route 1-A south, Jack slowed at each point where the ocean became visible. By the time they had reached Wallis Sands State Park, they were ahead of the boat, which was still tracking parallel to the coast.

"Looks like Ken will be right," said Jack.

"Keep going," said Max.

Just after Concord Point and before the road turned and disappeared behind the seawall that ran from Washington Road to Rye Harbor, he pulled off in another turnout and killed the lights to wait for the boat to come into sight.

"I can't believe how many people are out at this hour," said Jack as another car passed them.

"Me too. When we were moving, we saw no one."

"There they are," said Jack, pointing north. "We'll stay here until we see them make the turn into the harbor."

"What then?"

"We'll call Ken, and drive over."

"What if they see us?"

"Simple. We'll just go home, and then we can walk back to Ben's or wherever we need to be to meet Ken."

* * *

"Hey Ken, you were right. They just made the turn into Rye Harbor . . ."

"Okay. See you soon."

As they drove around the harbor, Jack could see the trawler moving slowly down the center channel. Instead of turning down Harbor Road, he decided to turn in at the entrance to the harbor and take the short road that ran past the commercial pier toward Harbor Road. That would give them a better view of the dock at Ben's.

"Change of plans," he announced to Max.

"What?"

"I'm going to park here on the commercial pier. We can see what they are going to do and watch for Ken. It'll be a while before he gets here, especially if he's coming from the Isles."

"But they'll see us."

"We'll hide by being in plain sight. If those guys know anything, they'll know that fishermen come in and go out at all hours. My truck is the perfect vehicle to blend in. As long as we stay out of any direct light, we'll be fine. And besides, it'll make it easier to meet up with Ken."

"I suppose, but I don't like it."

Jack leaned over and gave her a quick kiss that was meant to be reassuring.

"Don't worry. Things will all work out."

CHAPTER 78

EDSO STEERED *CHRISTINE* DOWN THE CENTER CHANNEL of Rye Harbor. During the entire trip, Courtney had remained with Edso at the helm while Gerhard sat in the back of the cabin watching them. There was no doubt that he disagreed with Otto's decision to trust either of them.

As they made that final turn, he joined them at the helm.

"So where to?" he asked.

Courtney pointed down the channel.

"All the way down. Then to the left, past the commercial pier, and we'll tie up at the dock in front of Ben's."

She breathed a sigh of relief when she saw that Ben's was closed and dark. It would have been hard to explain to her staff why she was arriving late at night with two strange men after being out of the office for a day.

As Edso brought *Christine* up to the dock, Gerhard said to Courtney, "The boat won't tie itself up. Get outside and secure us to the dock."

She started to protest that she wasn't a sailor and that she didn't know what to do, but he moved toward her, grabbed her arm, and pushed her toward the door.

"Gerhard!" shouted Edso. "That's not necessary."

Gerhard stopped. Still holding onto her arm, he looked at Edso and said, "You sniveling little shit. You lost your right to tell me what to do when you did not succeed in getting what your grandfather is looking for."

Then he turned back to Courtney and gave her a push out through the door.

"Get the boat tied up!"

Courtney struggled to tie up the boat. When it finally seemed secure enough, she went immediately to Edso's side.

"There. We're tied up as best I can. You might want to have Edso check how I did. We wouldn't want anything to happen to the boat."

Gerhard moved to the door, looked over the side, and returned to the cabin door.

"It looks good enough to me. Now, we go. Where to?"

* * *

Jack and Max watched the whole docking exercise, and while they couldn't hear all the words being exchanged on the boat, the voices carried well enough, and it was clear from the third person's tone that he was there to make sure that things went as they should.

Jack said, "Remember the nasty things Ken said about that Gerhard character. I think that's who's with them. I'm getting a bad feeling. I hope he gets here soon."

"Me too," said Max. "Where the hell is he?"

Jack looked toward the mouth of the harbor.

"I see some running lights. I think he's close."

Just then, Courtney and Edso—with Gerhard right behind—began moving up the ramp. The clomping sound of their shoes against the metal was magnified by the stillness of the night. Jack knew that there was no way to walk on that ramp silently, and he could only imagine how Gerhard was reacting to the noise.

"Let's go," said Max.

"Not yet. I see Ken coming in the harbor right now. We need to wait for him."

Max opened her door and slid out of the truck.

"Where're you going?" demanded Jack in a loud whisper.

"Look, they just went into Ben's. I'm going to go over there."

"No—"

But she had shut the door and was on her way before he could finish his sentence.

* * *

Once inside, Courtney flipped the light switch and began walking upstairs.

"Where're you going?" said Gerhard.

"Up to my office. You want the stuff I have? 'Cause that's where it is."

Edso let her get a few steps ahead before following, and as she expected, Gerhard was right behind Edso, pushing him along.

"Move. *Mach schnell.*"

Edso stopped just as Courtney reached the top of the stairs. He was about halfway up, and as she looked back, he turned toward Gerhard.

"Hey, asshole. Take it easy."

"*Schweinhunde,*" said Gerhard, and he gave Edso another push. "I will have no problem killing you right here. Now move."

At that point, they were most of the way up the steps, and when Gerhard pushed one last time, Edso spun around and kicked out, hitting Gerhard square in the chest, knocking him off balance.

As Gerhard fell backward, he cried out, "*Scheisse!* You are a dead man."

Craning her neck to see past Edso, Courtney got a glimpse of Gerhard crumpled at the bottom of the stairs. The expression on Edso's face was a combination of fear, triumph, and panic.

"What happened?" she cried out.

"Court, let's get out of here!" Edso yelled. Below him, Gerhard was beginning to move.

Courtney knew that returning down the stairs was not an option, but she wasn't sure which window would give them the best chance of escape. Then a better idea came to her.

"Edso, come. Hurry! He's moving!"

Edso sprinted up the last few steps, and Courtney grabbed his hand. "This way!"

Using only the dim light that filtered in through the windows, she led him through the warren of rooms that filled the area above Ben's dining rooms.

"Where the hell are we?" he asked when she finally stopped in front of a closed door.

"Tell you later. Stay close, and be careful. It will be pitch black in here, but he'll never find us."

"You weren't kidding," Edso whispered once they were inside and she had closed the door behind them.

She said, "Give me your hand, and follow me."

Edso tugged on her hand for a moment and pulled her to a halt.

"Court, I want you to know how sorry I am." Even whispering, his voice was like honey, and in spite of the fact that they were fleeing for their lives, she found herself remembering how skilled he was with his hands. Even in the darkness, she could feel herself blush.

"Keep moving," she said.

She moved forward slowly, her hand now acting as a blind person's cane as she felt for the opening she knew would take them to safety.

Finally, she stopped. "Listen. There's an opening in the floor here. We have to climb down. It's maybe a three- or four-foot drop. Then we'll be standing on a trap door that opens into the wood box next to the fireplace in the main dining room. We use it during the holidays so that Santa can come 'down' the chimney. There's an exit right next to the spot where we'll drop down."

"You're kidding."

"No. You ready?"

"I guess we don't have much choice. Hopefully he won't be there waiting for us, inside or out."

CHAPTER 79

JACK WALKED OVER TO THE FLOATS where Ken was just tying up his boat.

"So?" said Ken.

"They're tied up over there and they went inside Ben's a few minutes ago. We watched them from my truck, which is parked over by the commercial pier."

"Where's Max?"

"That might be a problem. She got impatient and headed over to Ben's to see what was going on."

"Why didn't you stop her?"

"I didn't dare yell after her. You were just arriving, and she's flat-out quick."

"Well then, we'd better get going."

"Come on. We can drive over and park across the street."

* * *

"*What the hell are they doing in there?*" wondered Max as she walked along the road that led from the pier to Harbor Road. She stopped and looked at the small window next to the door at Ben's. Someone had turned on the light inside, but from that distance she really couldn't see what was going on. She looked back and saw Jack and Ken heading to the truck.

She knew they'd catch up with her soon enough, so she kept going. Crossing the bridge on Harbor Road, she cut into the back corner of the parking lot. It was time to make a decision: watch and wait for Jack and Ken, or get closer and try to see what was going on. Considering that her best friend was in there with two dangerous men, the choice seemed simple enough, and she kept walking.

She moved across the parking lot like a hero in a Hollywood

movie. With adrenaline fueling her courage, she reached the bushes and trees that were planted to screen the kitchen end of the front porch. Then, one step at a time, she climbed onto the porch and—with back pressed against the wall—crept closer to the window next to the door that Courtney and her escorts had gone in.

* * *

"There she is," said Jack as he drove over the bridge. He saw Max creeping along the front of Ben's toward the one lit window.

"Is she crazy?" asked Ken.

"A little."

"If Gerhard's in there with Edso and Courtney and he catches her, he'll kill her."

Jack pulled into the parking lot across from Ben's. As he started to open his door, Ken said, "Hold on."

"But Max—"

"Listen, I know this guy. He'll eat you for lunch. Let me go. Then you follow in five."

"I'd rather—"

Ken cut him off again.

"Jack, I'm a lot better equipped to deal with Gerhard than you are. Trust me on that."

"Fine. But if you're not back with Max in five minutes, I'm coming after you. Clock's ticking."

"I'll bring her back."

Jack watched as Ken crossed the road and disappeared into the bushes that screened the kitchen from the front parking lot. A cat on the hunt couldn't have moved more swiftly or silently. Jack was about to follow when he saw the fire door from the main dining room open and two shadows exit.

He watched as they pressed the door closed and hurried in the direction of Courtney's cottage. Jack got out of the truck, ran over toward them, and called out in a loud whisper, "Court!"

* * *

Max crept across the porch and sidled up to the window. She planned to look inside and then report back to Jack and Ken. Suddenly the door flew open, and a man with blood dripping down his face ran out onto the porch and nearly knocked her down.

"Hey! What're you doing in there?" shouted Max.

Gerhard paused, and time seemed to stop as he stared at her. Then he snarled, "Who are you?"

"I work here. The question is who are *you*, and what were you doing in there?"

He continued to stare at her, as blood dripped from his head. Suddenly, Max saw the expression on his face change.

"I saw you at the marina. You were spying on us," he said.

"I don't know what are you talking about." replied Max, edging back from him. She recognized him then, and a chill went through her entire body. She thought of the things Ken had said, and suddenly she wished that she had listened to Jack and waited in the truck.

Before she could run away, he lunged for her. She dodged his first attempt, but he recovered faster than she did, and before she could escape, he grabbed her arm and pulled her close.

"Well, *fraulein*, I'm guessing that you're here to find your friend. I mean, why else would you be skulking around peeking in windows?"

"No, I told you, I work here. I forgot something and I just came back for it. Then you flew out the door. What are you up to, anyway?"

He did not relax his grip. "Nice try. Your friend has something I want, and now you're going to help me get it."

"Let go of me!" She twisted and wriggled, but his grip only got tighter.

"Do I have to hurt you? Be quiet!"

Max was about to scream when she saw Ken standing on the edge of the front porch.

"Let her go, Gerhard. It's over." Ken spoke in a slow, deliberate monotone that left no doubt that he could and would back up his words.

"Who are you?"

"A friend of hers."

"Well, friend, I suggest that you just leave us before someone gets hurt."

As if to reinforce his words, he squeezed Max's arm tighter and twisted it so she was pulled close in front of him.

"That's not going to be possible."

CHAPTER 80

AS SOON AS JACK REACHED COURTNEY, she turned and threw herself into his arms.

"Jack! Thank God you're here!"

"Are you all right?"

"Yes, but a real psycho is after us. We can't stay around here."

"How did you get out of Ben's?"

"Edso managed to kick him down the stairs. We made our way to the Santa door and came down. Gerhard isn't dead though. We need to keep moving!"

"And this is Edso?"

"Right. His grandfather wants those journals, and maybe something else, but we've got to get out of here!"

"Where is his grandfather now?"

"Out on *Vorspiel.* But Gerhard could be here at any mo—."

"Gerhard is still inside Ben's?"

"Yes! That's what I've been trying to tell you!"

"Courtney, *Max is over there.* Go sit in my truck. I have to find her."

Then he looked at Edso. "And *you,* stay right here. You've caused enough trouble already."

Cautiously, Jack made his way to the corner of the building. As he moved around the corner, he was able to get a look down the porch. The door that led upstairs was open, and in the narrow patch of light that spilled out onto the porch, he could see what could only be a body.

He froze, staring at the unmoving form. From his vantage point he couldn't tell who it was, and instantly he imagined the worst.

"Max!" he cried out as he rushed toward the body. Relief washed over him when he realized it wasn't her. It was Gerhard. Courtney had said the man wasn't dead, but from the way his head was twisted around in a most unnatural angle, there was no doubt that he was dead now.

Jack stopped and looked around, and another wave of fear and panic shot through him.

"Max!" he called out again. He moved past the body on the porch and stopped at the doorway. He looked inside, but no one was there.

"Jack!"

He heard her voice, but still overwhelmed by the past few moments, he couldn't tell where it was coming from. Then he heard a noise from outside. He spun around and stepped back out onto the porch, where he was nearly knocked off balance as Max launched herself into his arms.

"Oh, my God. Jack. I am so glad to see you!"

He held her tight, not daring to relax his grip lest she turn out to be an illusion.

"Are you all right?" he whispered.

"I'm fine, thanks to Ken."

"Where is he?"

Then he heard Ken's voice.

"Right here."

Jack eased his grip on Max and turned back toward the door.

"Ken? Where were you?"

"I was inside looking for Courtney and Edso."

"They're safe. As you went around front, they came out the back door of the dining room. They're waiting at my truck."

"Max!"

It was Courtney, who was certainly not in the truck. As she came running up onto the porch, Max let go of Jack and the two friends hugged. Edso was following a few steps behind, and when Jack saw him, he moved to put himself between the girls and Edso.

Ken grabbed his arm. "Easy, Jack."

Edso looked down at the body on the porch. "Gerhard?"

In a matter-of-fact voice, Ken said, "He's dead."

"How?" said Jack. He retreated back to Max and Courtney.

"Gerhard grabbed Max on the porch." He paused, and a hint of a smile came over his face. "Sylvie had told me Max was tough, but I had no idea how quick she was. She spun around kicked him in the balls so fast he didn't know what hit him. When he let go of her, she ran right into me, and she was so pumped up with fear, I nearly got the same treatment. Then Gerhard came at both of us, shouting threats while brandishing this knife." Ken reached behind and pulled the knife from his back pocket. With a hint of a smile he said, "Let's just say he won't be bothering anyone anymore."

"So, what now?" asked Edso.

Ken looked at him. "You okay?"

"Yes."

"We've got to get this mess cleaned up before anyone shows up."

"My grandfather is expecting us. Let's take him down to the boat," added Edso.

"You're right. Come on, give me a hand," said Ken.

Jack looked over at Max and Courtney who were still holding on to each other. "We'll be right back. Wait here"

Then he rushed to help Ken and Edso carry the body down to Edso's boat.

With Gerhard stowed safely on board, there was a moment of awkward silence as the three men looked at each other.

Edso broke the silence. "Let me take it from here. My grandfather is waiting for my return. He's expecting me, Courtney, and Gerhard, along with the proof he needs to confirm that his father and his father's friend had not failed in their mission but had instead died as heroes of the Reich at the hands of the Americans."

"And what's going to happen when you show up without Courtney, without the evidence, and with Gerhard's body?" asked Jack.

"I'll deal with it," he said.

Edso shook Ken's hand and then, catching Jack completely off guard, gave Jack a classic bro-hug, whispering in his ear, "Say goodbye to Courtney for me. Tell her that I was really falling for her and I'm sorry."

As Jack and Ken watched in silence, Edso climbed on *Christine* and started her engine while Jack and Ken cast her off. He was well away by the time Max and Courtney joined them.

The four of them were still standing in the parking lot when one of the town's cruisers pulled in.

Jack walked over to the car.

"Hey, Kevin. What's up?"

"Someone called to say that there was some suspicious activity going on over here. You see anything?"

"Only ones here are myself, Max, Courtney, and my buddy Ken. We were out on a friend's boat. He just dropped us off. Nice evening."

Kevin looked relieved that he wasn't going to have to deal with anything more serious. He shifted into gear and was about to drive off when Jack said, "Say hi to Tom for me when you see him."

Kevin gave Jack a wave and drove off.

As Jack rejoined the others, Ken said, "Timing is everything. Five minutes earlier and things could have gotten messy."

"I agree. We got lucky," said Jack.

"So, what happens now?" asked Max, looking straight at Ken. "Is it over, will Courtney be safe?"

"Max, Sylvie was right. You've got balls. It's been a pleasure getting to know you. I'll tell her you said hello."

"You didn't answer my questions."

"Yes, I believe that Courtney will be safe. People like Otto have their moments, but in the end, it is fleeting at best."

Before she could ask anything else, he turned to Jack. "Listen, I've got to get going. Give me a ride over to my boat?"

"Sure," said Jack.

Max and Court each gave Ken a hug good-bye. Then Court said, "All I want to do is lock up and go home."

"I'll help," said Max.

She gave Jack a quick kiss on the cheek and said, "See you at home."

CHAPTER 81

"YOU'RE NOT GOING BACK TO THE MARINA RIGHT AWAY, ARE YOU?" said Jack, as he stopped his truck by the dock.

"By asking, I think you know the answer to that. I still have some unfinished business."

"Can I ask you something else?"

Ken didn't say anything, but the nod he gave Jack said, "Go ahead."

"What's your connection with Sylvie?"

"We've known each other for years. We're just friends. We share similar skills and interests, and on occasion we help each other out. She had a conflict, so she asked if I would help her out this time."

"Tell her hello, and thanks."

"You know, she speaks highly of you. By the way, I think she's training for a marathon. That's where you two met, wasn't it?"

"Yeah, the Rockdog Run." Jack smiled as he remembered that perfect fall day.

"Well, I've got to get going. If I see her, I'll say hello from you."

* * *

By the time Jack got home, Courtney's cottage was dark and Max was sound asleep, her breathing deep and steady. He wasn't ready to sleep yet, so he poured himself a jigger of Blanton's single barrel bourbon whiskey and sat down on the couch. He was hardly settled before Cat insinuated herself into his lap. Under the influence of the bourbon and her purring, he began reflecting on life. The season was changing. They were already on the descent into what Max called the dark time. The days were getting shorter, the sun was no longer so warm, and too many days would be spent under the gloom of overcast skies.

Soon *d'Riddem* would be hauled out of the water, covered up, and put to rest until spring. Running would become more challenging—layers of clothes, hats, mittens, headlamps at night, and, when the snow came, narrower roads. It was a time for goals to be set, the attainment of which would be defined by strength of character and purpose.

"Cat, what do you think. Marathon next year?"

* * *

Jack did not remember climbing into bed, and the sun was well up by the time he awakened. His stomach grumbled. When his feet hit the cold floor, he nearly climbed back into bed, but hunger was a more powerful motivation, especially since Max was already up.

"Hey, Sleepyhead," she said when he walked out of the bedroom. "Courtney and I are going to Paula's for breakfast. You want to join us?"

"If you're ready to go, don't wait. I'll meet you there. I need a shower first."

"We'll save you a seat."

Thirty-five minutes later, Jack walked into Paula's Place. Most mornings there was a definite hum to the place, but this morning it seemed particularly charged. He saw Max waving at him, and as he worked his way over, Beverly said that she'd be right over with coffee.

Courtney looked subdued, but Max was all excited. "Did you hear?"

"Hear what?"

"A boat caught fire and burned out by the Isles last night."

"You're shitting me!"

Max shook her head.

Jack turned and walked back to the newspaper rack.

"He okay, Hon?" Beverly had clearly noticed the shocked look on his face as he walked off.

"He'll be fine," Max said as Beverly poured his coffee

"He'll have the stuffed French toast with sausage," said Max.

"Mornin' Jack." Tom flicked the paper that Jack was totally

focused on.

Startled, Jack lowered the paper and said, "Tom. Good morning. When did you come in?"

"Just leaving," then he lifted the to-go cup of coffee in his hand for Jack to see. "Kevin said he saw you last night."

Yeah. We had just come in on a friend's boat."

"You heard about all the excitement out at the Isles?"

"Max just told me." he said looking back at the paper. "What have you heard?"

"Not much. Some millionaire's yacht anchored out by the Isles caught fire. Pretty much a total loss I guess. Apparently it had been at the Wentworth Marina."

Jack had to ask even though he was pretty sure he knew the answer. "You know the name of the boat?"

"I heard it was German or something. *Vorspeck?* Something like that. Big blue yacht."

"Anybody hurt?"

He shrugged. "Haven't heard."

"If you hear anything, could you let me know?"

"Sure. Gotta' go. Say hi and bye to Max and Courtney for me. Have a nice day."

* * *

"Here you go, Jack," said Beverly. She placed a plate in front of him. "Thanks."

Courtney remained silent, but Max started right in, "So? What did Tom say? Was anyone hurt?"

"Tom didn't offer any more than was in the paper."

Obviously disappointed, Max looked at him, "How's your breakfast?"

"Good. Thank you for ordering for me. Maybe after breakfast we can drive over to the marina. I'd really like to talk to Ken."

Courtney finally spoke. "I'll pass. I have some things to do. Max, okay if I leave you here with Jack?" She stood up and grabbed her coat. "I'll catch up with you later."

"You okay?" asked Jack.

"Yeah, I'm fine."

As soon as she was out the door, Max said, "I don't think she's so fine."

"I agree," said Jack, as he took another bite of his breakfast.

CHAPTER 82

AS THEY WALKED DOWN THE STEPS TO THE BOARDWALK at the marina, Jack looked down the dock to see if Ken's boat was there. *Sylvie* was in her slip. He went over to the gate but realized that he didn't have the combination. Ken had always opened it.

"I'll wait here," said Max.

In the dockmaster's office, a short, stocky man was yelling at Jeremy.

"Listen, you little twerp, that is my boat and I intend to take her. Now give me the combination to the gate!"

"I'm sorry, sir, but I can't do that." Jeremy's tone remained patient. "That boat has been here all summer, and I can assure you that you are not the owner."

The man slammed his fist on the counter "What the hell are you talking about? I hired a delivery skipper to bring her up here, then my summer went to shit. Took me all season to get up here and now I'm here and I intend to use her."

Jeremy looked over his list of boats. "I'm sorry, sir, but we do not have a boat here with that name. I can't help you."

"I saw her!"

"Sorry."

The man mumbled an epithet and stormed out.

"Hey, Jeremy," said Jack. "What was that all about?"

"Hi, Jack. Nothing. That guy keeps trying to tell me that his boat is here in the marina, and it isn't. If he comes back one more time, I'm calling the cops."

"That's bizarre," said Jack.

"No shit."

"Anyways, I came to see if you could give me the gate combination. I just realized that Ken always opened it. I have something of his I want to return."

"Here." He passed Jack a piece of paper with the code written on it.

"Thanks. Hey, on another note, wasn't that something about *Vorspiel?*"

"Sure was."

"You hear anything about what happened?"

"Not really, but the Coast Guard was here asking lots of questions this morning."

"Well, thanks. Hope your day gets better."

"Thanks."

Jack was about to pull the door shut when he turned back. "Hey, Jeremy, did Edso ever come back?"

"Haven't seen him."

"Thanks."

He joined Max at the gate. As he punched in the code and the gate started to open, the angry man he had seen in the office ran over and pushed right past them.

"Thanks!" he called over his shoulder. "That little prick in the office won't give me the combination to the gate."

"No problem," said Jack as he and Max followed him through the gate. "Which boat is yours?"

"That one," he said, pointing toward *Sylvie*, and he hurried ahead.

As Jack and Max caught up with him, he was standing by her stern, staring, then he shouted, "What the fuck!"

"What's the matter?"

"Her name. Someone changed her name! *Sylvie!* Really! Her name is *Miss Demeanor.*"

"Good lookin' boat," said Jack as he stood next to the man. He knew that complimenting someone's boat would almost always get an invitation to board, and he needed to get a look around. "Can I take a look?"

The man's face softened at the compliment. "Sure."

Jack turned to Max. "Be right back."

The boat was clean, with absolutely no sign that Ken had ever been there. Clearly, this guy's story was true.

"Thanks for the tour," said Jack as he joined Max again on the dock.

"Hey, listen, if you're ever down in Port Charlotte, look me up. I'll take you fishing." He handed Jack a business card.

"I might just take you up on your offer. Thanks again."

As Max and Jack walked back up the ramp, she said, "I knew there was something fishy about Ken from the moment I set eyes on him. And then his association with Sylvie? I, for one, am glad he's gone."

CHAPTER 83

JACK SUGGESTED THEY SPEND THE REST OF THE DAY ON D'*RIDDEM*, and Max quickly agreed. When they got back from the marina, she spotted Courtney's car in front of Ben's.

"Let me out here," Max said. "I want to check on Courtney before we go out to the boat."

"I'll go feed Cat and then come pick you up."

* * *

"Hey, Court. How're you doing?"

"Depends. I'm really pissed at how Edso played me. But, now I know why I couldn't find anything out about him."

"Why?"

"Harding was his mother's maiden name. His real name was Jäger."

"That son of a bitch."

"But Max, in the end, he probably saved my life. Plus, now I know exactly what they were looking for, and I found it—or most of it, anyway."

"You do? You did?"

Courtney removed from her pocket the paper that she had taken from the desk on *Vorspiel* and handed it to Max.

"What's this?"

"It's a set of orders for a mission to land an agent here."

"Where'd you get them?"

"I saw Edso looking at a piece of paper on the boat. When he realized that I was watching him, he quickly tried to hide it. As soon as I had the chance, I grabbed it. Look at the date."

"September 29, 1942?"

"Exactly. Remember, that's the date in Ben's journal that had only a weather notation. Ben must have interrupted that landing."

Then Courtney pointed at the paper again. "Look. This is a list of what the German agent was supposed to take with him. I know it's in German, but I went online and translated the words in the list. He took several guns, documents, and—are you ready for this—a whole pile of cash and gold!"

Max gasped as Courtney continued.

"When I got here this morning, I went through more of Ben's stuff. In one box, I found this envelope."

Holding it up, she reached in and pulled out some of its contents. "Look: passports, maps, train schedules, and newspaper clippings. And everything's dated in the early 1940s."

Max looked at her wide-eyed, and said, "According to Jack, Gladys said that during the war, a German raft washed up on shore and really wigged everyone out. They found some guns in it, but nothing else—no documents, no money, no body."

"These have to be the documents," said Courtney. "Ben must have found the raft first."

"From what Edso told me, I'd guess that whoever was in the raft probably drowned. It was a pretty nasty night. It's possible that Ben could have run him down and not even known."

"I guess. But he had these," Max said pointing at the contents of the envelope.

Maybe he found the raft drifting around empty, took the stuff, and then let it go to wash up on shore."

"That could make sense."

Suddenly Courtney became strangely quiet as another possibility came to her.

"You okay?" asked Max.

"Yes . . . yes. I'm good," she said as she put those dark thoughts out of her head.

"You find any money?"

"No. If he had taken it, it wouldn't surprise me that he spent most of it."

"And what makes you think that?"

She told Max of the conversation she had with him shortly before he died.

"Wow," said Max. "I guess if he took the money, and he spent it slowly, and was careful, no one would be the wiser, but what about the gold?"

Courtney shrugged. "He probably spent the cash over the years. It must have cost a lot to get Ben's started. It certainly costs a lot to keep it going."

"But what about the gold?"

"No idea. I did a bit more research online, and it was illegal to own gold back then except in really small quantities. You could have a gold necklace, but that was pretty much it. If Uncle Ben really did have it, it would have been hard for him to use it. He might even have gotten arrested."

"So, you think it's still hidden around here somewhere?"

"It wouldn't surprise me, but I wouldn't even know where to begin looking. It's definitely not with the stuff upstairs."

"Can I tell Jack?"

"Jack, yes. But promise me you won't say anything to anyone else. Can you imagine if the 'boys' heard about this? They'd be impossible."

Max chuckled at the thought of Leo, Ralph, and Paulie speculating and prospecting for hidden gold.

"I promise."

"I'll keep looking," Courtney said, "but don't hold out much hope."

"I won't," said Max. "Listen, I've got to get going. Jack's probably downstairs waiting for me. We're heading out to *d'Riddem*."

"Sounds like fun," said Courtney with a teasing smile. "Have fun doing nothing."

CHAPTER 84

"YOU KNOW MAX, I'VE BEEN THINKING about what Courtney told you yesterday," said Jack.

He was outside staring at those boards again.

"Still think there's something on the boards?"

"I do. If Ben took the money and the gold, then there's probably something here. I've matched all of the boat names painted on the boards to names in his journals, except—"

"Except what?"

He pointed down at that lower corner of the boards, where most of the paint had rubbed off.

"The more I look at it, the more convinced I am that it's the name of a woman. Looks like *Jessica*. And these numbers. Look here. Four, Two, Nine, Two, Nine. Her phone number? You hear of anyone around here with that name?"

"No. . . Wait. I have seen it. It's the name on that boat model in the bar. I was cleaning it not too long ago and I remember thinking what pretty name for a boat."

Jack looked at her.

"Thinking about it, something else I noticed, it's really heavy."

That caught Jack's attention. "Heavy?"

"Yeah. I mean, I can pick it up and all, but it's a lot heavier than it looks."

"Let's go look."

* * *

Max was right. The model of *Jessica* was a lot heavier than it looked. Jack lifted the model and its cradle off the shelf and placed it on the bar.

Then he heard Courtney's voice calling from the stairs.

"Is that you, Jack? What's going on?" She joined them at the bar.

"We're looking at your model," said Max pointing at the sailboat.

"Where did you get it?" asked Jack.

"I don't know. It was just always here. I found it upstairs after Ben died. Seemed fitting to put it out here."

She looked at it more closely. "*Jessica*? You know, when I was going through those boxes I found upstairs, I found a picture of the actual *Jessica* under full sail. There was a note on it that she was lost during the hurricane of '38. Maybe I should frame it and hang it by this model. Boy, it's a mess. I didn't realize she was so beat. Maybe I should get her fixed up, too. There might even be some more."

"Models?"

"Yeah. Where I found that picture, there were a couple of boxes in the back of the closet labeled *model boats*. They were on the bottom of the pile, so I didn't even try to get them out. I was more interested in trying to find answers.

"OK if I check them out?"

"Sure, but you're on your own. I have to go out, but I'll tell you where they are. Looking more at Max, than Jack, she said, "You know how to get to where the trap door is that we use for Santa at Christmas?"

Max nodded 'yes'.

"Well to the left of the door that leads to the trap door, there's a kind of a small closet. That's where I found the boxes of stuff I've been going through. They're in there. Listen, I've got to go out. Have fun."

CHAPTER 85

JACK PEERED INTO THE CLOSET.

"She wasn't just kidding."

With much grunting and colorful vocabulary he finally exposed the boxes he wanted.

The first one didn't want to slide out so he cut the tape and opened the flaps. Inside, it was filled with crumpled newspapers. He pulled some out and looked at the dates. They were all from the 1940's. As he burrowed through the crumpled papers, he found a model—a lobster boat. As he lifted it out, he was struck by just how heavy it was.

"Can you get this," he asked as he passed it back to Max." It feels like there's another. Careful, it's heavy."

Max took it from him. "Woah! Why does it weigh so much?"

Slowly he backed out of the closet with the second model, this one a sail boat.

She looked at him, her expression blank at first. Then slowly, he could see it change as she had the same thought he did.

"You don't suppose?" she said.

"We'll find out."

Jack took the model from her and began to study its construction. After a few minutes, he was able to pry off the deck.

"Holy shit," he whispered as he looked inside.

"Oh my god. Is it . . .?" said Max.

"It is."

Jack carefully put the boat on the floor and began to pry out one of the small gold bars that was wedged inside. It was about one inch by three inches and a half-inch thick, a little bit bigger than a small chocolate bar.

"This feels like about a pound," he said, holding it in his hand.

Stamped on one face was the German emblem.

Jack took five more bars out of the boat and handed one to Max.

She stared wide-eyed at the small bar of gold. Finding her voice, she whispered, "We found it. How much do you suppose it's worth?"

"I don't know," Jack said, "but I'm guessing a lot. And here's another boat, and there's at least one more box in there labeled *boat model*."

* * *

Max and Jack were sitting at the bar when Courtney returned. They were all grins and giggles.

"What has gotten into you two?" she asked and then looked at Angela.

She shrugged and said, "No idea. They've been like this ever since they came down."

"Hi Court," said Max, and then she started giggling again.

She turned toward Angela, "How many has she had?"

"Only two. And they had something to eat as well."

"Okay, you two. What's up?"

"Oh, Court. Have we got a surprise for you."

She looked at them, trying to figure out what could get this kind of reaction from them. That's when she began to smile. "So is it something worth celebrating?"

"I guess you could say that," said Max after trading looks with Jack.

He smiled and took a slow sip of his beer.

"You're not going to tell me, are you?"

Max shook her head, trying to not smile and took a sip of her drink.

Court stared at them, then noticing that Max was keeping her left hand hidden under the bar. "OK, so that's the way it's going to be. Angela, could you make me a Stoli Razz and soda?"

Courtney sat down next to Max and turned her bar stool so that she was facing her. "Max."

"Court."

"Max, What aren't you telling me?"

"Guess."

"I don't want to guess."

"Come on. Just one."

"Will it make me happy?"

Jack looked at Max, then said, while looking at Courtney, "I'm pretty sure it'll make you happy."

"Is it big or small?" She was beginning to get into the game.

"Sort of small, wouldn't you say Jack?"

He smiled and nodded.

"How small?"

"Smaller than you would think."

"Is it shiny?"

"Oh, yeah, it's shiny," said Jack.

"Max, let me see your hands."

"Why?"

"Because. I want to know if you two got engaged."

With that, an awkward silence came over them.

"Engaged!" Jack blurted out.

Max looked panicked and raised both her hands in front of Courtney's face. "Nope."

Obviously disappointed, Courtney said, "I give up. What?"

* * *

"Come. Sit," said Max.

On the floor in front of the closet were several boxes, each with a model boat sitting on top, some sail and others lobsterboats. Some were finished and others partial.

"Court, these models are exceptional and I think quite valuable. They would look nice on display somewhere downstairs."

"Those were in those boxes? I had no idea Ben had these."

"But wait," Jack said in his best infomercial voice. "There's more."

"What the hell are you talking about Jack Beale?"

He put a model on her lap.

"Notice anything?"

"Not really."

"Nothing?"

"It's kind of heavy, I suppose."

"Very good. Do you know why it's so heavy?"

"Jack, I really don't care."

Max couldn't contain herself, "You will, Court. You will."

Jack took the model from her.

She said, "You two are making no sense at all."

That was when Jack popped the deck off of the boat.

"Jack! What are you doing? You were just telling me how cool these models are and now you're breaking it."

"Court. Stop. Pay attention. Look."

He pulled out one of the small gold bars and handed it to her.

She stared at it while the color left her face. "Wh . . . Jack . . . Is this . . . "

"Court!" Max shouted as she caught her friend.

EPILOGUE

"JACK," COURTNEY SHOUTED.

He looked up and shut the table saw off. "Hey, Court, what's up?"

"I'm taking you and Max out to lunch."

Several weeks had passed since the burning of *Vorspiel.* There had been little information available about the tragedy. Several bodies were recovered, all crew members, but no sign of either Otto or Edso.

Courtney had asked Jack to find a way to display the boards at Ben's. The boat models were packed away and Court, Max and Jack remained the only ones who knew about their true value.

He glanced at his watch. It was lunch time. "Thanks. What's the occasion?"

"You two have done so much for me, and I can't possibly repay you for all of it, but I can take you out every now and then."

"Max know?"

"She's getting ready right now. Come on."

* * *

"Where're we going?" asked Jack.

"You'll see."

The gravel crunched under the tires as they drove through the gate to Great Bay Marina. "I hope they're still open," said Courtney.

"Lexie's Landing? I love this place," said Max.

"I had a wicked craving for a really good burger and their Bistro fries last night."

"I would have thought you'd avoid this place," said Jack.

For a moment, things got really quiet in the car. "Why do you say that, Jack?"

"Didn't things kind of get started with Edso, here?"

"We had lunch here once, and just because he turned out to be a creep, that doesn't mean I can't still enjoy their burgers."

There was a buzz of activity as boats were being hauled out of the water and their bottoms power washed in preparation for being moved to their winter spot. A sign in the parking lot announced that Lexies would be closing for the season the next day.

"You two go on ahead, I see someone I want to say hi to," said Court.

They stopped and watched her walk out onto the docks toward a motor yacht tied out on the end.

"Isn't that the *Christine*?" asked Jack.

"I don't know."

"Come on. I'm curious."

By the time they got out to the end of the docks, Court had stopped and was talking to an older man next to the boat. "Jack, Max, I'd like to introduce you to my friend Rusty. We met briefly that day I met Edso for lunch. He offered to take me out on the bay to see the foliage."

Rusty looked at her, surprise on his face. "Edso? Is that what he told you his name was?"

"Yes. Why?"

"Told me his name was Stuart. Stuart Winne. He's the one who chartered my boat. Three weeks, Paid up front, then returned her three days later, insisted that I keep the entire fee."

Court stared at him. "Stuart. You're sure?"

"Positive."

"Was he alone when he returned the boat?" asked Jack,

"Actually, no. There was this old guy with him. Surly, looked like he had been in a fight. Definitely had an attitude. They didn't stick around either. Got right off, car picked them up and they were gone."

"Had to be Otto," mumbled Jack under his breath.

"You OK?" asked Rusty, looking at Courtney.

"Yeah. I'll be fine."

"I don't mean to give you more bad news, but I won't be able to take you out on the bay to see the foliage. No sooner did those two drive off, I got a call from some gal, wanted to charter *Christine* for the entire winter. Already paid. Said she had heard about *Christine* from a friend, some guy over at the Wentworth by the Sea Marina. I'm leaving tomorrow, heading down the waterway."

"Do you mind if I ask what her name was?" asked Jack.

"Give me a minute, I'll think of it."

Jack glanced over at Max.

"Hey guys, It's lunchtime." said Courtney.

"Wait, I've got it!" said Rusty. "It was Sylvie."

Reality in the fiction of *Jessica's Secret*

p. 61   Great Bay Marina – Newington, NH
        www.greatbaymarine.com

p. 61   Lexie's Landing – Newington, NH
        www.peaceloveburgers.com

p. 61   Nellie and Joe's Key Lime Juice – Key West, FL
        www.keylimejuice.com

p. 61   Hannaford's (Pic N' Pay) – Portsmouth, NH
        www.hannaford.com

p. 106 Pulpit Rock Tower – Rye, NH
        www.friendsofpulpitrocktower.org

p. 106 Odiorne Point State Park - Rye, NH
        www.nhstateparks.org

p. 109 Latitudes – New Castle, NH
        www.wentworth.com/latitudes-waterfront/

p. 131 Wallace Sands State Park – Rye, NH
        www.nhstateparks.org

p. 183 Green Bean Dockside
        www.wentworthhmarina.com

OTHER BOOKS BY K.D. MASON

HARBOR ICE (2009)

The winter has been brutally cold, leaving Rye Harbor frozen solid. Finally, the weather warms and the ice begins to breakup and drift out to sea. That's when a woman's body is found under a slab of ice left by the outgoing tide. Max, the bartender at Ben's Place recognizes that it is her Aunt's partner and that begins a series of events that will eventually threaten Max's life as well. It is up to her best friend, Jack Beale, to unravel the mystery.

CHANGING TIDES (2010)

Fate, Chance, Destiny . . . Call it what you will, but sometimes life changing events begin in the most innocent and unexpected ways. For Jack Beale that moment came on a perfect summer morning as he stood overlooking Rye Harbor when something caught his eye. In that small space between the bow of his boat and the float to which it was tied, a lifeless body had become wedged as the tide tried to sweep it out to sea. That discovery, and the arrival of Daniel would begin a series of events that would eventually take Max from him. Who was the victim? Why was Daniel there and what was his interest in Max? Was there a connection? And, so began a journey that would take Jack from Rye Harbor to Newport, RI and, eventually Belize, as he searched for answers.

DANGEROUS SHOALS (2011)

Spring has arrived in the small New Hampshire coastal town of Rye Harbor and all seemed right in the world. Jack Beale and Max, the feisty red haired bartender at Ben's Place, are back together after their split up the previous year and are looking forward to enjoying a carefree summer together. Then, someone who they thought was just a memory reappears, pursued by a psychotic killer. When he ends up dead, Jack and Max become the killer's new targets. What should have been an easy, relaxing summer for Jack, Max and his cat, Cat, becomes a battle of wits and a fight for survival.

KILLER RUN (2012)

Malcom and Polly were living their dream, running a North Country Bed & Breakfast they named the Quilt House Inn. The Inn was known for two things, the collection of antique quilts on display and miles of running and hiking trails for their guests use. Jack, training for his first trail marathon, The Rockdog Run, heard about the Inn and hatched a plan whereby he and Max could enjoy a romantic get-a-way and he could get in some quality trail training. For his plan to work, Dave and Patti joined them at the Inn. Meanwhile, in the weeks leading up to the marathon, a delusional antique dealer developed a fascination with one of the quilts on display in the Inn and It wasn't long before Malcom and Polly's dream and the four friends became forever entwined in a deadly mystery spanning two hundred years and 26.2 miles. Running a marathon is challenging enough by itself. Doing so on trails and starting before sunrise, in the dark, on a cold November day is even more daunting. When Jack trips and falls, landing on the lifeless body of an unknown runner, the race becomes a true "killer run."

EVIL INTENTIONS (2013)

Unseen forces at play may dramatically change the quiet seaside town of Rye Harbor forever. It's early spring, and one of the town's oldest homes, the Francis House, has just gone up in flames, revealing a badly burned body in the ashes. With help from an unexpected source, Jack and his friend Tom, the Police Chief, unravel the mystery fueled by a broken heart, a secret real estate deal, and a deadly double-cross.

UNEXPECTED CATCH (2015)

A summer heat wave blankets the New Hampshire seacoast. In an attempt to beat the heat, Jack's best friend, Dave, arranges for a day of fishing far off shore on the boat *Miss Cookie*. Even though they land only a few fish, they pronounce the day a great success—until Jack spots smoke on the horizon and they convince the reluctant captain to bring them to investigate. What they find will have a profound effect upon all of their lives as they deal with the consequences of an Unexpected Catch.

BLACK SCHOONER (2016)

Jack and Max hire a delivery skipper, TJ, to bring her catamaran from Belize to Rye Harbor, New Hampshire. TJ takes on a mysterious woman as crew in Florida, but after she jumps ship in Gloucester, TJ enlists Jack's help for the final leg of the delivery. In Gloucester, TJ, an incorrigible woman-izer, reconnects with a former lover and crew mate, and that chance meeting triggers a search for a black schooner from his past—along with the chance it affords for closure and revenge. His search takes him through Kennebunkport, Boothbay, and Camden, Maine, and finally to the Isles of Shoals, where TJ and Jack's friend Tom, the police chief of Rye Harbor, become targets of an unknown killer.